MEDDLING MAGES

THE LAST LUMENIAN SERIES

BOOK IV

S.G. BLAISE

info@thelastlumenian.com.

First paperback edition December 2023

Book design by Tim Barber from Dissect Designs
Map Illustrated by Clif Chandler
Edited by Julie Tibbott and William Drennan
Publisher: Lilac Grove Entertainment LLC

ISBN: 979-8-9885265-0-6

www.sgblaise.com

To receive exclusive content, sign up for the S.G. Blaise newsletter at sgblaisenews.com

To Alex:
the best alpha, beta, etc., reader in the Seven Galaxies.

To Gabe:
this book is much shorter than the third (just saying).

To My Mom:
yes, there will be that many books in the series.

To all of you, Dear Readers, who love this series as much as I do—I hope you enjoy Glenna's story.

MAP OF RAGHILD

PAUCITY

CHAPTER 1

GLENNA

Gasping, I hold my right arm close to my body to ease the pain from my dislocated shoulder. It hurts like the two burning suns of Uhna, combined with the large sun of Evander.

Exhaustion beyond the physical presses down with unbearable weight. Corruption climbs in my throat. I struggle for air.

This is it. This is how it ends. I thought I had more time to . . .

My knees buckle. I drop into the mud, crying out from the white-hot agony that jabs into my injured shoulder.

Freezing wind tangles my once-dark crimson hair. The white streak swallowed up most of the dark red, leaving a slight hint of the original color. The wind blows long strands across my face, a few getting stuck in the blood seeping from my eyebrow. Cold cuts through my torn and bloody cloak. A shiver racks my body.

Get up! Get up!

But I can't muster the energy.

Battle and fire rage around me. The smell of smoke burns my lungs, mixed with scents of blood and dirt.

I am outnumbered.

Get up! Get up! Move! But I can't.

A malicious and victorious laughter echoes in my mind.

The dark and imposing fortress crashes behind me with an ear-shattering boom.

Screams of pain, anger, and desperation add to the cacophony of chaos. Debris shower around me, burying many where they stand. But it doesn't stop the Turned. They swarm like sandroaches that flock to the carcasses of the fallen.

With my left hand, I dig into the ground, trying to draw strength from the soil, but my reward is an annoying and insistent buzzing that peppers my mind from hundreds of thousands of points originating deep below the surface.

I sway, trying to block that nagging buzzing.

I am so tired.

"Glenna!" Ragnald roars. "Watch out!"

CHAPTER 2

FEW WEEKS EARLIER—GLENNA

Leaning a hand on the wall of the beaten green shuttlecraft, I hesitate to step down from its landing platform. I don't want to be here on Raghild, but I am out of options.

Trying to hide my disappointment, I exhale. For a few moments, my breath hangs like a puff of fog in the cold wintery air. I look around with curiosity.

The sky, what's visible beyond all the dark clouds, seems unhealthy. It appears pale, gray-hued, and hostile. I might be biased being a healer on the mages' planet, but even the weak yellowish sun hides behind the dark gray clouds as if it's too ashamed to show anything cheerful in this gray and disheartening world. It doesn't help that the trees look dead without their leaves to hide their white-grayish bark. Even the falling grayish snow seems to add to the desolate atmosphere that blankets this place.

The distant sound of thunder breaks into the hustling and bustling city noise, unnoticed by its citizens. Men and women attend to their business, trampling the dirt road into a muddy lane. They scurry with their heads down, holding their worn cloaks close to their bodies. Their gazes never stay long on the shuttlecraft that clicks and clangs cooling down, or on me—a newcomer. Maybe they're accustomed to seeing a lot of crimson-haired women with matching eyes.

Shouts from the port to the far right ring out in alien languages, too muffled for my genetic translator to pick it out. Burly men unload large metal crates of wares from wooden ships that rock from side to side on the choppy water of the dark sea. Already, high waves crash into all the ships lined up at the dock as a coming storm builds.

On my left, rickety buildings line roads that branch into all directions. There is something precarious in the way the houses look—old and ready to collapse, yet somehow still standing.

I pull out a pair of glasses I "borrowed" from Ragnald and place them on my nose. The orange-tinted lenses make my eyes water for a second, then the crisscrossing layers of Fla'mma and T'erra elemental magic covering every inch of the structures almost blind me with their brightness.

Of course it's magic that holds up all the houses, but it does not quite prevent them from falling apart, as missing roof tiles and broken windows can attest. The mages are famous for infusing their magic with technology, with architecture, and even with weapons—though they have not done the latter since the Magical Cleanse War ended with them being banned from the Pax Septum Coalition and stripped of their membership. That is, until the ma'ha and ruler of Uhna—where I lived and worked as a palace healer—invited a mage, Ragnald, to reestablish diplomatic channels. That didn't turn out well.

I put the glasses into the pocket of the dark gray traveling cloak Ragnald insisted I wear to blend in. Whenever I pushed its too-warm hood off my hair, he kept pulling it back on, explaining that winter can get harsh at a moment's notice.

"It's not that cold," I mutter.

A frigid blast of wind pricks the skin on my face and hands while also assaulting my nose with scents of brine and trash.

Gagging, I wrinkle my nose. How can anyone live in this horrid place? Raghild is so bleak. I know my best friend, Lilla, would agree with me.

A tall man coalesces out of dark smoke next to me.

"But Lilla is not here," he says, crossing his arms over a white shirt tucked into black pants and boots that mud cannot touch. "You abandoned your so-called best friend when she needed you the most. You abandoned so many, including me."

I stare at the visage of a man who resembles my beloved Nic with his athletic build, dark hair, and handsome face. I know Nic is dead. I couldn't heal him and watched him die in my arms.

"I did not abandon you. I don't know who you are, but you are not my Nic."

"Oh, but you know who, or *what* I am," the man says, smiling, but no warmth reaches his dark brown eyes.

Covering my mouth, I realize that the corruption—embedded in me by the Archgod of Chaos and Destruction back on Uhna during our fight with Him—became so powerful that it can now manifest in the guise of my Nic.

Gods! I thought I had more time to deal with the corruption.

"You are running out of time," Corruption Nic says in a singsong voice.

"Leave me." I concentrate on achieving just that. The corruption dissipates with a theatrical puff of smoke. I have a feeling it's not gone.

Ragnald pokes his head out. "I heard you talking. Is everything okay?"

I manage a nod, but Ragnald is too busy taking in our surroundings with a proud smile on his lips. He let his long silver hair down, reaching almost to his elbows. His black mage cloak—with the six light elements: A'qua for water, Fla'mma for fire, A'ris for air, A'nima for all living things, T'erra for soil, and Lume for light and energy embroidered on its lapel—gapes open. I have no business admiring how his shirt stretches over his well-shaped chest, or how his thigh muscles push against the material of his pants. He is a mage, and thus an archnemesis of healers such as me. But I cannot stop my gaze from roaming his face with sharp cheekbones and a straight nose, snagging on kissable—I mean lush—lips.

Ragnald turns to me, and we lock eyes. The smile disappears from his face as his storm gray eyes darken.

I hold my breath in anticipation.

He leans closer to me and opens his mouth to say something.

Panicking, I turn my head away, breaking the moment.

There cannot be any attraction between us, no matter how handsome he is. It's best to stifle that idea before it can take root.

Ragnald clears his throat and steps off the spaceship's ramp. Then he turns to me and extends his hand. "Welcome to Raghild, my beautiful world and the home of the Academia of Mages."

I accept his hand. It envelops mine as I jump down, but he doesn't release me just yet. Warmth spreads from his rough skin, heating mine. My fingers curl around his as if I've always known his touch.

What am I doing? Anyone who gets close to me dies.

I pull my hand back and hide it in my cloak's pocket. "Aren't you full of yourself, your Academia, and your desolate world."

Ragnald's expression shuts down.

I got the intended result; then why do I feel guilty for being so mean to him? I don't have any feelings for him.

"You are such a pretty liar," Corruption Nic whispers in my mind. "Of course you felt that spark of connection with the old mage."

He is not old! He's two hundred and forty—that's the equivalent of a thirty-year old healer, seven years older than I am. Mages tend to age a lot slower than healers. No one knows why.

I take a step away from Ragnald and sink ankle deep in the muck.

"That's where you belong," Corruption Nic says, laughing in my mind, "in the mud. You get it?"

I shake the mud off my boots, ignoring a strange buzzing that makes my head hurt.

The sooner I get to the Academia of Mages, the sooner I can rid myself of the corruption, and the pesky mage with a fetching smile.

CHAPTER 3

"Give me a few minutes to settle our fare," Ragnald says, then retreats inside the shuttle.

Carefully, I make my way around the ship, avoiding the puddles that cover the road. I miss my best friend, Lilla, an ex-princess-turned-rebel-turned-sybil. We always confided in each other, even after she became the right hand to the Archgoddess of the Eternal Light and Order, one of the two ruling archgods in the Seven Galaxies.

"I doubt you miss her," Corruption Nic says as it appears by my side. "She lied to you. Not to mention, you never approved of violence."

Why is the corruption back so soon?

"It was a matter of miscommunication. She was worried about what I would think about her, is all."

I head toward a cluster of houses, letting my feet carry me.

Corruption Nic snorts. "No wonder she worried—you are very critical for a healer. You're supposed to have boundless compassion and empathy."

"I am not judgmental or perfect."

Thanks to the corruption, I can't be by my best friend's side when she needs me to assist her in the Era War.

Whenever the Balance shifts between the ruling archgods, an Era War breaks out in the Seven Galaxies. It's the Omnipower's way to restore Balance. Even if it means cultures and worlds disappear as collateral damage.

Now I'm stuck here, seeking help from the charlatans.

"Oh, poor you! I'm sure you also think you didn't deserve me, gifted to you by the Dark Lord of Destruction."

"This corruption DLD 'bestowed' upon me is not a gift," I correct it, using Lilla's nickname for the archgod that helps take some of the power back from the menacing archgod. I had the misfortune of meeting Him in person in the dungeons of the Crystal Palace, and I do not care to repeat *that* experience.

"You earned His gift by your misguided actions. Aren't you supposed to not harm others?"

It's true; healers are forbidden from harming another being. We can't even wield real weapons—other than a slingshot powered by our A'ris elemental magic—to defend ourselves. I got carried away and did something reckless for the first time in my carefully controlled life. I regret giving in to that impulsiveness but would do it again if I had a chance.

I raise my chin. "It was an innocent mistake. Besides, Ragnald survived, which means there was no harm done."

"I like how you pick and choose what supports your beliefs. Did you know that delusion is another form of lying?" Corruption Nic takes a sniff of the air around me, becoming more substantial, and asks, "Guess what I'm smelling."

Great. *Any* form of lies makes it stronger. I better be careful around it.

Corruption Nic sniggers. "I admire your ability to fool yourself. How can you still think that you are in any way in control over this situation you got yourself into? Is that why you resist me? Don't you want to be the most powerful healer in the Seven Galaxies? Imagine all you could do with that much magic at your fingertips."

I stop for a second and close my eyes as my mind conjures the image of being the strongest healer in the Seven Galaxies. A dream my family harbored generation after generation—to be the most famous healer, as strong as the infamous mages everyone kept talking about.

I never cared for the mages or their self-proclaimed importance.

I open my eyes and resume my trek, shaking off the temptation. If only I could get rid of whatever causes that buzzing in my mind.

Besides, that's not how corruption works. If I ever give in to it, I will become one of the Turned—nightmarish creatures, mindless and pure evil. Nothing but a cruel weapon in the hands of DLD, who uses them to level civilizations, killing anyone and anything in His way. I'd rather die than become one of the Turned.

A child's troubled cry makes my head snap up. I wave the corruption away. I search for the direction of the cry, originating from the nearest alley between two three-story houses.

I pick up my pace and hurry to the end of the alley. I stifle a gasp at the scene that greets me.

Children of all ages, from many worlds, are chained together by the neck; their hands and feet are in shackles. They shuffle down the landing platform of a humongous red spaceship. The children cower under the cold gaze of dozens of large men with scales covering their bald heads, wearing uniforms of black overalls with yellow belts. Many children cry or scream, while others stare into space.

My heart sinks into the mud seeing them, some still toddlers. How can this be happening? Why are these children here?

I watch local men and women bustle past the long lines of children—as many as two hundred—and not feel anything for them, not even pity. They disregard the sights and sounds as if those children are invisible.

When an old woman nears me, I stop her with a hand on her arm.

"Why are those children in chains?" I ask and point at the lines. "Why isn't anyone doing something about this?" This must be a crime! I have never seen anything like this. Even the charlatans, I mean mages, wouldn't sanction something like this, would they?

The elderly woman blinks at me, as if just noticing me now, then jerks her arm out of my grasp. "Bah! What is wrong with you? Are you so stupid to question the mages out in the open like this? Risking my life?! Or are you just a fool who wants to die?"

"I—"

The woman huffs, then hunkers down deeper into her cloak and shuffles away, mumbling to herself as she looks around nervously.

I swipe the hood off my head. "That's not the answer I was looking for."

The skin on my left forearm itches, and I scratch the teardrop-shaped bump that protrudes from among older smooth and fibrous scars.

I turn back toward the lines of children, but even I am not such a reckless "fool" to attempt a rescue on my own, facing so many guards equipped with laser rifles.

9

With a muffled curse, I head back to Ragnald. The mage better know what to do.

After a few turns, I stumble to a halt in the tight alley.

Four masked men block my way with sharp daggers pointed at me.

CHAPTER 4

RAGNALD

Ragnald eyes the man who piloted the shuttlecraft to Raghild and forces himself to be patient. His hands itch with the beginning of his Fla'mma magic. He stifles the familiar impulse that made him, as a young mage, do many regrettable things, but he learned to have more control over his magic.

"We agreed on the fee before we left," Ragnald says in a cool voice. He curls his fingers into his palm to prevent the heat leaking and glowers at the pilot.

The short man, wearing black overalls, rubs his pointed chin with long strands of hair sticking out from various moles on his pale orange-hued skin and looks away from Ragnald's cold gaze. "Those credits were, uh, for *one* passenger."

The pilot is not wrong. Ragnald didn't put Glenna's name on the passenger list when he booked the trip—he wasn't sure what the situation would be on Raghild, since he didn't leave on good terms a year ago. That's why he took precautions. Now it's time to pay.

Ragnald counts out the requested amount of hexagon credits then hands them to the man. "Fine, take it."

The pilot shoves the payment into one of his pockets and turns away from Ragnald. "Pleasure piloting you and—"

"Just me," Ragnald cuts in and the pilot shrugs.

A bang sounds at the side of the spacecraft and the pilot jumps.

"Ragnald, my mage," a man says. "Is that you in that ship?"

"Deliver our bags to The Inn and you can leave," Ragnald says as he heads to the back of the ship and steps off, bypassing the landing platform. He softens his landing by using his T'erra magic.

"I see you haven't changed a bit since you left," a tall and wiry man says, laughing. "You always were a showoff."

Ragnald grins at the young man who used to be a follower, the lowest rank of mages, at the Academia a long time ago. "Tag! What are you doing here? I thought you left when I did."

Tag looks away. "No, my mage. I couldn't. You know how it is, those credits the thieves' guild pay—"

"Will kill you one day," Ragnald interrupts him, but Tag just lifts a shoulder and runs a hand through the long black hair that covers half of his red-hued head.

Tag leans close to Ragnald. "You're not supposed to be here. The mage elders are watching every new arrival. Any one of us who sees anything suspicious is supposed to report it." Tag raises a hand and adds, "But I won't report you, my mage. You saved me many times during my years when I ran away, never being harsh to me. I will never forget and will return all those favors."

Ragnald crosses his arms. "I've told you before, Tag, you don't owe me anything."

"I do, and don't try to convince me otherwise. But that's not why I'm here. I came to tell you that the ban is back, and—"

Ragnald frowns. "Are you serious? Why didn't Mage Leader Alaisdair do something about it? It was he who eliminated the ban fifty years ago." A ban that forbade all healers on Raghild. He cannot let Glenna learn about this or she would have a fit. Thanks to the corruption, her temper and actions are unpredictable. Though he cannot deny how exquisite she looks when her dark red eyes flash with ire and a flush of fury brightens her cheeks.

"There is so much more to tell you," Tag says, and glances around. "I can't stay any longer. There are spies everywhere. I'll find you later. Watch your back, my mage. No one is safe." He darts away, disappearing in seconds.

Ragnald trusts the young man not to betray his presence to the mage elders. He wonders what made them so cautious to bring back the ban. What more could be happening? Was it a mistake to come back to Raghild?

He shakes his head, dismissing the annoying questions.

The forty mage elders and the mage leader, who rule the Academia, have always been hungry for knowledge and power. But he learned how to navigate the dangerous politics, until he made a misstep.

All he needs is a bit of time to find his footing, come up with a plan, and then he can help Glenna.

Where is she anyway? I asked her to stay put, didn't I?

Ragnald scans the ground for clues, finding Glenna's bootprints in the mud, heading away from the spaceship. He follows them to a nearby alley.

He almost collides with a group of masked thieves—Raghild is plagued by many of them, all part of guilds and eager to make a living under the forgiving eye of the mage elders.

Behind the group of men, he finds Glenna glowering.

"What is the meaning of this?" Ragnald asks and shows the embroidered lapel of his mage cloak to the thieves.

The thieves note the mage symbol and scurry in the other direction. At least that didn't change since he left Raghild. Mages still trump thieves.

"Are you okay?"

"Never mind that, mage. I have something to show you."

Without waiting for his answer, Glenna grabs his arm and pulls him after her.

CHAPTER 5

VENERATOR MAGE

The Venerator Mage curses as he sprints across the street, away from the group of thieves and ducks into an alley with dirty walls. He was about to confront the red-haired woman, when those thieves turned into cowards and almost ran over him thanks to Ragnald flashing his mage symbol at them.

I should have never sent those incompetent thugs to do my bidding!

There was something familiar about that woman. Then he felt that tingle of magical power that made the hair on his arms stand up. A feeling he hadn't sensed for a hundred years at least. He thought he would never find it again. He never gave up, kept searching for it, but with each passing year he was less hopeful of ever getting it back.

Once close to her, he confirmed both his suspicions—she is a relative of someone he'd known, and indeed, she possesses what once belonged to him.

"Never ask someone else to do what you can do better," he says and hits the wall with his fist covered in Fla'mma magic to protect his bones. Plaster shatters from the impact and showers over his black boots.

I was so close!

He could have taken it back from her, and no one would have been the wiser.

But no, that sniveling follower Ragnald had to show up. Who, by the way, isn't supposed to be here on Raghild, but then again, that mage never did what he was supposed to do.

Isn't that interesting?

Even more interesting is that Ragnald is with that red-haired woman.

But why? Does he want the same thing I want?

The Venerator raises his fist to hit the wall again but stops when a thought occurs to him.

If Ragnald knew about it, he would have taken it for himself.

Which means the Venerator still has time to get it back.

When he entered the godsforsaken City of Paucity this cold morning, he had no real purpose other than spending another day wasting his talents by doing the same old petty things the mage elders forced him to do—harassing the citizens of Raghild to show off the mages' power and to ensure everyone knew where they belonged. That didn't mean preventing crime per se. It was more like reminding everyone that the mages ruled Raghild above all else.

But with the presence of Ragnald and that red-haired woman, the Venerator has a new purpose—he will find a way to use them to his benefit and regain what was supposed to be his in the first place.

CHAPTER 6

GLENNA

Ragnald glares at me as he pulls the hood of my gray cloak over my head. "What were you doing so far away from the shuttlecraft?"

"Nothing," I say, and poke him in the chest. "Tell me about the children."

Ragnald frowns. "What are you talking about?"

I grab his strong forearm and drag him to the mouth of the alley. Then I point at the line of shackled children being unloaded from the space vessel. "What kind of crime is happening here?!"

Ragnald sighs. "That's nothing to concern yourself with."

My anger rises. Corruption Nic laughs with pleasure in my head.

"Explain this right now, *mage*, or I will march over there and—"

"All right" Ragnald says and puts a hand on my shoulder, channeling his Fla'mma magic to counteract the corruption brewing in me. The pressure from the corruption relents a bit. "I will explain it to you, but not here."

He leads me away from the children, toward a dilapidated four-story building with a sign reading The Drinks and Damages Inn.

"I'm listening, *mage*."

"What you saw are children heading to the Academia of Mages to—"

"They are handcuffed!"

"—to become followers and work their way through the ranks of mages as part of the family."

I rub my temple. "What kind of *family* treats children like this?" I've never had a humming headache like this one.

"I was one of those children when my parents sold me. The mages gave me a home and I am grateful for that. Many of those children are not wanted thanks to possessing magic their world fears or does not respect. If not

16

for the Academia's welcoming arms, these children might be killed. But mages, like my Mentor, made sure to prevent that by offering rewards to anyone who brings magically inclined children to us. He pays for the children and their passage to Raghild. It's very generous and safer this way."

I gape at Ragnald. "Of course the mages call this arrangement generous and safe."

Corruption Nic laughs in my head. "Your stubbornness to see reason is delicious. You're blinded to reality and want to change it to fit your misguided views of how the world should work. But not everyone operates the way you do, my little healer."

"It's propaganda," I say both to it and to Ragnald. "The mages justify their actions by hiding behind so-called good intentions. It does not make how they treat these poor children right."

All the Academia cares about is how much magic these children have, and what use they will be to the mages. That's why the charlatans never cared for healers—our magic is too weak for them and makes us more susceptible to corruption. We also tend to overuse our magic when we are in the midst of saving someone's life without caring for our own.

Ragnald raises an eyebrow. "I didn't realize you were an expert at all things mage-related."

In response, I shrug his hand off my shoulder.

Ragnald purses his lips and lets his hand drop.

Corruption Nic hoots in laughter. "I marvel at your ability to offend that poor mage. Or is this a charade to push him away from you?"

It's not a charade. Healers and mages don't mix.

Corruption Nic claps. "Oh, delusions galore!"

Taking a deep breath, I try not to get riled up. There is no point making the corruption stronger than it already is.

We cross the trampled, muddy street. Across from us another group of thieves pickpockets the pedestrians.

"Why did those thugs run away when they saw your mage emblem?" My gaze tracks the thieves roaming the street across from us.

Ragnald runs his fingers over the embroidered circle. "Because we rule Raghild, though we don't use titles such as ma'ha or king to preserve order."

My jaw drops. "There is crime everywhere, and you call this order?"

At The Drinks and Damages Inn, Ragnald waits for the short shuttlecraft pilot to run up to us, holding our bags. He takes them, then turns to me. "There is no killing on Raghild or any other serious lawbreaking. The thieves know what boundaries they cannot cross when it involves a mage. I'd say that's order, more than any other world can offer."

I reach for my small bag, but Ragnald refuses to release it. With a huff, I put all my weight behind pulling at its strap until he lets it go.

With a sigh, he opens the door. "After you."

Raising my chin, I enter.

Overbearing warmth hits me in the face from a large fireplace that takes up the back of the main room.

I raise my hand to push my hood off, but Ragnald grabs my fingers. "Leave that on. I'll talk to the innkeeper and reserve two rooms. Don't go anywhere. Don't talk to anyone. Don't trust anyone."

Without waiting for my answer, Ragnald cuts through the crowd that parts in front of him.

I glare after him. "You know, 'please' and 'thank you' go a long way."

I glance around.

Every rickety wooden table in the rectangular room is occupied by more people than should fit around them. The citizens of Raghild hold their wooden mugs with a forlorn look, gazing into their purple, foamy drinks as if searching for life-altering answers.

"What a delightful crowd," Corruption Nic says, appearing next to me. "I just love the aromas of guilt, greed, and shame."

I hate to admit it, but the corruption might be more observant than I thought.

Obnoxious laughter rings out from near the fireplace.

Men, wearing similar outfits as those guards with the shackled children, bang together their big metal mugs, sloshing foam to the hardwood floor.

How dare they celebrate hurting children for credits?

Heat burns my cheeks as I curl my fingers into my palms, fighting the urge to do something about them.

"Go ahead," Corruption Nic says, nodding toward the men. "You could poison their drinks or spike their hearts to scare them. Teach them a lesson."

It is tempting, so tempting.

Closing my eyes, I take a few deep breaths—following the same advice I gave multiple times to Lilla whenever she dealt with claustrophobia-induced panic attacks. It does not seem an adequate means to handle my anger over the injustice. My temper recedes, but the buzzing headache intensifies.

With a final exhale, I turn my back on the jovial men and head toward the unsound-looking staircase by a swinging door that must lead to the galley.

Young and gaunt-looking servants rush into and out of the kitchen, carrying trays laden too heavy for their small stature.

On my right, Ragnald engages in a heated conversation with an oversized man, the innkeeper.

A yelp of pain sounds, coming from the kitchen.

I drop my bag and push the swinging door open without hesitation.

Corruption Nic sniggers. "Oh, this is going to be good. I love watching you meddle."

I ignore it and enter.

Everyone stops to stare at me as I wade through the kitchen overflowing with cooking pots that rattle their tops from the heat. The fifty servants hesitate, standing around wooden counters, amid preparing, washing, or plating food.

I search until I find my patient in the back by a wooden chopping block.

Tantalizing scents of stews and soups waft to my nose as I make my way to a small boy who tries to wrap his bleeding hand in a dirty dishrag.

Urgent whispers, too quiet for me to understand, strike up behind me as I take the rag and reach for the hand of the servant boy.

His skeptical brown eyes go wide under unwashed strands of black hair. The boy, who cannot be older than ten, tries to hide his injured hand.

It pains me to see him like that, but as my adoptive father, Great Healer Robley, used to say, *Everyone deserves healing*—a motto I agree with.

"Show me, please," I say in a gentle voice. "I won't hurt you. I promise."

Corruption Nic shakes his head. "You healers always promise no pain, but it's such a lie. I didn't realize you were a walking cliché."

My smile wobbles at its jab, but I nod at the boy, waiting to see what he'll do.

The boy looks around. No one says a word to help him or discourage him. He decides to show me his hand.

"It's a deep cut," I say to him with a smile meant to be reassuring, "but there is nothing to worry about." I hold his hand in mine and channel a small amount of my A'ris magic into the cut, helping his body's natural healing to stop the bleeding and close the wound.

I let go of his now healed hand. "There, that should do it."

All the servants rush toward the boy, chattering in all kinds of languages as they try to get a closer look. I leave the kitchen smiling, letting the door swing shut behind me.

When I look up, I find the innkeeper sulking down on me.

"Now you'll get what you deserve," Corruption Nic says with excitement in its voice.

"Did you come from my kitchen?" the innkeeper asks, reaching for my arm.

"No, uh . . ."

"Lie," Corruption Nic says with glee.

Ragnald lunges between the innkeeper and me, shoving the large man's hand aside. "She's with me. Let her be."

The innkeeper backs away. "Yes, uh, mage sir."

Corruption Nic leans close to me. "Saved by a mage. How this must sting!"

I didn't need Ragnald's help. I could have handled it myself.

Corruption Nic bursts into a laugh. "If you say so, my little liar."

"Right this way, mage sir," the innkeeper says. "Allow me to show you to your—"

Ragnald picks up my bag, hoisting it next to his. "Don't bother. We can find our rooms without your guidance."

The innkeeper wrings his hands in his stained apron, then turns on his heels and ambles away.

"Ragnald, I—"

The mage points toward the stairway. "Our rooms are on the next level."

I snap my mouth closed and climb the rickety stairs to the second floor.

Ragnald strides down the corridor with windows on one side and closed wooden doors on the other. Conversations or muted shouts drift through the thin and dingy walls. Scents of old food, soap, and dirt permeate the stale but cold air.

"What kind of name is 'Drinks and Damages' anyway?" I ask, hoping to break the awkward silence.

Ragnald stops in front of an open door leading to a modest-size room with a bed, table, and chair grouped near a tall window. "That name started out as a joke—if you come here and drink too much, you'll do some damage to your credits. But it became too cumbersome and now everyone just calls it The Inn, since it's the only one in the City of Paucity." He holds out my bag to me.

I accept it. "Oh, I see. Listen, I didn't mean to cause any trouble."

Corruption Nic snorts, leaning on the wall by the doorway. "Yes, you did."

Ragnald raises an eyebrow.

I look away from him for a second to gather some courage. "I'm not going to apologize for healing someone who needed my help—"

Ragnald grabs my upper arm. "You will not heal anyone anymore. You will not leave your room. Not without my permission. Do you understand?"

Not another order!

Raising my chin, I enter my room, turn to look him in the eye, and slam the door in the mage's face.

CHAPTER 7

An unrelenting series of knocks wakes me.

I blink my eyes open and that persistent headache jabs into my mind. I grimace and try to remember where I am. Oh, right. I'm on the charlatan's home world, Raghild.

Judging by the almost pitch dark in the room, it's still the middle of the night.

I yawn and stretch.

Maybe I imagined the knocking. I close my eyes, drifting back to sleep.

Another set of knock sounds.

I get out of bed. "Ragnald? Is that you?" Though what the mage would want at this hour is beyond me.

I open the door to a crack and peek out.

The servant boy I healed stands in front of me. "I need you, uh, to, uh, come. Quick!"

Without waiting for an answer, he dashes to the end of the corridor.

Corruption Nic yawns in my mind. "Is it time for you to make more trouble?"

"He must need help."

When the boy realizes I am not behind him, he turns around and points to his now healed hand, then gestures toward the stairs to follow him.

"Ah! Someone needs healing." I hold up a finger. Then I go back into the room, get dressed, and kick my discarded clothes on the floor out of the way, searching for my gray cloak and a belt containing my herbs and potions. When I find them, I put them on and leave my room, hurrying to him.

He rushes down the stairs, then out the back door, heading to a spacious barn behind The Inn.

When we enter, I stop and stare.

Instead of livestock, I find hundreds of children huddled or sleeping on every available surface—on the hay-covered ground, in the empty stalls, on top of hay bales, even in the hayloft.

The boy heads to the back. I follow, making sure not to step on anyone. Sleepy gazes of children blink up at me, but many go back to sleep, while others look scared at the sight of me.

The boy squats by a sobbing girl, who muffles her cries with an arm. The other arm has something sticking out of it. As I lean closer, I realize it's a bloody bone shard.

Oh, my gods!

I drop on my knees by her, gathering a thick thread of A'ris to me and focusing on the task ahead. This will take a lot of magic to heal—breaks are always difficult.

After an hour, I sit back on my heels and wipe the sweat off my forehead. The little girl, pale and shaking, seems to be doing better now that the break is taken care of.

Someone taps on my shoulder. I look back.

A teenage girl stands behind me. "Who are you?" she asks in a broken Common Seven language. "Are you a mage?"

All the kids around us gasp out of fear.

An older girl scoffs. "Leah'na, you can't ask that!"

"I am not a mage," I say with a placating smile. "I am a healer."

Corruption Nic sits next to a sleeping boy. "An infected healer, to be more precise."

Leah'na turns to the others. "See? I told you she wasn't a mage. I saw her help Jon'ah. She didn't hurt him or cut his hand off so he could go back to work."

I blink. "Are you telling me that the mages' way of treating injuries is to hurt the patient or cause more harm?"

Leah'na nods. "They cut off the limb that's broken," she says, counting it off her fingers, one of them missing half a digit. "They also cut off fingers if they bleed. When one of us gets sick, the mages often resort to killing to prevent the spread of disease among the others."

These charlatans are even worse than I thought!

I shake my head. "Everyone deserves healing. No matter who they are, what they are, or where they rank in a society." The mages deserve a taste of their own medicine, but I am under my healer oath and won't be able to teach them *that* lesson.

Corruption Nic tilts its head. "You must admit, it's efficient though."

No, it is not!

"Why haven't you run away?" I ask, looking at the children who stare back.

Leah'na shrugs a shoulder. "Many died trying. There is nowhere to go where the mages won't find us. And when they do, they often kill that child to scare the rest of us. Right. Reh'ba?"

The older girl nods. "When we didn't get selected at the Academia, the mages kicked us out. Many perished from starvation on the way back to the city. Others ended up on the street, homeless or as slaves to the Haulers. We made it here. We are the lucky ones."

Corruption Nic smiles. "I like her; she knows her place."

"Lucky? How can you say that?" I ask.

Reh'ba hugs Leah'na's shoulders. "Working at The Inn is not so bad as working at some other places. We have plenty of food, and a shelter against the weather. The job is not that hard if you are careful. Besides, I met Leah'na here, and once we earn enough credits, we will buy fare off Raghild to somewhere . . ."

Leah'na kisses Reh'ba's cheek. "Somewhere where there are no mages."

A couple of children line up in front of me, one of them sporting an eye swollen from infection.

I wave at the closer child and gather my A'ris magic to me.

"How long have you been here, Leah'na?" I ask while I remove the infection from the eye.

Leah'na looks at Reh'ba. "I arrived here when I was four, so that makes it fourteen years for me, and you were two, so that would make it twenty."

Reh'ba smiles. "Twenty-one. I had my birthday yesterday, but we were too tired to celebrate."

Leah'na ducks her head.

Next in line is a boy, pointing at his inflamed cheek—an infected tooth. I channel my A'ris magic into his cheek, trying to hide my astonishment at Reh'ba's words. They have been here for a long time, and they still haven't earned enough credits to leave.

Then a teen boy limps toward me, his left foot enlarged.

My A'ris magic finds the source of the swelling—a thorn stuck between two of his toes.

Once done, I wipe my hands on my cloak. "All done."

"What about them?" Leah'na points behind her at an even longer line of children waiting.

I twist my hair into a knot and gesture toward the closest child. "Who's next?"

CHAPTER 8

Stifling a yawn, I push at the back door of The Inn. It's stuck. Again. Just like that throbbing headache that's been bothering me ever since I set foot on Raghild. No matter how many dried herbs I chew in hopes of curing it, it won't budge, as if it's lodged in my mind.

I spent the past five nights healing children in servitude to the cruel innkeeper. He inflicted many wounds on them or let their infections fester.

Using my shoulder, I put more pressure on the door.

It swings open, crashing into the wooden stairway with a loud bang.

Corruption Nic appears, bending over his knees and laughing.

Rolling my eyes, I slip inside. I tiptoe toward the stairs, but a tall and wide-shouldered man I've seen lingering around the main room of The Inn steps in front of me. He winks and turns his back, blocking my way.

I open my mouth to argue with him when I hear the innkeeper's voice.

"What are you doing slamming my door?" the innkeeper asks. For a second I worry he is asking me, but then I realize he can't see me.

The tall man puts his hand in the pocket of his brown cloak. "Why do you care?"

"How dare you . . ." the innkeeper's voice trails off when the tall man pulls out a wooden pipe and taps it on his palm.

"I figured it's best not to smoke inside, lest your inn would burn down," the tall man says.

"Bah! You figured," the innkeeper grumbles. Then I hear receding footsteps.

The tall man puts his pipe away and turns to me. "I'm Angus the Wanderer. Swift travels and much happiness upon reaching your destination."

I gape at the handsome man with long dark brown braids framing a rectangular and tanned face. Kind brown eyes glint above a crooked nose and wide mouth.

Corruption Nic points at Angus. "You're supposed to say the greeting back to him."

"Uh, yes! Swift, uh, travels to you as well. And, um, thank you, for the, uh, rescue."

Angus smiles. "It was my pleasure to help a fellow traveler. What were you doing outside?"

Ragnald's warning about not talking and not trusting others flashes in my mind.

Corruption Nic grins. "To lie or not to lie. What will she do?"

Lying would mean following Ragnald's order and avoiding more trouble. However, lying also means giving strength to the corruption. It's already too strong for my liking.

With a deep exhale I say, "I was out healing the children."

I glance at Angus, getting ready to run by him in case he tries to shout for the innkeeper.

To my surprise, Angus smiles wider. "Good on you, uh, I didn't catch your name."

"Oh! It's Glenna."

Angus nods. "Good on you for helping them, Glenna. I am no Weaver of Life, but even I could see their suffering from various illnesses."

Weaver of Life? What a curious term for healers. I like it!

"Don't forget broken bones and parasites. There are always more children each day who need help. I just hope . . ." my voice trails off as my vision blurs and I waver on my feet.

Angus catches me by my shoulder. "There, there." He leads me to the stairs, and we sit down.

I raise a hand. "One moment, please." Then I lean forward between my knees, fighting the urge to faint. Once the dizziness passes, I straighten back.

Angus pats my back. "Are you okay, lass?"

Corruption Nic puts his elbow on the stairway's banister. "She is overusing her magic."

I glare at the corruption. Angus follows my gaze, frowning.

"It's nothing, just a bit of exhaustion," I say, glad that Angus can't see or hear the corruption.

"That would do it, lass."

"What are you doing up at this hour?"

Angus looks away. "Couldn't sleep."

I study his face, detecting dark circles under his eyes. "You're either in physical pain or in emotional pain."

Angus rubs his chest and moisture wells in the corners of his eyes that he wipes away surreptitiously.

Emotional pain it is.

I put a hand on his arm. "I didn't mean to disturb you in your grief."

Angus nods. "You didn't, lass. It's my sister. She was taken from us a year ago, but there are days that this pain strikes me anew. Like tonight, when the moon is clear. It was her favorite night of winter. She loved watching the moon, anticipating the snow to come."

"She must have been a wonderful person."

Angus nods. "She was the kindest lass you could have ever met."

"Glenna?" I hear Ragnald's voice from above us.

Angus gets to his feet. "It's best I go. I bid you good morning and a bright day."

I get to my feet. "Same to you, Angus Wanderer."

Angus strides away just as Ragnald's footsteps come closer.

"You are up early," Ragnald says, looking well rested. "I knocked on your door, but you didn't answer. I should have known you were heading for breakfast. Raghild's fresh air has that effect on many guests—brings out the appetite."

Corruption Nic bursts into laughter. "Talk about delusional!"

"Yes, that must be it." It's not a lie, just a bit of stretching the truth.

Corruption Nic inhales. "But it still counts as one."

I rub at the teardrop-shaped scar on my left arm, trying to stay calm. Who is so good that they never tell even a little bit of a white lie?

Corruption Nic points at me. "Evidently not you. Your loss, my gain."

Ragnald puts a hand under my elbow and leads me to a worn but clean table. I try to ignore how nice it feels to have him touch me.

In the soft sunlight of the morning, the main room of The Inn looks dark and outdated. Many tables are already taken, with more people entering, bringing with them the cold city air full of smells of garbage and grime, mixing with the aromas of baked pastries and soups.

The wooden chair creaks under my weight and tilts to the left when I settle in. I worry it will buckle under me, but it stays upright.

My gaze tracks the servants, some of them I just healed, others I couldn't get to due to the hours of the night running out. I wonder how much longer before I drain all my magical reserves. Before the corruption gets too strong.

Ragnald, as if sensing my thoughts, puts his hand on my shoulder and channels the morning dose of his Fla'mma magic. For a few minutes I pretend I don't enjoy his touch, then it's over too soon.

Corruption Nic's visage flickers, but it stays otherwise unaffected. It leans so close to me that I can make out the pores in its face, including the small scar my beloved Nic had on his cheekbone from a deep cut while shaving. "You are brimming with so much magical potential," it says. "You could unlock your true self."

I rub my tired eyes.

I heard about my magical potential all my life—first from my great-grandfather, then my grandfather and my father, all the way to my adoptive father, Great Healer Robley. They kept telling me that I was holding myself back from achieving the height of my magical healing career. I never believed them or cared much about it. But I cannot help but find it strange how the corruption uses that tidbit from my past against me. At least I have no doubt what would happen if I were to give in to it—I would become Turned. No, thank you.

"Go away," I mutter and Corruption Nic dissipates into a puff of smoke.

Ragnald looks up from the wooden tablet with food choices listed on it. "What did you say?"

The innkeeper stops at our table and Ragnald rattles off two orders of the morning special of pastries and egg soup without asking for my input. I don't mind; I am so ravenous I could eat anything just to replenish my magical and physical energy.

"Liar," Corruption Nic purrs in my head. "You do care about not being asked."

When the innkeeper leaves, I ask, "How much longer do we have to stay in this fog-cursed, I mean, Raghild?" I've had enough. I'm ready to go to the Academia to get rid of the corruption before it gets too powerful and overtakes me.

Ragnald clasps his hands on the scratched tabletop. "I've explained this before, but I will say it again—we leave when I say we leave."

Arrogant mage! I push the hood of my cloak off my head. "I am tired of waiting."

Ragnald jumps to his feet and pulls the hood back over my head. "Stop that! Just trust me a bit longer."

"You're asking a *healer* to trust a *mage*? Are you jesting?" All those unwarranted killings the mages committed against the healer community in the name of erasing any possibility of Turned left us with trust issues and tragic scars on our families, including mine.

"This animosity between you and that mage is such a boost for me," Corruption Nic says in my mind.

Anger rises in me. I push back my chair and get to my feet.

Ragnald reaches over and clasps my fisted hand. I ignore the tingling sensation where his hand covers mine and try to pull away. He won't let go.

"Glenna, please sit down."

I glance around the room. Many patrons stare at us. Corruption Nic laughs in my head, enjoying my embarrassment.

Sighing, I obey.

Ragnald lets go of my hand. "We can't just go to the Academia arbitrarily. It's more complicated than that. There are procedures we must follow."

"Leave it to the mages to complicate something as simple as visiting them."

Leah'na brings our food without looking at me. I nod at her and take my steaming wooden bowl. Then I dig in with gusto, even lifting the bowl to my mouth, drinking the last ounce of liquid to Ragnald's satisfaction.

A commotion sounds behind me at the entrance of The Inn. Everyone in the main room goes silent.

I put my bowl on the table and careen my neck to peek.

A mountain of a mage stomps inside, wearing a robe covered with long brown and gray fur. Scars pepper his squarish and gray-toned face, framed by long, greasy black hair. His cold gaze takes in the room, hinting at no emotions as he marches to the back, toward the fireplace.

The scarred mage stops at a table that's already taken. Three men out of four scramble away from the table, but the fourth is asleep and does not move. The mage grabs the sleeping man's shoulder and shoves him out of the chair, then takes the now-empty seat, facing the room.

"What an unpleasant man," I whisper, but Ragnald cuts me a glance as if to say, *Be quiet.*

After a long moment, the silence blanketing the main room gives way to chatter, though much more subdued than before. A palpable fear hangs over the patrons, one that Ragnald never brought out of them before. These people must have had a bad experience with that scarred mage.

Ragnald puts his elbow on the table and nods at the closest servant. He shows two fingers, indicating he wants two metal mugs full of a foamy purple drink.

I wrinkle my nose. I am not a fan of the local alcoholic beverage, Pumy, that is made of the stomach contents of ferocious vermin, the size of a small dog, that run free on the streets like k'raats. The locals catch them and thanks to an accident of storing the corpses, they learned that the grains fermenting inside the vermins' stomach is a great alcoholic drink that should not be allowed to go to waste. The purple color is due to the grains changing color from the stomach acid of the creature. Yuck!

Ragnald accepts the mugs and pushes one toward me, spilling purple foam on the tabletop. "That's why we had to wait." He nods toward the other mage.

I glance back. There is already a line of people waiting in front of the menacing-looking mage.

"Do you know him? Can't you just go over to him, get what we need, so we can leave for the Academia?"

Ragnald shakes his head. "I've never met him, though I may have seen him once or twice."

At my incredulous glance, he adds, "There are more than five hundred thousand mages that come and go, live off-world for decades, and visit the Academia for a short time after they graduate from student ranks—followers, disciples, and adherents—to one of the higher ranks—prowler, combat, venerator, and elementalist battle mage—with the highest rank being mage elder. Not to mention, we must have graduated twenty years apart—that mage is pushing three hundred at least."

I shrug, uninterested in the inner workings of the Academia. "I still don't understand why we need him."

"We need him, just like those people, to get a magical passport. That is the identification the Academia accepts from visitors."

"What kind of magical passport?"

"It's a magic stamp on the forehead," Ragnald says, "nothing outrageous. I believe Mage Leader Alaisdair simplified the process a few years ago from getting branded to getting a stamp of magic."

How nice.

Corruption Nic smirks. "Maybe your mage is wrong, and they still brand people."

That would be awful! I can't believe mages did that, but I shouldn't be surprised by now, seeing how callous they are.

I push my chair sideways so I can watch the slow-moving line but can't see much happening. "Then what are we waiting for? Let's petition for one."

Ragnald winces. "It's not that simple."

I frown without taking my eyes off the fraught-looking petitioners. "What do you mean? Or are you worried we won't get one?"

"Pray that my worry won't come true," Ragnald says and takes a big swig of his foamy drink.

"Why?"

Suddenly the big mage slams his fits on the table, making it rattle. The people around him recoil in fear. Then the scarred mage flows to his feet, much faster than a man of his size should, bearing down on the old man in front of him.

The older man tries to back away from the mage, but the crowd behind him prevents any escape route.

Without any warning, the mage engulfs the cowering old man in fire and watches him burn to ashes with delight dancing in his cruel black gaze.

CHAPTER 9

RAGNALD

Ragnald crushes the need to comfort Glenna. Her compassion is too vast to handle watching someone executed on the spot. He, on the other hand, is used to the mages' harsh and swift punishments—the scars on his lower back, inflicted by a A'qua whip, are reminders of his life as a follower. There isn't a mage who has not received a punishment like that, when they started out at the Academia.

The Inn's patrons yell and scream in shock as the innkeeper jogs around trying to calm everyone while the scarred mage stares at the scene he caused.

The smells of ash and charred meat hang heavily in the air and Ragnald waves a hand in front of his nose. "It's best we don't find our passport declined."

Glenna gapes at him, then red patches appear on her cheekbones. "Are you telling me, *mage*, that our success depends on that merciless charlatan?!"

Ragnald grabs her hand before she can jump up. "Don't be so loud, or you'll attract unwanted attention. But yes, we need that, uh, mage."

Nevertheless, Ragnald agrees with her outrage. So much had changed since he had left Raghild.

Glenna mutters under her breath but the noise inside The Inn covers it.

It's a good thing, as anyone could be a spy.

"What are you going to do about this, *mage*?"

Ragnald leans back. "I will do nothing. We will do nothing. I have a plan; all I need is more time." More like he is waiting to come up with a plan, but she does not need to know that.

"I can't wait to get rid of the corruption and you!" Glenna snaps, her dark crimson eyes flashing with ire.

Ragnald ignores her verbal jab. He's heard her say much worse, back on the Pada world. But sometimes he cannot tell whether she says what's in her heart, or what the corruption makes her say to inflict the most pain and chaos possible. He's never met a Turned before, and by gods he won't let her become one.

"As I said, we cannot go to the Academia uninvited," Ragnald says.

"Not even you, *mage*?"

Ragnald doesn't respond to that. He won't tell her that he's not welcome here, after he botched his previous post on Uhna—a last resort to earn redemption in the eyes of the Academia. At least that's what his Mentor promised him, but he failed both his Mentor and the Academia.

Glenna studies him, and he wonders if she can read his mind. "What are you hiding, *mage*?"

Too many secrets.

"Nothing. All I ask is a bit more patience."

Glenna looks away and mutters—a new behavior she started to exhibit after they arrived on Raghild. He notices dark circles under her eyes.

Why is she so tired? Is the corruption hurting her? Is she not getting enough sleep because of it?

Ragnald places a hand on her shoulder, channeling another dose of his Fla'mma magic into her for a few minutes. He tries not to think about how often he must do that for her now.

She is running out of time.

Glenna glares at him. "Why can't we just board a shuttlecraft and fly to the Academia right now?"

"Still uninvited. Being shot out of the sky by Fla'mma magic is a terrible way to die," he jokes, but Glenna does not find his humor funny.

Another bang comes from the scarred mage, screams of fear rise, then fire envelopes a different petitioner, this time an older woman.

Glenna's eyes widen.

Ragnald reaches for her hand, but she avoids his fingers.

She springs to her feet and runs out of The Inn.

CHAPTER 10

GLENNA

"There is nowhere to run," Corruption Nic taunts, appearing beside me and keeping pace as I burst outside. I elbow the mass of people who try to make their way inside The Inn.

"You are trapped," it says.

"Oh, shut it," I mutter, running across the street. Once I am far enough from The Inn, I lean a hand on a house, trying to calm my racing heart. My head pounds with the never-ending headache that got even worse outside.

The smell of burned meat hits my nose and my stomach roils. I throw up my half-digested egg soup next to my boots.

Wiping my mouth, I straighten and spit the bitter taste to the side.

I don't understand how the citizens of Raghild can live like this.

"Oppression comes in many forms," Corruption Nic says, "but the beauty of it is that people who are eyeball deep in it don't even realize how oppressed they are. At this point they are no better than sheep, which in turn makes their own oppression easier. It's a perfect cycle."

More like a malicious cycle.

"Let me be," I mutter, though I should not engage with its mind games. But witnessing another innocent person being burned alive broke something inside me. I didn't become a healer to watch people die. No, not die. Murdered for a fog-cursed magical passport or stamp or whatever it is. As if it's a normal part of life on Raghild.

I cover my face. "I've had enough of mages. I don't know how long I can take this."

I wish I could go back to Uhna, but the Crystal Palace is no more, and

I have no idea where my home is anymore. Gods, I miss Lilla and my friends! She would know what to do.

"Oh, lass, don't despair," Angus says from somewhere nearby.

I remove my hand from my eyes.

Angus holds out a handkerchief for me.

I take it and wipe my eyes. "Swift travels, and uh, much happiness, uh, upon reaching your destination."

Angus bows. "You remembered! Same to you, Weaver of Life."

I blush at the honorable title I don't deserve. I hand him back his handkerchief.

Angus smiles. "It's yours. May it bring you much happiness."

I nod in thanks and put it in the pocket of my cloak. Then I lead Angus away from the puddle of vomit that smells unpleasantly, though he is too polite to mention it.

"Why were you so upset?" Angus asks once we stop at another building. He leans a shoulder on a once ornate-now-worn column that supports its peaked roof.

I explain what happened inside The Inn.

Angus rubs his chin. "I gather you want to go to the Academia of Mages as well?"

I lift a shoulder in answer.

I trust him since he saved my healer hide, but don't want to go into details as to *why* I need the mages' help. On one hand, I cannot bear seeing disappointment in his kind gaze. On the other hand, I wish I could stay longer at The Inn and heal more children, but I worry I don't have long before I become a danger to them as a Turned.

Corruption Nic makes a *tsk, tsk* sound. "You should not be ashamed of your condition."

"It's not like I'm pregnant," I mutter. Physical pain jabs into my heart. Nic and I never had a chance for happiness together.

Angus tilts his head at me.

I clear my throat but have no idea what to say. I'm sure I look like a crazy person.

Corruption Nic snickers. "That's because you are one."

"Is everything all right?" Angus asks. "Did that silver-haired mage threaten you or hurt you?"

What? "Oh! No! Nothing like that. Ragnald would never do that." That mage orders me around, forbids me to use my healing magic, and annoys me, but he would never hurt me—I know that much.

Angus pats my shoulder. "I'm glad. When you ran out of The Inn, as if you were escaping him, I was worried. Are you sure it wasn't the mage you ran from? You can tell me, you know."

"I am sure and thank you."

"As someone who travels a lot, I can understand homesickness better than anyone. Is that the cause of your sadness?"

I sigh. "I do miss my friends."

I wonder what my friends are up to. How is Lilla handling her sybil duties to the Archgoddess of the Eternal Light and Order? Or how she deals with her grumpy father-in-law, the praelor and emperor of the dangerous Teryn Praelium? How far has the Era War progressed while I am derailed here?

Corruption Nic whispers into my ear, "I bet they don't miss *you*."

I try to look away to hide my hurt, but Angus brushes an errant tear off the corner of my eye with the tip of his finger.

"I wish I could say it will get better," he says, "but that would be a lie. If you ever need help, just call my name." With a gentle smile, Angus nods and strides back into The Inn, almost bumping into Ragnald as the mage crosses the street toward me.

"Who was that man?" Ragnald asks when he reaches me.

"Never mind him."

Is that jealousy I detect? Ragnald must know that there can be nothing between a mage and a healer.

He extends a hand toward me. "Come on, let's go back inside."

I step back from him. "Please don't try to convince me to get in line and risk my life to get that so-called passport, because I won't do it."

Corruption Nic laughs. "You are such a coward!"

Maybe I am, or maybe I'm just smart.

"Glenna, you must—"

I grab his hand, and all his attention focuses on me. "Please don't make me. There must be another option."

Ragnald squeezes my hand. Then his gaze snags on something, and he lets it go. "There might be something I can try. Wait here."

I nod and watch him stride down the street toward the port, passing by an old homeless woman. He drops a few credits into her metal mug, then continues his trek.

Snowflakes fall from the dismal sky, whirling on the wind that rolls garbage down the street. I notice the homeless woman's feverish gaze and decide to examine her.

When I reach her, I squat beside her. My hand goes to my belt, but it's empty of my herbs and potions—I used them all up healing the children and hadn't have a chance to replenish them. Not that there is much growing in this barren city.

"What are you doing?" Corruption Nic asks, bending over to study the older woman, then me.

I hand my flask, full of water, to her and channel a tiny bit of A'ris into her so I can make a diagnosis. But she is too far gone with many serious ailments. All I can do is give her a bit of water and not much else.

The homeless woman takes the flask with shaking hands, sparing me a quick grateful nod as she gulps the water.

"Take your time," I say to her in a soft voice.

Corruption Nic shakes its head. "You can't save everyone."

I straighten. "Everyone deserves healing. No matter who they are."

Corruption Nic snorts. "You just prolonged her suffering. She could have been free in a few hours—"

"You mean dead."

Corruption Nic shrugs. "Same difference."

I shouldn't try to reason with it.

"Go away." The corruption turns into smoke, leaving me.

I turn around.

A farmer coming out of a nearby alley, hawking his produce attracts my attention. He stops by me with his barrow, packed full of orange, purple, and green fruits, and some root vegetables.

The farmer with a bald head and long white beard beams at me, showing off missing teeth among his blackened ones. "Radish-apple, fresh picked for the pretty lady."

I laugh at the "pretty lady" and search for a credit in my pocket. When I hand it over, he grabs it out of my fingers and gestures toward the produce. "Pick any one of them, pretty lady."

I peruse the fruits and chose an orange one in the shape of a diamond. I rub it on my sleeve to clean it a bit.

The farmer leans close. "If you want to visit the Academia, me know the safest way for pretty lady. Me not like those greedy Haulers. Me cheap."

Frowning, I bite into the fruit. It has soft flesh with sweet and tart flavors. I chew it, taking my time to come up with an answer. My instincts do not warn against this emaciated farmer in his tattered overalls, but I also don't feel that I can trust him.

"Who are the Haulers?" I ask instead. I take another bite from the fruit.

"Bah! The Haulers are no good, pretty lady. Stay away from them," the farmer says, shaking a crooked finger at me. "They take your credits, they do, and then stab you in the back. All they do is deliver young ones to the mage lords. Not good for pretty lady. If pretty lady needs the safest way into the Academia, then choose me. Me can meet you at the rise of the moon. Me will help you, free of charge for pretty lady."

But I don't pay any attention to him after I realize who the Haulers are.

My temper rises, and I see red.

Fuming, I march toward Ragnald.

CHAPTER II

VENERATOR MAGE

The Venerator Mage, disguised as an old farmer with a white beard, laughs with satisfaction as the petite red-haired healer with wrath burning in her red eyes tramps to Ragnald, foiling the mage's plans.

He enjoyed upsetting her more than he could have imagined. He even planted seeds of "help" so she would come to him. Now that she was so close to him, he confirmed his suspicions beyond any doubt—she does indeed possess the artifact that was once his a long time ago.

The Venerator abandons the cart and heads back into the alley, stepping over the dead body of the original owner. He plans to cut Ragnald and Glenna off near the port. He shakes off the disguise from one step to the other.

Who knew that the old Academia game of how to disguise oneself with the help of Fla'mma magic would come in so handy?

There is no denying he was always the best among his peers. He would go as far as to say even better than that sniveling Ragnald. Of course there was another reason, not just his Fla'mma magic that assisted him in becoming such a brilliant and skilled mage. He will never be able to reveal that secret to the mage elders.

He nears the end of the alley and puts his back to the wall, peering out.

As he hoped, the little healer tears into Ragnald, then into the bulky Hauler with such vehemence that the Hauler steps back from her fury. Then she tries to attack the leader of the Haulers, with her fingers poised to take an eye out.

He chuckles under his breath.

Ragnald's head snaps toward the alley, and the Venerator ducks back.

There is no way Ragnald heard me, is there?

He waits a few moments, then leans forward again.

Ragnald is busy trying to calm the healer.

He didn't see me. There is no danger of him recognizing me. I don't understand how the mage elders picked him over me for the elder rank—Ragnald is nothing special.

As if his thoughts attracted the mage elders' attention, white-hot pain bursts in his forehead.

The Venerator squeezes his eyes shut against the agony, to no avail. The forty mage elders' order flows into his mind, paralyzing his muscles.

"There are two unknown newcomers on Raghild. Find out who they are. Report back to us when you do."

Then the oppressing presence of the powerful elders' lifts. A new talent they acquired last year.

The Venerator doubles over, spitting bile to the garbage-covered ground. Blood drips from his ears onto one of his black boots.

He straightens and punches the wall with a Fla'mma-covered fist. The wall cracks.

How could the mage elders already know about Ragnald and the healer? I didn't report them. Someone else did. But who?

He takes a deep breath but can't calm down.

I planned to kill Ragnald first, then the little healer, once I took back what's mine. Then there would be no stopping me getting the promotion to elder rank. Now I have to change my plans.

The Venerator raises his eyes to the sky but there are no answers scratched into the dark clouds.

For now, he must follow the mage elders' order. For defying them is a death sentence.

CHAPTER 12

RAGNALD

Back at The Inn, Ragnald stops in front of the door leading to Glenna's room. He tried to stay composed as they walked back, but every time he glanced at her, his patience evaporated anew.

Glenna cuts a sharp look at him, condemnation shining in her gaze.

She just can't appreciate all that I am doing for her. Can she?

"I was this close"—he shows the small distance between his thumb and forefinger to Glenna— "to book a trip to the Academia, complete with false authorization papers."

Paleness replaces the angry blush on Glenna's face as she looks away.

That's right. I had negotiated it. For you.

A guest walks down the corridor. Ragnald and Glenna step aside, waiting for the older man to pass out of hearing distance.

Ragnald continues, "Offending the leader of the Haulers was an impetuous act even for you. It cost me a lot of credits to smooth his ego and erase your offense. You risked both of our lives."

Glenna's head snaps up. "How can you do any business with someone so . . . so . . . despicable? Aren't you ashamed of yourself?"

Why does she have to be so pejorative? And why do I care what she thinks of me?

"I gave you my word that I will get you to the Academia," Ragnald says, "and I meant it."

Glenna raises her chin. "I don't need your help anymore, *mage*. I've found another way."

She has no idea how beautiful she looks right now.

"Let me guess—someone offered a 'free trip' to the Academia, out of the goodness of their heart, one that would get you there 'safely.' Does that sound familiar?"

Glenna purses her lips. His gaze lingers on them for a second; in his mind he is already kissing her to ease the pain that gleams in the depth of her dark crimson eyes.

He clears his throat. "The mage elders have their people patrol the city, ambushing anyone who is careless enough to try to sneak into the Academia."

Glenna crosses her arms, looking unsure whether to believe him.

Ragnald spreads his arms. "Of course, you are welcome to try your luck. I won't hold you back."

Glenna narrows her eyes.

He reaches for her shoulder to administer his Fla'mma magic, but she pulls away.

"I cannot bear your touch, *mage*. Not after seeing how complicit you are when it comes to those poor children sold into servitude. You are no better than those Haulers."

For the love of magic! Not with that again!

Ragnald drops his hand, trying hard not to show his irritation. "Stay in your room. And no healing!"

"Fine!" Glenna snaps and slams the door, rattling the door frame.

Ragnald curses under his breath as he enters his room, shutting the door behind him with a click.

He knew Glenna would not wait until he could discern the situation regarding admittance to the Academia. When he learned they needed a mage's approval for a passport, he did not rush to meet that mage—he wanted to see what that approval entailed.

I'm glad I was cautious, or Glenna would be one of those piles of ashes taken out to the back to be scattered to the wind.

Ragnald paces in his room, striding past a small flea-infested bed that stinks of old sweat and hay. Past the dark blue high-backed chair with its stuffing sticking out of the worn and stained fabric. Past the tottering coffee table with a Fla'mma-infused oil lamp on top of it. He stops and peeks out the grimy glass pane of the cobwebbed window, watching the bustling street below and waiting to feel at home. But being on Raghild does not infuse his mind with the warmth as it used to. He pulls the stained lace curtain closed, as if he could close that line of thought as well.

Ragnald did not anticipate the vehemence of Glenna's dislike for Raghild. He had no illusions that she would learn to care for a mage, but he hoped she would warm up to his home world. He should feel offended, but even now he must fight the urge to storm into her room, pull her into his arms, and comfort her.

He smiles recalling how outraged she was on behalf of those abandoned children.

Did anyone fight for me when I was one of those young ones?

He does not remember much outside of a vague sense of being scared. His parents are a blur. Did they love him? Is that why they chose to sell him to the mages? To protect him? Or did they want the credits?

No one but his Mentor cared for him at graduation when Ragnald showed a rare major triple affinity in three elements—Fla'mma, A'qua, and T'erra. No one in many millennia had possessed such major affinity at the Academia. Many had two major affinities—meaning active and powerful control over an element—with one or two minor affinities—meaning passive and not perfect control over an element. Ragnald had a minor affinity in A'nima, which he should have learned to develop more, but never cared for it.

Just like the Academia never cared for "skills" that have roots in many-generation-dulled minor affinities, often the sad result of thoughtless breeding. These skills could manifest as the ability to slightly manipulate someone if it's relating to the Fla'mma element; cure superficial wounds and nondeadly illnesses if it's relating to the A'ris element; reinforce building materials if it's related to the T'erra element; being a talented fisherman if it's relating to the A'qua element; and gaining animals' loyalty if it's relating to the A'nima element.

Ragnald learned that the Academia hoards all magical knowledge. However, the lesser ranks have no access to these important scrolls and tomes. When Ragnald was promoted to mage elder—right after his graduation from adherent to elementalist battle mage—he didn't waste any time trying to soak up as much magical knowledge as he could. His Mentor seemed to cherish and support Ragnald's thirst for knowledge, and the two of them spent many months reading in the Academia's vast library, often going days without speaking to each other. Those were the good days.

But when Ragnald asked the elders to teach him more, they refused him. Ragnald felt betrayed. He had a burning desire to become the most powerful mage, which led him to the H'rarh Dynasty, where he studied under a Pada monk. It was his first disobedience against the Academia's wishes—going outside for magical knowledge. The mage elders overlooked that but gave him a warning.

The second time . . .

Ragnald closes his eyes as memories of fire, screams, and smells of ash, smoke, and those sickly sweet scents assault his oratory sense.

The second time, the mage elders did not forgive his disobedience.

I was fortunate they didn't kill me outright when they stripped me of my elder rank.

His Mentor's interference saved his mage hide. At the time, Ragnald felt devastated when he was stationed on Uhna. But he met Glenna there. Now all he needs to do is to regain his elder rank; then he'll be able to convince the forty mages and the mage leader to help him rid the corruption brewing in Glenna.

Knocks sound.

Recognizing the pattern, Ragnald opens the door. "Tag, shouldn't you be anywhere but here, helping a known offender?"

Tag scoffs. "You helped me when I was that so-called known offender, didn't you? Besides, this couldn't wait any longer."

Ragnald clasps the other man's forearm. "Tell me more."

The mischievous smile disappears from Tag's face. "The mage elders require a magical passport from everyone who wants to enter the Academia. They search for A'ris magic traces, and if anyone has them, they kill the petitioner on the spot."

"I know that." He can still smell that burned scent from the victims.

"What you don't know is that the elders have acquired a mysterious device. They gave it to the guards at the Academia's gate, allowing them to search out even the most minuscule amount of A'ris in those who already possess passports."

Ragnald shakes his head, disbelieving. "That's bad news."

Tag nods. "I'm afraid so. One of the thief houses tried to steal a device—there are a handful of them—but the mages eliminated everyone connected to that house as punishment. They even burned down the building, cordoned off the street, and killed anyone who inquired about them. Now no one dares do anything. There is a rumor that once the mages are done with the passport holders, they will launch a widespread search for A'ris not sparing *anyone*, including mages and citizens of Raghild. This is a war on A'ris."

Ragnald curses. "I cannot believe they would kill hundreds of thousands because they have trace amounts of A'ris." The weakest of all six light elements.

What are the mage elders up to?

"You better believe it, my mage. As I said, much has changed since you were gone. Remember, no one is safe anymore."

With a nod, Tag slips out of the room on silent feet.

Ragnald steeples his fingers under his chin, digesting what he heard.

If I were to sneak Glenna into the Academia, then I better have a fool-proof disguise for her. I cannot do this on my own anymore.

But he knows where he can find more help.

He strides to the window, shoves the lace curtain out of the way, and sends a complicated Fla'mma, T'erra, and A'qua mix of a magic symbol—his personal calling code to his mage brothers.

CHAPTER 13

GLENNA

"There," I say to the lanky teen servant in the kitchen of The Inn. "The skin will be sensitive for a few days and may scar a bit, but you'll be fine." The teen nods, looking embarrassed as he pulls down his shirt over his stomach and picks up his stained apron.

I sneaked out of my room the second Ragnald went into his. I didn't even bother to grab my fog-cursed cloak, nor did I mean to enter the kitchen during broad daylight, but when I heard a painful squeal, I forgot all caution. I rushed in, and it was a good thing too, as I saw the teen boy splash boiling water over himself.

Leah'na hisses, watching the swinging door. "You shouldn't be here!"

Corruption Nic materializes by me, nodding. "She is right, my little infected healer."

Ignoring it, I push back the white strands of my hair. "Yes, of course. I'll leave right away." I get to my feet, stumbling a bit from the loss of expended magic.

Reh'ba snaps at the others. "Bah! Don't stare at her! We have work to do. Or do you want the innkeeper to come investigate why we're so quiet?"

Everyone goes back to work with urgency.

The discord of cooking gets louder with more pots banging, metal spoons scraping, and water bubbling. The mouthwatering scent of mushroom stew drifts to my nose as I make my way to the swinging door, cursing my impulsiveness. But everyone deserves healing, even if it means I must risk my life to do it. No exceptions.

One of the servant girls with long blonde hair lifts a finger when I near the doorway. She glances outside, then nods.

I take it that it's safe to leave and steal out of the kitchen, heading toward the main room.

Out of nowhere the innkeeper leaps at me.

"I knew it!" he shouts into my face and grabs my forearm. "I was right all along!"

Corruption Nic laughs. "Oh, this should be interesting."

"Shut up," I mutter.

The innkeeper glares at me, aghast at my words. "You won't be cheeky when I'm done with you," he says and drags me through the crowd of guests drinking and chatting in the main room.

"Let me go!" I yelp, pulling my arm away from him, but the innkeeper is stronger than I thought. He tightens his sausage-like fingers on me, digging his filthy nails into my skin.

The conversation dies around us as people realize there is something amiss. Many put down their foamy drinks in a hurry, spilling purple liquid on dented tabletops.

We wade through the now-silent crowd, with the innkeeper pulling me, and I pushing against him.

As last resort, I scratch at his face, drawing lines of blood on his right cheek.

The innkeeper yells in pain and backhands me with his meaty mitt.

Pain bursts behind my eyes. I cover my stinging face with a shaking hand.

"Nice try, my little infected healer," Corruption Nic says. "You should have been more careful."

"Insolent A'ris wielder," the innkeeper grumbles. "Wait till the mage lord sees you."

My stomach sinks. I can't let him take me to that mage who burned people to ashes!

With all my strength, I buck against the innkeeper's hold.

"Stop it!" he shouts as my arm slips out of his fingers. I take a few steps away from him when he grabs a bunch of my hair and pulls on the long strands.

Shooting pain bursts from my scalp, my eyes watering from it as I jerk to a stop.

The innkeeper wraps my hair around his fist and yanks again.

"Ow!"

Corruption Nic shakes his head. "Are you going to let him treat you like this? If you want more power to fight back, you know what to do. I'll help make this problem go away. I swear."

"I'll never give in," I mutter.

The innkeeper frowns. "Don't try to beg," he says and shoves me into a table, knocking the air out of me. "You deserve no clemency." He bows to the mage and adds, "Lord mage, I found this woman *healing* in my kitchen."

The huge mage, wearing that unpleasant fur-covered cloak, gets to his feet, towering over me by at least two heads. "I'll take it from here," he booms in a deep voice.

The mage gives the innkeeper a small bag full of credits and dismisses him with a flick of his scarred hand.

Then the mage turns his cruel gaze on me.

I gulp when I glimpse my death in his eyes.

CHAPTER 14

RAGNALD

Muffled shouting attracts Ragnald's attention.

Now what?

With growing suspicion, he steps out of his room. Ragnald tries Glenna's room, but it's empty. Other than her scattered clothing on the ground, she is nowhere to be found.

Why can't she just do what I ask? Just once?

Cursing, he sprints back into his room, grabs the small bag he kept packed, then rushes down the corridor to the stairway, taking the stairs two at a time. All the while imagining the worst—Glenna as a pile of ash.

Gods! Don't let me be late!

He bursts into the main room, finding all the guests on their feet, gawking.

"Move!" Ragnald snaps. The patrons jump out of his way as he cuts a path through them. He heads toward where everyone is looking—all the way to the back.

Ragnald takes in the scene—the massive mage looming over Glenna, ready to strike her down.

Not today, he won't!

Acting on reflex, he grabs a thick thread of Fla'mma magic, letting it erupt from his fingers as a gust of fire. It strikes the other man in the chest. The mountain of a mage falls backward.

Glenna startles and jumps out of the way.

Ragnald nods toward her, then advances on the other mage, who lies on the ground. unconscious.

Scared mutterings erupt from the guests of The Inn, but no one moves to interfere with a mage.

Ragnald reaches for Glenna when a muscle on the other mage's face twitches.

With a grunt, Ragnald drops to one knee and shoves a huge amount of his T'erra magic into the hardwood planks. The planks shatter as the huge mage sinks under the ground.

Using another thread of T'erra magic, he smooths the floor of the main room until nothing but a patch of packed dirt remains.

Ragnald glances around, noting how the terrified onlookers back away from him and winces. Then he turns his attention back to the fresh dirt spot, and sighs.

This won't stop that mage for long, but at least it will buy us some time.

Time they need to get on the run.

This is not how he wanted Glenna to experience Raghild, but nothing has gone the way he wanted since they arrived.

The innkeeper approaches them with a purple face, ready to argue. Ragnald cuts a sharp look at the stout man, who cowers.

Ragnald extends a hand toward a gaping Glenna. "We must leave, now!"

She blinks at him, hesitating.

I never wanted her to see this side of me—the battle mage who invokes fear in others. But saving her was worth it. I just hope she won't become afraid of me.

"Come on," he urges her again.

She nods, takes his hand, and they bolt out of The Inn.

CHAPTER 15

GLENNA

We erupt out of The Inn, then slow our steps so as not to attract any attention. Corruption Nic waltzes beside me, whistling.

Ragnald stops for a second, looking down the muddy street as if trying to decide whether it's a better idea to go toward the port or deeper into town.

"Wait!" Angus shouts as he trots to us with a knapsack thrown over his round shoulder. "This way!"

Ragnald frowns, but I tug at his hand to follow Angus.

Corruption Nic snorts. "Why are you always so trusting?"

I ignore the question. I've always been trusting, except when it came to mages. I learned the hard way never to believe in them.

"Yet you trust *this* mage," Corruption Nic comments.

I don't want to think about that fact for too long.

Angus takes to the alleys with the expertise of someone who has done this a few times. We hurry after him, zigzagging through the streets and filthy side streets until one dead ends into a foreboding forest.

Ragnald shakes his head. "You can't be serious."

Angus grins. "Do you have a better idea? We can't hide in the city—the mages have full control, not to mention their spies are everywhere."

"Anything is better than the Forest of Loss and Darkness," Ragnald says. Then he drags a hand through his silver hair and adds, "I dislike your idea but I concur. We have no other viable option. Lead the way, whomever you are."

"Introductions can wait," Angus says and breaks into a run.

Ragnald and I pick up our pace and enter the forest too. We jump over twisted roots and duck under low-hanging vines dangling from gray branches

52

overgrown with fungi. Our steps disturb layers of rotting leaves, and a disgusting smell trails us.

Branches get stuck in my hair, with stinging and biting insects falling on my neck and down my shirt. Yuck!

But with each step we get farther away from the city, the insistent headache lessens.

Corruption Nic paces with me with its hands clasped behind its back. "Isn't this place wonderful? Reminds me of the forest where your best friend and her entourage got lost not too long ago."

Chills run across my back, raising goose bumps. "I am so tired of running through forests," I say, recalling the frightening woodland in the Spirit Realm.

Menacing growls from dozens of throats sound around us, making me feel like a prey, though I have no idea where the predators lurk.

I shiver and stay close to the men.

When we slow down, I introduce them to each other, then ask, "Why is this place called the Dark Forest of something or other?"

Angus smiles. "It's the Forest of Loss and Darkness, and it earned its name—"

"Because of all those who never came back," Ragnald cuts in, "or if they did, they were lost to darkness, meaning insanity."

"How nice," I say and rub the teardrop-shaped scar on my left arm as I glance around at the lush greenery, imagining all kinds of danger waiting for us.

"How can someone so small cause so much trouble?" Corruption Nic asks. "You are a walking threat to anyone around you. There is a high chance one or both men will die here. Because of you."

"Leave already," I whisper, and the corruption retreats into my mind, laughing.

Angus winks at me. "Don't worry, lass. As long as you're with me, you'll be safe here."

Ragnald focuses his storm gray gaze on the other man. "Are you inferring that I cannot protect her?"

Angus grins wider. "You are a mage, aren't you?"

Ragnald glowers back at the tall man.

The smile disappears from Angus's face. "There is your answer. On Raghild, no one is safe from the mages."

CHAPTER 16

"We've wasted enough daylight," I say into the uncomfortable silence, hoping the men won't come to a fist fight.

Ragnald grunts, then gestures for me to go ahead of him.

Angus picks an invisible path through the thicket of plants and trees. The weak sunlight wanes the deeper we trek, with narrow swashes of light shining down on us, until it turns so dark I cannot tell whether it's day or night anymore, yet Angus seems sure of his destination.

Ragnald steps beside me, glaring at Angus's back. "I don't know what you see in him."

I snort. "Are you jealous?"

"Of this oaf? Never!"

"Then is this a mage quality—to be so suspicious toward everyone?"

"In my two hundred and forty years, I have learned that everyone will betray you for one reason or another. The question is not *if* they will do it, but *when*."

"That's a strange way of looking at life," I say to him, wondering how many had, indeed, betrayed him and how.

Up ahead, Angus jumps over a six-foot-wide gap.

I stop. I don't think I can jump that far.

Ragnald grabs my elbow, then uses his T'erra magic to bridge over the gap and leads me forward.

"Thank you," I mutter, then pull my arm back before I can get used to his touch.

To distract myself, I wonder what he experienced in his long span of life. Does he look down on me because I am a healer? Maybe he feels pity for me now that the corruption is overtaking me. Does he think my A'ris magic is useless and weak too, like most of the mages do? I want to ask him why he is so helpful to me, but I am afraid of his answer.

"You are such a coward," Corruption Nic says in my mind.

I'd rather be a coward than get Ragnald killed too.

The tip of my boot gets caught in a rock stuck in the forest floor. I stumble and fall forward.

Ragnald catches me by my waist, preventing me from falling on my face.

He pulls me into his body for a moment. Warmth seeps into me, and my skin tingles where his hand rests on my waist.

Oh gods! Why does he have such an effect on me?

I pull away from the mage with heat rising in my cheeks.

"You are pathetic," Corruption Nic laughs in my head. "Having a crush on a mage? Is that how low you've sunk?"

I don't have a crush on Ragnald, but I avoid looking at him.

Angus notices that we fell behind. He halts and leans on a tree waiting for us to catch up.

Cold winter wind blasts through the forest, scented with snow and that pungent T'erra scent of nature. It cuts through the thin material of my long white shirt I wear over black pants. I wish I would have grabbed my gray cloak with its nice faux-fur lining. I wouldn't even fight to wear its hood. At least I have my boots on.

I rub my arms, trying hard not to shiver from the cold.

Sleet begins to drop, then pour.

Ragnald pulls me under a tree crown and rummages in his bag. "Take my spare cloak before you freeze to death."

I accept the black cloak and pull it on, tucking my hair into its hood. Then I realize I see him holding one large bag instead of two. "Where is mine?"

Ragnald chuckles. "Your room was a mess. I had no time to clean up and pack for you."

What?! "But you have yours!"

"I always have my bag ready so I can leave at a moment's notice. Unlike you. I had no idea you were so untidy. I thought healers were more organized than that."

Oh, the arrogance!

"Is everything okay back there?" Angus asks.

I raise a hand in the wanderer's direction. "Give us a moment, please." Then I turn to Ragnald and add, "I wasn't planning on getting arrested today, *mage*."

Ragnald leans close to me until our noses almost touch. "And I warned you not to heal anyone."

"More like ordering me." I turn away from him and head toward Angus, pushing a branch out of my way. I smile with satisfaction when I hear it hit him. No mage has the right to look as good as Ragnald does.

"Just so you know, *mage*, I've been using my magic for *days*."

Ragnald mutters a few choice words, stomping behind me. "Well, I hope you're happy. Instead of staying in a nice warm inn, we'll have to rough it in this godsforsaken place."

"Are you saying this is my fault?" I whirl on Ragnald, but he doesn't pay any attention to me. Both he and Angus are staring back, from where we came.

A dangerous light flashes across Angus's dark brown irises when he glances at Ragnald.

Ragnald nods and Fla'mma fire covers his hands. "We are being followed."

CHAPTER 17

THE VENERATOR MAGE

It takes him a long time to wake up, but whatever is going on downstairs is loud enough to raise the Venerator Mage from his stupor—he had a few too many drinks, celebrating how close he was to his lost artifact, and got a bit carried away.

He sits up, wrestles with the sheet tangled around his strong body, and realizes he is still dressed in yesterday's clothes—black shirt and pants. At least he had enough brains to kick off his mud-covered boots.

He sniffs his armpit, left then right, and decides that there is no reason for him to change.

More shouts, muffled, drift from below him.

Yawning, he puts on his boots, drags his fingers through his long hair, and leaves his room.

He descends the stairs, listening, but can't make out words.

At the bottom of the stairway, the innkeeper waits for him.

"Lord mage! Thank the gods you are safe!" the innkeeper says, wringing his hands.

"Why wouldn't I be safe?" the Venerator asks.

As if the patrons of The Inn sense his presence, everyone falls silent.

The Venerator scans the main room, trying to deduce what had happened, but no one would even look at him.

"What is going on? Speak!"

"Yes, mage lord, sir. It was a healer and, uh, another mage."

The Venerator turns a sharp gaze on the innkeeper, who is tripping in his own feet, backing away from him. "Spit it out already or I swear I will burn you to ashes."

The innkeeper begins to recount what he witnessed, stumbling over his words in his haste, and making no sense whatsoever.

The Venerator notices the bulging money bag, with the mage's symbol embroidered on it, hanging from the innkeeper's belt. He pieces together the events earlier—the innkeeper caught the healer using her magic, arrested her, dragged her to the Prowler, and got paid for it. Somehow Ragnald was alerted to the trouble, and by the time the innkeeper returned from the kitchen the Prowler was gone.

The Venerator takes out his green magic–sensing glasses and puts them on. He ignores the older threads of elemental magic, following the trail of a bright thread of Fla'mma magic, then on the circular patch of ground a sizable amount of T'erra magic.

He puts the glasses away and strides through the cowering crowd, all the way to the fresh dirt spot. He squats and touches the dirt.

The Venerator straightens and studies the main room. There is no other sign that Ragnald used his magic—the walls, most of the furniture, and the hardwood floor outside the dirt patch are all as they were before. Not a speck of stray T'erra dust on them.

With a bitter smile, he admires Ragnald's handiwork.

That mage was always a master of T'erra, never doing more damage with his magic than necessary. Yet something made him lose his control. No, not something. Someone—that petite healer. Interesting.

The Venerator heads to the exit, already forming new plans in his head when sharp pain jabs into his mind and his muscles lock up, petrified.

Gods! Not now!

But there is nothing he can do to stop the forty mage elders' voices piercing his mind. *"You failed to report to us information about the return of Ragnald, along with his healer. You will work with Prowler Mage Bruth, and together you will bring those two known offenders to us. You have five days to complete your task or suffer the consequences of your failure."*

The moment the elders' hold ceases on his mind, the Venerator bends over, panting. Two lines of blood drip down the sides of his face from his ears, down his neck, and into his shirt. He wipes them off with impatience.

For the love of Fla'mma balls! I can't waste time working with that dumb Prowler. But what choice do I have?

With a frustrated sigh, the Venerator heads back to the smooth dirt patch. *Now I know who snitched on me.*

And now he must help that very mage. How ironic!

For a long moment, he considers letting the Prowler stay where he is buried, pretending that it was too late to save him. But at that second, a hand bursts through the mound of dirt, grasping for a hold.

Those darn prowlers! They are like caveroaches—you cannot stomp them out, burn them, or drown them. They are always back for more, like this sniveling follower. They are nothing if not tenacious.

The Venerator points at a group of men wearing overalls from a factory nearby. "You three! Go help him. Now!"

He goes back to his room, picks up his black cloak and his packed bag. Then returns to watch the frightened men struggle to pull the large Prowler out of the ground.

I despise working with prowlers. They are all psychopaths, and this one takes insanity to a whole new level with his games. I better watch him, or he will backstab me, or use me to his own advantage. I plan to do the same to him.

The Prowler's head and upper torso emerge from the ground. "You left me there long enough, Venerator Mage—"

"Do not call me by my name, Prowler. You have not earned that privilege yet." He forms a Fla'mma ball in his right hand.

The three factory workers scatter. The other mage glares at him with hatred.

The Venerator smiles, then shoots the other mage with the Fla'mma ball across the face.

It slaps the Prowler's head to the side.

It's important to put the Prowler in his place, right from the start, so he'll know where we stand—he is not equal to me and never will be.

Then the Venerator extends a hand toward the Prowler, and he accepts it with a grunt.

Once free, the Prowler shoves the other mage's hand away, and wipes the dirt off his furry cloak.

How that sniveling follower can wear that vile cloak is beyond me.

"Pull yourself together," the Venerator says. "The elders gave us an order. You will do my bidding, as I tell you. Are we clear?"

The Prowler nods.

The Venerator raises an eyebrow.

"Clear as a crystal," the Prowler grumbles with hatred glinting in his black eyes. Many A'nima mages acquire such unsettling eyes, like the animals they have control over. It's still bizarre to see.

The Venerator tilts his head toward the exit.

The Prowler, with pursed lips, squats and sniffs the ground.

Bah! Such an animal!

It's not long until the Prowler picks up Ragnald's trail. They follow it out of The Inn, then through the alleys and side streets, zigzagging until they reach the edge of the Forest of Loss and Darkness.

The Venerator finds three pairs of footprints in the otherwise undisturbed ground, heading into the forest.

The Venerator wonders at the stupidity of Ragnald, daring to enter the unpredictable and often lethal place most mages tend to avoid.

Sleet begins to patter the ground. Then it pours, washing away the trail in seconds.

Great! Just what we needed. At least this makes Ragnald's life as miserable as it does mine.

There is nothing else to do but to follow Ragnald into the forest.

He nods to the Prowler to enter first, then follows him.

There is no way I will ever let that brute be at my back. Lest he gets some ideas.

The Venerator smiles, already forming a plan to get back his artifact, get rid of Bruth, and then Ragnald.

CHAPTER 18

GLENNA

We trek through a thicket of trees into a strange clearing. Large rectangular stone tiles in pristine condition make up the hexagonal area. Not a single weed grows around the tiles. A well stands in the middle of the tiles, under an ornate stone arch. The triangular wooden huts around the clearing, on the other hand, have not escaped the passing of time—many are overgrown with vegetation. The ones closest to the tiles seem to be in better shape.

I swipe water off the sleeve of my borrowed cloak.

At least the sleet stopped.

Corruption Nic steps out of a puff of smoke and studies the area. "I don't like it here," he says, then takes shelter in my mind, radiating an indignant silence.

I like it here and won't miss its grumblings.

"Shouldn't we worry about whoever is pursuing us?" I ask and rub the teardrop-shaped scar on my left arm under the sleeve of the cloak.

"The sleet did us a favor," Ragnald says and puts a hand on my shoulder. "But once we've made camp, I will go and muddle whatever tracks have survived. That will buy us some time to rest and continue at the first light of morning. Don't worry; I won't let anything happen to you."

But I do worry. I put these men in danger with my mere presence, and now we are on the run.

Angus treads to a small hut on our right. "This will do." He pats its wooden side and murmurs words too quietly to be audible, as if praying.

Ragnald enters the hut, ignoring Angus.

I wander around the well, picking up seeds and herbs, then pocketing them. There is a strange pull emanating from the well—a mix of tranquillity and something ageless I can't quite explain. Even the air smells cleaner with a sweet hint of flowers.

I touch the smooth ledge of the well and peer into it. Blackness looks back, yet I feel more connected to Raghild than when we were in the City of Paucity. Closing my eyes, I let myself absorb it. In my mind's eye, I see a bright sunny spring day. Underneath the clear blue sky, a verdant field bursts with colorful blossoms and other signs of life. In the distance, a beach with soft yellow sand stretches, butting against a snowcapped mountain.

Peace envelops me for the first time since I was infected months ago. My eyes fill with tears, dripping down my face and falling into the well. I remember how different my life was back then before the corruption. Simpler and happier. All I cared about was healing my patients. But nothing lasts forever.

After a moment, I open my eyes and wipe my face. I step away from the well, hoping that the men did not witness my moment of vulnerability.

Ragnald steps out of the hut. "There is one large room and one small private room inside, which should be for Glenna," he says. "Angus and I will sleep on the floor in the common area." Angus nods. The mage turns to me and adds, "I placed my spare woolen blanket on top of the bed—it seems clean and in good condition. I'd wager it'll be more comfortable than our beds at The Inn."

I smile in thanks.

"I'll go and hunt for dinner," Angus offers. "I have some salted radish-apple and sugared mushroom caps, but it won't feed the three of us."

Ragnald blocks his way. "How did you know about the existence of these sacred altars?"

Angus scoffs. "The mages may have forbidden us to celebrate our Guardian Goddess Cyn'rha and her three giant protectors, but we have not forgotten about them. Cyn'rha might be sleeping for now, but she will return to take back what is hers. There are primordial powers at play that you mages will never understand nor will ever respect."

I look at the abandoned settlement in a whole new light—the mages must have made the inhabitants leave. How cruel!

Angus shoves Ragnald out of his way and heads back into the forest.

Ragnald stares after the other man.

"Why do you have to be so rude to him?"

"This place has been abandoned for more than a hundred years, long enough for many to forget its existence, let alone the history behind it. Yet, Angus led us here. I think that's suspicious."

"I don't see any problem with that. Angus is a wanderer and must have come across it during one of his journeys."

"That might be so," Ragnald says after a while.

A rustling sound attracts our attention.

Angus returns holding three small animals that have long bodies, reminding me of the sand rabbits of Uhna. He places the animals on the grass while he takes out a metal pot from his bag. Then he prepares the animals and throws the meat, along with some spices, into the pot.

"Over there is a fire pit," Ragnald says and strides toward our hut where a circular stone pit, complete with a hook to hang a pot from, awaits. Using his magic, he starts a fire and waits for Angus to place the metal pot on the hook.

"I'll go back to the stream for some water," Angus says, but Ragnald shakes his head.

"I'll take care of it," the mage says and fills the pot with water, using his A'qua magic.

"Two elements," Angus comments as he drops some root vegetables into the water. "Remarkable."

"It's three elements," Ragnald corrects him and boosts the fire with his Fla'mma magic until the water boils in a few seconds.

Angus glowers at the mage before focusing on our meal.

Ragnald wipes one of the curved wooden benches that run the perimeter of the stone pit and waits for me take a seat before settling next to me.

I pretend his closeness doesn't bother me and extend my hands to the flames to warm them. The mage leans a hand on the edge of the bench behind me, his arm bracketing my back.

Corruption Nic laughs in my mind. "The way you two dance around each other is pathetic. Just get on with it, will you?"

Ignoring the corruption, I glance at the mage's face, but he looks straight ahead, though a muscle jumps on his jawline.

Soon our dinner is ready. Angus serves the cooked and spiced meat on pieces of bark he had in his bag, adding a portion of salted radish-apple and sugared mushrooms as well. We eat in silence until our appetite is sated. Then Angus cleans the pot, while Ragnald wraps the leftovers in leaves the other man left out for that job.

I get up too, feeling guilty for not helping them with dinner preparation, but then mixing healing potions. I am not a great cook. Deidre, who was the head chef at the Crystal Palace, spoiled Lilla and me with her amazing dishes and pastries. Until DLD killed her, when He tried to turn her into one of His mindless minions, called dark servants, that make up most of His army. A fate I almost encountered too and am trying to avoid now.

"Is everything all right?" Ragnald asks, stepping to me.

I put a hand on his forearm and look up at him. "I, uh, never thanked you." His muscles turn to rock under my fingers.

He frowns. "Thank me for what?"

"For taking care of me after I got, uh, you know, ill," I say. "It must have been difficult for you to help me." It's getting harder to resist the urge to run my hand up to his shoulder and into his hair.

Ragnald takes my hand in his. "It was not difficult at all. I would do it all over again."

"Ragnald, I . . ." My voice trails off as my heart speeds up from the caressing look in his storm gray eyes. All thoughts flee my mind.

"I love the way you say my name," he says in a deeper voice and cups my cheek. "I admire your perseverance and your passion. You intrigue me, Glenna." He brushes his thumb over my cheekbone and leans down.

My breath gets stuck in my throat. My body feels hot all over as a few inches separate our lips. I can feel his kiss on my lips . . .

Corruption Nic sneers in my mind. "How adorable the two of you are! Too bad the mage will die soon because of you."

"Stop it!" I snap at the corruption.

Ragnald recoils, with hurt flashing across his eyes.

"Wait! I, uh, didn't—"

"I must go now and hide our tracks before night falls," he says, looking away from me as he marches toward the forest.

CHAPTER 19

RAGNALD

Ragnald curses into the insect-noise-filled night as he cuts through a grove of trees.

Just when I open up to her, she crushes me. I should have known better by now.

He focuses on their tracks, smoothing them out with his T'erra magic and breaks into a sprint to rid himself of his burning anger. He jumps over twisting roots and fallen trees, uncaring of the scratches the woods inflict on him, while erasing any traces of their footprints.

He stops after an hour, breathing hard. *This is as good a spot as any to lay down a few false tracks.*

Using his A'qua magic mixed with a large thread of T'erra, he creates a false set of footprints, one of them leading toward a small stream and across it—the exact opposite direction from their camp—while the other set leads toward a hidden canyon.

Satisfied, he examines his work.

That should do it.

Sharp pain jabs into his right arm.

Ragnald turns to find a red and triangular flower gnawing on the sleeve of his cloak, trying to chew through it with dozens of sharp, thorn-like teeth.

With a grunt, he punches the flower until it lets go of him.

The flower screeches, some of its thorn-teeth bloody, then coils backward, hiding between two large frond-like leaves.

What kind of heinous flower attacks a mage?!

With a splash of A'qua magic, Ragnald cleans his sleeve from sticky pollen and blood residue, then continues his way back to the camp, obscuring any old track he missed on the way here.

He stays alert for any more of those carnivorous flowers and can't help but imagine what Glenna would say about it. He has no doubt she'd love it at first sight. Because that's who she is—always trying to help those who are injured, risking her life while the corruption gets stronger in her.

Ragnald sighs.

She is the most amazing woman I've ever met. No one has ever made me feel what I felt with her.

She makes him want to do things for her, just to see that beautiful smile light up her face. Instead of that angry person that the corruption twists her personality into, altering her to become someone cruel, almost like a Turned. Nothing like her true, kind self.

Ragnald shoves a low-hanging vine out of his way as he realizes what happened.

Of course it was the corruption!

It's been hours since he administered his Fla'mma magic regimen to her. Then he closes his eyes for a second out of irritation.

I shouldn't have overreacted.

It's clear Glenna needs him, now that her condition is getting worse.

A thorny dark green leaf slaps him across the face, blowing a yellow-green puff of pollen into his eyes and nose.

Ragnald engages his Fla'mma magic, burning any pollen particles off his face, then turns the blaze on the offending plant as large as a sapling.

It squeals in a high tone, emitting a bitter smoke that makes him grimace. Before the fire could spread over the whole forest, he douses it with his A'qua magic.

The scents of smoke and ash bring back memories. For a second, all he sees is a terrified young girl, her blue eyes in her tanned face full of pain and grief. The night sky behind her flares in an unnatural orange-reddish light.

Another terrible squawk brings him back to the present, warning him of more predatory flowers or animals.

For the love of magic! What is wrong with the wildlife in this cursed forest?!

He glances up, seeking answers. The moon rises above the treetops, dominating the dark sky like a silver orb, but does not offer any wisdom for him. He picks up his pace, pushing branches out of his way.

A loud creaking-scraping noise sounds behind him.

He peeks over his shoulder.

Hundreds of triangular red flowers bare their thorny maws at him.

Ragnald swallows and sprints away.

CHAPTER 20

GLENNA

"You were quite rude to poor Ragnald," Corruption Nic says, appearing in the form of Lilla. "I loved watching every second of it!"

Hiding my alarm at its growing abilities, I snap, "Go away!"

"Don't you wish it would be so," it mocks, grinning like Lilla does, showing her white teeth, then morphs into smoke, drifting away.

With a huff, I turn to face the wooden wall of the hut, fidgeting on the feather-filled bed, and searching for a comfortable spot to no avail. I pull the wool blanket higher, tucking it under my chin. I shiver from the cold winter night air that seeps into the small room through the cracks of the wood shutters over the window.

My conscience aches when I recall the pained look on Ragnald's face. I wasn't trying to be rude to him, at least not on purpose. Ragnald must know that.

But how could he? He looked so hurt.

I toss and turn to the other side, facing the open door with darkness beyond it. I would erase that memory if I could, but there is nothing I can do to change what happened.

As a healer, I swore to do no harm—I always took it to mean both physical and emotional. Well, apart from what happened on Uhna. I wasn't prepared for all the buried emotions to overwhelm me when the mage showed up at the Crystal Palace.

Wind picks up, bringing scents of smoke from our cooking fire.

This smell of smoke transports me to the day when everything changed. The night I lost everyone who mattered to me.

It started out as a beautiful bright summer day, too hot and humid for the adults, but perfect for my siblings and me. We had just returned from swimming in a fast-flowing stream, still dripping wet when they struck.

Seven elementalist mages descended on my family in our small, cozy cottage.

My three older sisters and I screamed, rushing to the attic, but the mages caught them before they could escape. I made it into the small cupboard in the back corner of the roof, hiding.

I didn't see what happened. I heard their pained screams and the crackling and sizzling of the fire that engulfed the cottage.

With a sob lodged in my throat, I open my eyes, staring into the dark.

I have no idea how I survived the fire. The days I wandered in the Evander Forest are blurry—all I can recall is the feeling of starvation and going half insane from the burn injuries. According to Great Healer Robley, he found me on the brink of death and healed me at the last second. He took me in and raised me. He couldn't heal the angry-looking welts that cover both of my forearms—a small price to pay to be alive. Unlike my family. They died because I couldn't refrain from healing the hapless critters, alerting the mages to our presence. I knew better, but I always found an excuse to break the promise I made to my parents—to avoid using my magic unless in an emergency.

I swipe the tears away.

Corruption Nic sneers in my mind. "You don't deserve to feel such self-pity. Your tears won't bring back your family. You'll have to live with the consequences of your careless actions."

"I don't feel self-pity." Though why I bother to argue with it is beyond me. I tried to live my life after the tragedy and help anyone who needed healing. Then Ragnald showed up on Uhna.

I was not prepared for how upset the mage's presence made me. I was furious. I wanted revenge on the mages for what they did to my family. I didn't care whether it was Ragnald who committed the murders. I just wanted to excise the pain of my grief. I bribed a few servants to gather information. When I learned that the mage liked to take a bottle of boomberry wine up to the library every week, I decided to act. It wasn't anything ominous—just a few herbs mixed into the wine. Harmless to most, but somewhat toxic to mages. It wouldn't have killed him, but it was enough to satisfy my vengeance.

Then I waited, imagining the physical pain the mage would suffer and waited to feel relief. But it never came.

As the hours ticked by, so did my determination evaporate. I couldn't continue to act as if I didn't commit a horrible infraction. A crime that almost broke my healer's oath, creating a fertile ground for the corruption to take root in me later.

By the time I rushed to the library to undo what I've done, it was too late. Ragnald was already gone. So was Lilla.

I had no idea that Lilla had to rescue a drunk Ragnald, who almost drowned in the Fyoon Ocean.

That act of vengeance didn't bring me relief but guilt.

Just like how I feel now—remorseful for hurting the mage. Except I didn't do it out of vengeance, but by accident. I wish I had been more careful!

I turn on my back, staring at the peaked ceiling, and not feeling even the tiniest bit tired.

What is wrong with me? I cannot fall for Ragnald. No self-respecting healer ever had a romantic relationship with a mage. It's just not done.

Then why can't I stop thinking about him and me together? As if he is the forbidden herb I know I shouldn't pick but can't resist.

My lips tingle just remembering how close he came to kissing me. I recognized desire in his eyes; the same passion that burned in me, asking for that kiss. A kiss I was ready to return.

Oh, gods!

Feeling overheated, I kick the blanket off.

I must stop with this foolishness. I experienced true love with Nic, but he passed away, taking my happiness with him. That was it for me. I have no business wanting more from Ragnald. There cannot be anything between him and me. It's safer that way. I cannot have the mage's death on my conscience too.

The door of the hut opens. I listen, hoping it's Ragnald.

Footsteps approach.

Pretending to be asleep, I peek through my eyelashes.

Ragnald enters the room and places something on the small table by my bed. Then pulls up the wool blanket, making sure to lift my right, then left arm when he tucks the blanket. He hesitates a moment, then slides his fingers down my right arm with the slightest touch before leaving the room and closing the door after him.

I look over to the small table to find a Fla'mma-infused candle.

Does this mean he is not upset with me anymore?

I turn to face the wall, trying to ignore the tingling warmth on my arm where he touched me.

CHAPTER 21

The angry sounds of a blizzard wake me in the middle of the night. A gust of wind batters the side of the wooden hut with force.

Snoring sounds through the closed door from the common area.

With a sigh, I try to drift back to sleep.

A loud bang reverberates from outside, as if a lightning bolt slammed into the ground right outside my room.

I sit up and bump my head on the empty wooden shelf above me. Dust showers on me, and I cough. The Fla'mma-infused candlelight flickers, making shadows dance on the wall of the room.

I shiver.

Another gust of wind rattles the wooden shutters over the window.

Will winter win and break this hut into pieces? Burying us under a ton of pristine whiteness?

"You won't have such a serendipitous end," Corruption Nic croons, squatting by me, then glances toward the window. "The Archgod of Chaos and Destruction will have you soon enough."

A sharp rambling sound tears through the quiet, gaining volume as if something terrible is hurtling toward the hut. Toward me.

"Leave me," I say to it and the corruption dissipates.

There is nothing to worry about. Just go back to sleep. Who knows what tomorrow will bring?

An even stronger blast of wind crashes into the hut, extinguishing the candlelight. Only the weak moonlight streaming through the cracks of the shutter remains to combat the near pitch darkness.

Chilling cold sweeps through the room, sucking all warmth out. Frost spreads on the ceiling—thick, white, and crackling. Two-foot-long icicles form in the corner of the room and by the doorway, right before my eyes. More frost unfurls, like wildfire, on the planks of the floor, then all the way up the walls, trying to swallow the room and me.

My panting breath comes out like a small cloud of fog every time I exhale, searching for calm. This is not normal, my instincts clamor, but I don't know what to do. Fear paralyzes me and I cannot move.

"I see you, my corrupted healer," a deep and powerful male voice booms inside the room.

I squeeze my eyes, shutting the voice out. I know with every fiber of my body that this is DLD speaking.

"You cannot hide from me," the archgod says, His voice dripping with darkness and terror. "I am coming for you."

Corruption Nic appears laughing with anticipation, his eyes black orbs, with black veins pulsing on his pallid face, turning into a dark servant in a blink, then disappearing as a cloud of smoke.

The light disappears, pitching me into complete darkness.

"No!" I force my body to move and jump out of the bed. Slipping on the ice-covered floor, I throw the door open. Icicles shower around me as I dart into the common area.

Ragnald is gone. Angus sleeps by the entrance, undisturbed.

I drop down on my knees next to him and shake him. "Help me, Angus!"

But he doesn't wake.

"No one can help you, my corrupted healer."

"No!" I hunch down over my knees. Presenting the smallest target to the archgod as I pray to the Archgoddess of the Eternal Light and Order for assistance.

"The Lady won't help you, my little corrupted healer. You are mine. Give into the inevitable and join my side."

"Never!"

Something touches my shoulder.

I flail my hands with all my strength.

My fist connects with something, and I hear an "Oomph."

"Glenna, wake up!" a male voice insists, nothing like the archgod's.

I open my eyes, panting.

In the weak moonlight, I find myself in my room, untouched by frost or icicles, my body twisted inside the woolen blanket. The Fla'mma-infused candle's flame flickers on the nightstand.

Ragnald, with a bruise darkening under his right eye, perches on my bed. "Are you okay? You were yelling in your dream."

"Where were you? I couldn't find you . . ." My voice trails off and I tremble, still under the hold of the nightmare.

Ragnald brushes my hair. "I stepped outside for a few minutes to walk around the hut."

My body shakes and my teeth chatter, but I can't seem to calm down. All my fear and shock turn into a sob.

Ragnald embraces me, and I throw my arms around his neck.

"It was just a bad dream," Ragnald says, rubbing my back. "You're safe. I'm here now."

I pull back from him. "I thought . . . that DLD was here to take me as a Turn—" I bite the word off. I don't want to say it out loud.

"It's the Forest of Loss and Darkness. It plays with your sanity. Some see their worst fear, while others . . ."

I wipe my face, feeling calmer. "It was just a dream." I struggle to believe that what I experienced was imaginary. I can still feel that bone-chilling cold and the menacing darkness enveloping me.

Ragnald gets to his feet and lifts my blanket so I can lay back down. "Just a dream."

"Sorry about the, uh, black eye." Touching his arm, I send a bit of A'ris magic, clearing it up. It's the least I can do.

Ragnald smiles. "Go back to sleep. Morning is almost here."

I return his smile with relief now that the nightmare has no more hold over me.

He tucks the blanket around me. "Sleep well." He touches my face for a second, then leaves the room, shutting the door after him.

My eyelids turn heavy as I turn on my side, facing the door.

Then my gaze lands on a broken icicle in the corner.

CHAPTER 22

Early at dawn, my boots slide on the fresh snow-covered ground as we hike through the forest with Angus in the lead and Ragnald at my back.

After seeing that icicle, I couldn't go back to sleep. The icicle was gone by morning; not even a telltale puddle stayed behind as proof. The restless night has taken its toll on my body—all my muscles ache from the mad dash through the woods the day before.

I drag my feet, tripping over roots hidden under the layers of whiteness and curse.

The pale sunlight reaches the ground in streaks through the thick crowns of trees. I glance at the sky and note the numerous dark gray clouds that threaten with more snow. Splendid, just splendid.

A spot in the middle of my back, between my shoulder blades, itches. A feeling of being watched raises goose bumps on my skin.

I listen for any sign of being followed, but the racket raised by the occupants of the forest indicates that whoever hounds us is much farther behind us. The animals would be quieter if someone was close to us. I've learned to rely on the creatures as the best warnings for the first sign of danger—let it be an approaching storm, a predator, or the dangerous presence of a hunter.

It's best if I focus on getting out of this fog-cursed forest, going to the Academia, and then getting rid of the corruption.

"You are so naïve," Corruption Nic says, kicking the snow next to me, though its foot passes through it without leaving a dent.

If I ignore the corruption hard enough, maybe it won't be able to gain strength from me.

Corruption Nic laughs. "That's not how this works. Besides, you can't ignore me forever. I am part of you, my sweet darling."

My temper boils hearing the pet name my Nic gave me on the night we first made love. How dare it remind me of a time when I was happy. A time when Nic was alive, dreaming of a future we'd spend together.

"You can't bury your past," Corruption Nic says.

"Watch me."

Corruption Nic inhales with pleasure, its eyes glowing black. "Don't say I didn't warn you."

I glare at it, wishing it to go away. After a moment, the corruption complies.

Angus veers to the right, avoiding a patch of disturbed ground with loose soil. Either some kind of animal had just burrowed deeply into the ground, or it's a home for a predator that lives underground waiting to spring on its prey. I've seen both types of animals in Evander—I agree with Angus that it's best not to find out which kind lives here.

A breeze brings the scents of dirt and soil mixed with decomposing vegetation. Scents so familiar to me that they remind me of my childhood and a different forest peppered with giant trees and a cloudless blue sky.

I recall the day when I ran through the Evander Forest with my three older sisters, but I was hungry and separated from them, deciding to sneak into the kitchen where my mom left a few baked mushroom pies to cool.

Opening the back door to a crack, I entered the kitchen on silent feet. Before I could reach the closest pie, resting in the middle of the homemade table, I heard my mom exclaim, "I am tired of moving again, Josh'ia!"

I tiptoed to the arched doorway and peeked inside the living area.

My mother, looking worn with her shoulders bent forward, perched at the edge of a wooden bench. Her dark crimson hair fell forward, and she twisted the strands around her finger. Wrinkles cut deeply around her dark crimson eyes as she wrinkled her nose in distress. She looked a decade older than her youthful age of twenty-six.

My father stepped behind her and began to massage her neck. "Amel'ee, my dear love, you know we cannot stay in place too long. It's already been five years and any day now the mages could—"

"I've had enough of the mages!" My mother covered her face with both hands, stifling a sob. "Your great-grandfather warned us about that heirloom, but you didn't listen. Now we can't find peace, running from the mages, lest they find us and take our precious heirloom. You never should have accepted it, let alone given it to our youngest daughter. Now she has the same fate awaiting her!"

I touched the teardrop-shaped scar, the incision still red and painful days after the surgery my father did to insert the heirloom under my skin.

My mom continues, "It's thrice blessed, for it made your family lucky for generations, helping amass great fortunes no healer had possessed before—but it's also twice cursed, for that's how many times their luck ran out, losing every credit whenever the mages found them. Always hiding, always starting over. You knew all of this, and yet you accepted it anyway, waiting for our daughter to be old enough to receive it."

"Amel'ee, you know I did it because I believed that by skipping a generation, our little Glenna could benefit the most from it, even break the cycle of misfortune." My father pulled her hands from her pale face and added, "I am just as tired of the mages as you are, but I won't let them stop us from living our best life. They might be able to hunt us in the name of corruption and preventing Turning, but it won't last long. The tide will turn, and we, healers, will show them what true magical power looks like. I believe in our Glenna. Don't you?"

My mother frowned. "I believe in her more than anything I believed in my life, but Josh'ia, we still don't know what that heirloom does!"

"I showed you the scroll that mentioned the magical powers of these ancient heirlooms. They are good luck charms, as my grandfather can attest. But he didn't know about the recommendation to insert the heirloom under the skin to gain the most benefit. I thought it would be best to insert it under Glenna's skin—she has the most magical potential of all of us. She is already ten times the healer I was when I studied at the Healers' College, as she cures all the injured animals around us without showing any signs of fatigue."

My mother crossed her arms, looking unconvinced.

"Our daughter could have been a great mage with such power if the mages wouldn't be so prejudiced against our A'ris element," my dad said. "But with the help of this heirloom, she will be able to protect herself, and prove that the healers are a force to be reckoned with—"

"None of that will matter when the mages come to kill her," my mother said with tears rolling down her face.

"Have more faith, my dear love! Our Glenna has more affinity to A'ris than the two of us combined. She won't be killed. She will become the most famous healer. She will be our legacy. This day will be a distant memory we'll laugh about, worrying over nothing."

As I child, I didn't understand that conversation between my parents and went back to the kitchen to steal the pie. My mother laughed when she caught me with the empty plate, holding my stomach in pain. Later that night, my father held my hair while I threw up.

A branch hits the top of my head.

Ice-cold snow showers on me, snapping me out of the past.

Look at me now; I am nothing but a disappointment to my family's dream—I have not achieved anything to be proud of.

I touch my left wrist. I never thought twice about the tear-shaped heirloom my father inserted under my skin, until now.

Now that memory has more meaning, and as a grown-up I agree with my mother. My father had no right to make that decision for me. I've never felt any luckier than others, nor did I make a fortune. I lived on the basement levels in the Crystal Palace, alongside other servants and was happy with my life.

I try to recall if they ever talked about this family heirloom in more detail, regarding how it worked, but find nothing else in my memory.

Even now, the heirloom lays dormant under my skin. The one "benefit" I've had from it is that it helped me to self-soothe in stressful moments when I rubbed it. That's all.

But now I wonder. What will happen if I thread a bit of my A'ris magic into it?

I raise my arm and take a deep breath. Concentrating, I select the smallest ribbon of A'ris and touch it to the heirloom. It sucks my magic in with great hunger, swallowing it. Nothing else happens.

"It must be long dead," I mutter, staring at my arm. It is an ancient heirloom, left behind by one of the cultures that did not survive the devastation of an Era War—a war between the two ruling archgods.

"You'll never be your family's legacy," Corruption Nic mocks in my mind. "Not until you give in to the Archgod of Chaos and Destruction."

"I can live with that," I mutter. Better to be a failure than be a Turned.

A soft mewling sound catches my attention. I forget all about useless heirlooms and unachievable family expectations. I veer to the left, listening.

Angus stops. "Glenna, lass, do not venture into the forest. It's not—"

"Shush," I say and bend down. I know in my heart that whatever made that noise is dying. I've heard too many animals make that distraught sound to mistake it for anything but a last-ditch cry for help.

Ragnald turns to me. "Glenna, stop this folly. Let us go."

I spare a glare at the mage—healing is not foolish!—and drop down onto my hands and knees, crawling inch by inch and searching the undergrowth until I find the source.

With the utmost care, I reach and cup the small creature in my palms.

The creature, a red triangular flower hybrid, shivers, mewling. It sounds even weaker.

"Good gods," Ragnald says as he stares at the flower babe. "That thing is carnivorous. Let's just leave it and—"

"I will do no such thing, *mage*," I say. "Everyone deserves healing." Then I examine the tiny flower, trying to figure out its ailment. Underneath the normal-looking flowerhead, the sepals are more developed, like a predator's maw with teeny thorns in it, like fangs. That's what the flower uses on its prey, proving that Ragnald is right about it being a carnivore. Two pairs of small orbs, eyes, blink at me.

Then what could be the problem?

"Oh, poor you," I whisper to it, petting its red petal with a fingertip. It tries to raise its head but falls back, its roots flailing to grasp onto my wrist.

I glance up and notice the grown-up versions of the flower all around us, attached to the trees with their robust root system, coexisting. Carnivores they might be, yet they don't attack us, staying still as if not to scare us. Maybe waiting to see what I'll do with one of their offspring.

I return my attention to my patient. I cannot find any obvious injuries. Whatever ails it must be internal.

I thrust my other hand out. "Water, please." One of the men gives me a flask.

I drip some water into the flower's green maw. It swallows it but rejects more. Yet it still mews.

I glance around. "Could it be that you're hungry?" I find a dead insect with pale wings, and I add, "I know you prefer live ones, but it's the best I can do for now."

A theory forms in my mind as to why this youngling ended up down here.

Just as I suspected, the flower presses its green maw closed against the dead insect.

I dig into my pocket. "There is one more thing left to try." I pick out a few seeds and drop them next to the flower on my palm.

The flower babe's green sepals snap open. It dives for the seeds, gobbling them up. Then it mews for more.

I smile. "Aha!"

Angus puts his hands on his knees, looking at the plant, then at me. "What just happened?"

"This little one is a vegetarian carnivorous flower," I explain. "That's why the others couldn't help it. They didn't know how."

As if to prove my words, a large green vine sneaks out of the closest adult flower, with a red petal the size of my head, heading toward the little plant. It touches one of the babe's petals for a moment, caressing it, then retracts.

"I will take care of it," I promise to the older flower, knowing full well that this youngling cannot live among its family, being too different from the rest.

Corruption Nic scoffs in my mind. "More like you'll take care of it until you get bored, then you'll abandon it."

Grinding my teeth, I do not respond. Instead, I gaze down at the flower babe, which already looks better. "Welcome, little Mia." At least I think it's female. It's hard to tell at first glance.

Angus chuckles. "Would you look at that?"

Ragnald crosses his arms, looking unimpressed. "Now can we go?"

CHAPTER 23

RAGNALD

Ragnald marvels at Glenna's cleverness, wishing he would have told her that instead of snapping at her for holding their progress back. But he knows that a prowler-ranking mage—judging by the characteristic fur cloak that mage wore—is not far behind them.

He is not sure whether he can take out the Prowler on his own *and* keep Glenna safe at the same time. He suspects that Angus can take care of himself but can't tell where the wanderer's loyalties will lie when the unavoidable confrontation comes to a head.

Unlike Glenna, I don't trust Angus. That man harbors a grudge against mages, but then again almost all Raghild's citizens have that kind of attitude.

Yet there is something about the wanderer that makes Ragnald protective of Glenna, and it's not just jealousy.

He glances at Glenna, who cuddles her new pet, Mia, murmuring comforting words to the carnivore plant that doesn't eat meat. She just can't resist helping everyone, now can she?

Is that what she sees in me? Someone who is broken by his past and needs healing? Someone she can pity?

"Enough with the defeatism," Ragnald hears Devotee Zavier's patient voice in his memory. "It won't change anything."

Ragnald instantly transported into his past, to the day he studied with the Pada monk.

Ragnald nodded. "I want to learn everything."

Devotee Zavier smiled and clasped his hands in front of his dark blue robe with two sashes running in front of his chest—one sky blue for A'ris and the other dark brown for T'erra. "Then it would be my pleasure to offer you knowledge."

Ragnald blinked in surprise. He was expecting much more resistance from the wide-shouldered and bald monk.

Devotee Zavier laughed. "You forget that the mage elders are the ones with insatiable hunger for all magical knowledge without the desire to share said knowledge."

Ragnald snorted. It's the nicest way anyone ever put the hoarding tendencies of the mage elders when it comes to magic.

Devotee Zavier's dark brown eyes sparkled with humor. "One who can see both sides of a matter will finish this life the wiser."

"You mean, having perspective?"

Devotee Zavier nodded. "When we lose the ability to have perspective, then that is the day we lose compassion. For nothing is what it first seems."

Ragnald crossed his arms. Did the monk think that the mages are unfeeling? "The mages took me in, gave me a home. You cannot expect me to turn my back on them and not—"

Devotee Zavier raised a hand. "It is not betrayal to notice others' mistakes, even if they are our family, and learn from them. Blindness will turn one into a zealot. Do you understand, young mage?"

Ragnald prepared to defend the mages, but something in the depth of the monk's gaze stopped him to blurt out the usual answer. He suspected that the Pada monk would not tolerate any superficial denial and would refuse to teach him. Instead, he stayed quiet.

Devotee Zavier grinned. "Good! You are not a lost cause. Now let us begin."

"May I call you mentor?" Ragnald asked.

"No need, young mage. I am but a humble teacher who derives pleasure from the simple act of teaching magic to those who want to learn and nothing more."

Ragnald shakes his head, returning to the present. He learned so much from the Pada monk, even if the mage elders gave him a warning when they learned of his apprenticeship.

I wonder if Devotee Zavier's teachings were the inspirations behind my disobedience at that last order from the mage elders that caused me to fall from their favor.

A disobedience that led to him being stripped of his elder rank and exiled to Uhna.

Ragnald experienced loneliness on that oceanic world—thanks to the general hatred toward mages—leading him to drink boomberry wine every night to drown his troublesome emotions. But he didn't regret his post on Uhna. For one, it led him to Lilla, the last of the legendary Lumenian race, who needed magical guidance he was happy to provide; and for another, he met Glenna, who nestled herself into his heart with her first glare.

Ragnald chuckles under his breath recalling how upset he was knowing that it was Glenna who meddled with his wine but couldn't prove it at the time.

Glenna gives him a questioning look.

The chain of events that came after that wine incident led him on a path back to his beloved Raghild and to the Academia. He knows that he can regain his elder rank with the help of his Mentor and find a way to help Glenna. He just has to find a way inside the Academia first.

Angus stops. "We can't go this way."

Ragnald steps around Glenna. He studies the half a dozen sizable fallen tree trunks blocking their way. "We can't go around them."

On the left, there is a steep mountain wall that would be difficult to climb under the best of times, but now with ice covering its rocky surface it's nearly impossible. While on the right, a vertical canyon drops dozens of feet deep.

"What should we do?" Glenna asks.

Ragnald raises both of his arms. "Step back."

With a thought, Fla'mma threads flow out of his palms and engulf his hands in fire.

For a second, he is transported to the past, to that same terrified young girl from before, illuminated by an unnatural orange-reddish light in the dark night. Behind her, Fla'mma fire raged everywhere—on top of straw cabins, covering villagers who scuttled around screaming in pain.

"Ragnald?" Glenna asks, cutting into the nightmarish vision. "Is, um, everything okay? You are scaring baby Mia."

He clears his throat. "That's not a baby." Then he lobs the flames at the tree trunks, controlling the fire's spread, ensuring that the trunks burn up and nothing else.

Angus tilts his head at him. "I guess mages do have their use."

Ragnald wipes his hands. "I guess so."

Glenna peers up at him with a concerned expression, then follows Angus, stepping over the ash on the blackened ground.

As he strides after her, a pit in Ragnald's stomach aches, reminding him that his past is about to come back with a vengeance.

CHAPTER 24

THE VENERATOR MAGE

"For the love of Fla'mma balls!" the Venerator exclaims, propelling his arms backward to regain his balance and prevent falling into a gaping canyon that seemed to appear from one step to another.

His fingers brush against dry leaves. He grabs onto them.

Thorns cut into his palm, but he ignores the pain.

Small price to pay for not dying by breaking my neck from that twenty-foot-deep fall.

Next to him, the Prowler regains his footing as well, and pulls himself away from the deep chasm by holding onto the branches of a tall sapling, partially uprooting the young tree.

The Venerator glares at the other man. "You sniveling follower! You almost led us to our death! What kind of tracker are you?!"

"I didn't tell you to take the lead, did I?"

"I did not take the lead," the Venerator says. "You slowed down on purpose, didn't you?"

The Prowler smirks.

The Venerator gathers a wide thread of Fla'mma magic to him, forming it into a whip. Then he lashes out, singeing half the furs on that horrible cloak the Prowler prefers to wear.

The other mage shouts a curse and raises his arm to attack the Venerator but then decides against it. Instead, the Prowler curls his clawed fingers inward—a disfiguration many mages with major A'nima affinity have.

"I do not care for your explanations," the Venerator says, letting the fire dance over his hand, enjoying the discomfort of the other man. Just like the dumb animals the Prowler controls, the mage has acquired an instinctual fear of fire.

"What are you waiting for?" the Venerator snaps when the huge mage stands around impersonating a mountain. "Find their tracks. Now!"

The Prowler sends one last glare at him, then leaves, muttering under his breath.

The Venerator knows he made an enemy, but always believed that fear is the greatest motivator. That is why the mage elders were able to suppress that weak guardian goddess of Raghild, whatever her name was, and erase any proof she ever existed. Now, generations after the purge, many original inhabitants have long forgotten that the mages were not the ones on Raghild first.

Wiping the blood stain from his palm with a round leaf, the Venerator shakes his head.

I underestimated Ragnald's affinity in T'erra. He must have practiced more with that element, gaining better control of it.

Ragnald was always the favorite in the eyes of the mage elders and of the mentor. Ragnald became the youngest mentee in three hundred years. That's why Ragnald got promoted over the Venerator to elder rank—he received unfair advantages.

It's not right that Ragnald had all this fortune, while I had nothing of the sort! I am more talented and better at following orders than he is!

Yet, none of that mattered to the mage elders.

Making sure the Prowler is out of sight, the Venerator strides in the other direction, pulling on his green-colored glasses—he would not fall into another trap Ragnald made. This also allows him to pick up any magical traces that sniveling mage left behind.

It doesn't take long to find Ragnald's faint A'qua, Fla'mma, and T'erra magical signatures. The Venerator increases his pace until he races through the forest. He ignores the false trails the other mage laid down—they're much weaker than the one he follows. Let the Prowler distinguish the tracks, busying himself and staying out of the Venerator's way.

I don't have much time to find Ragnald and the pet healer. I need to get to the artifact without letting the Prowler know about it. I won't let that psycopath get his claws on what is mine.

Night falls, but he doesn't stop until he nears a clearing with a thin layer of snow on it. His gaze passes over the well under a triangular stone arch in the middle of an oval clearing and searches the multitude of huts. Smoke trails from one chimney.

Found them!

He puts his glasses away and rubs his chin.

The Venerator has one major elemental affinity in Fla'mma, with a minor affinity in A'qua. But those are not what he needs now. He reaches for his skill originating from A'ris. It is a trace amount, and before that black device the mage elders acquired, no one could have detected it in him.

This skill is the true reason the mage elders kill anyone on Raghild who possesses the smallest amount of A'ris. They don't care about the healers, or any healing ability tied to A'ris. No; what they care about is the once-lost skill that allowed a whole culture to train invisible assassins who do not leave any footprints behind. Nothing can reveal them, not even scent-tracking animals. The Second Era War decimated that world, and most of that knowledge had been lost to all but to the mage elders.

This skill is more powerful than triple major elemental affinity. Yet I couldn't disclose it to the mage elders and expect to survive long. But when I get my hands on that artifact, then I can pretend I got this powerful new ability from it, while still using the artifact for its own purpose, whatever that may be.

The Venerator spent many years searching scrolls about the artifact. He learned that before the Omnipower took over, there were Ancient Powers that ruled the Seven Galaxies. The tears of these dying powers became the rare artifacts known as Tears of the Ancients, scattered all over the Seven Galaxies. Many became incorporated into expensive jewelry, with the owners none the wiser.

That's how the Venerator found his—it was part of an ornate necklace.

As to their use, according to the tattered scroll, there were many aspects: some would store elemental magic for later use, such as a battery; others would neutralize elements rendering the owner indomitable; yet others could amplify the owner's magic. There were many more other uses, but parts of the scroll were missing, and he could not find out more.

The Venerator nears the hut and hesitates.

Two male voices sound, then Ragnald opens the door. The silver-haired mage walks around the hut first, then extends his patrol circles until he enters the woods.

The Venerator approaches the doorway when the door opens again. This time a wide-shouldered man strides out, holding a long-stemmed pipe.

The Venerator sidesteps the tall man and slips inside before the door closes on him.

The Venerator looks around the room and finds the petite healer sleeping under a woolen blanket near the crude fireplace in the corner—the source of the curling smoke.

He squats by the healer and moves his hand over her until he finds where the stinging sensation is the strongest—over her left forearm, coming from underneath her skin.

How strange! I never would have thought to insert the artifact under my skin, but that's healers for you—they are always thinking about ways they can cut you up and stuff you with "medicine."

He curls his fingers above her arm, fighting the temptation to kill her and cut out the artifact, but he doesn't want to fight that big man, giving Ragnald a chance to return and ambush him.

The Venerator must be smart about this. Patience is key.

At least he can figure out what the artifact does.

He chooses a thin Fla'mma thread and threads it into the artifact.

It rings hollow, as if unused, then quaffs his magic down.

Which means it's either a storage artifact or a neutralizer. Both would be of great use to me.

Before the Venerator can do anything more, the door opens, and the tall man returns. The mage slips out, unseen, planning ways he can get his hands on that artifact as the door closes.

As he sneaks around the hut, he notices a few bundles left outside on top of a flat stone.

He opens a package made of leaf, to reveal salted meat inside—their provisions for the coming day.

The Venerator grins as he pulls out a vial of noxious dried herbs he always carries. It has saved him many times when he needed a getaway and used them in wines, killing its drinker overnight. They are nearly impossible to detect due to their scentless state and the fact that they turn transparent once they mingle with drink or food.

The mage elders didn't state whether Ragnald and the healer must be alive or not.

Finished, he returns to the forest.

This visit wasn't such a waste.

CHAPTER 25

GLENNA

An argument drifting from outside rouses me from a dreamless sleep. I sit up and shiver from the cold. The fire has long died out in the small fireplace and the frigid winter air replaced whatever little warmth it generated the night before.

I shake out then fold the wool blanket and place it next to Ragnald's bag, which is already packed. Then I pull on the black mage cloak and pick up the sleeping Mia, with her roots wrapped in a now-dry rag. I pour some water on the rag and place her into the front pocket of the cloak, adding a few seeds next to her in case she gets hungry when she wakes up. Then I stretch my arms above my head, wincing as my body aches from sleeping on the floor.

The argument outside gets louder. I decide to investigate.

My boots crunch on the fresh snow as I walk around the hut, toward the back where the two men stand facing each other with a hostile air around them.

Ragnald points at Angus. "Admit that it was you!"

"For the last time," Angus growls the words, "why would I do such a thing?"

"What is it?" I ask and glance around.

The abandoned huts with broken or caved-in straw roofs look as desolate as they did the night before when we made camp. The clearing holds no obvious clues either. A pristine thin layer of snow sparkles on top of the stone tiles, almost translucent in the morning light.

When the men look at me, I worry that I did something.

Corruption Nic laughs, materializing by me. "Wouldn't be the first time, my little corrupted healer."

I ignore it and note the dark gray clouds hurrying to take over the pale sky, ready to unleash another snowstorm. The wind picks up too.

"It's nothing," Angus says.

"It's *not* nothing," Ragnald protests.

How can two intelligent men make so little sense? I study them both, waiting. It seems that's the extent of their conversation.

My stomach grumbles. I reach for one of the leftovers from yesterday's dinner.

"No!" both men shout in unison.

I recoil. "For the love of mushrooms! Will one of you tell me what is going on?"

Ragnald lifts a wrapped package and shakes it. "This happened!" One of the corners looks chewed on a bit. It's still salvageable in my opinion. Waste not and all that.

"Did Angus chew on the corner?"

Angus chuckles. "No, lass, I didn't. But that poor thing did." He points to his left, where a wolf-like animal with shaggy black-and-white-striped fur lies on its side not too far from the stone. Its tongue hangs out, puffed, its four legs curled inward, and its two pairs of antennae lay flat on its elongated head.

"It's dead," I say and turn back to the men, hoping neither of them killed it.

Ragnald nods. "That's correct."

I take the ruined package from Ragnald and open it up. I raise a hand when the mage tries to interfere. "I have been trained to detect all kinds of venom."

At the Healers' College, the professors had a hands-on approach to teaching toxins and poisons, both nature-made and man-made. I don't tell them that healing myself with my own magic is not as reliable as another healer's A'ris magic. Instead, I sniff the meal.

I don't detect any bitter or strange sweet scents—a good indicator of many toxins derived from flowers. That leaves the undetectable ones with no smell or taste. I touch the surface with my pinky finger, then lick it.

The men shout in protest.

I raise a finger. They quiet.

Focusing inward, I swirl the saliva in my mouth. I don't taste anything out of the ordinary, just the spiced meat. Then a tingling numbness bursts on the tip of my tongue—numbness that I recognize. I spit the poison out before it can spread. Using my A'ris magic, I neutralize any toxin left behind.

Now it all makes sense.

I put the unwrapped meal back on the stone top. "You think it was Angus who poisoned our food." It would have been so nice to eat it for breakfast. I glance at the rest. There is no reason to test them. They must be all ruined too. Not to mention, I have my limits.

Angus grimaces. "I've told him, *many times now*, that I have no incentive to do such a thing. But your mage won't believe me."

He is not my mage!

"Ragnald, what has gotten into you? I don't believe for a second that Angus would try to poison us. If he wanted to kill us, he could have done it many times over, in much more creative ways too."

Corruption Nic raises its eyebrows. "Do enlighten me, my little corrupted healer, what do you mean by 'more creative ways'? I'm dying to know!"

"Go away," I whisper, willing it to leave. Thank the gods it complies.

The mage crosses his arms. "I have a hard time believing Angus. If it wasn't him, and it wasn't you or me, then who did this?"

The three of us stare at each other, then we all turn to face the forest. There is nothing to see, no other signs jump out at us to explain what happened.

Could someone have gotten close enough to poison our meal? Close enough to even kill us? But how?

"There are no footprints outside of ours and that animal's," Ragnald says, echoing my thoughts and watching Angus, "which is why I thought it was him in the first place."

Angus glares at the mage. "Do not start again, mage. How do we know it wasn't you? I have not scented anyone around the hut except you. It would be impossible for anyone else to get so close with neither of us the wiser. I doubt that the mages have new magical abilities, allowing them to turn invisible, or they would have unleashed even more terror on us."

"Why would *I* poison our food?" Ragnald asks. "And we do not 'unleash terror' on anyone!"

Angus pokes the mage in the chest. "Really? How many families have you hurt in the name of the Academia? How many grieve a loss of their family member or friend because of you, mages? You are all murderers!"

Ragnald takes a step closer, pushing against Angus's hand. "Take it back."

Angus growls. "Do not test me, mage."

Ragnald narrows his eyes. "Are you afraid of this 'murderer'?"

With a huff, I turn away from the men. I don't have time to waste on soothing their egos. We need food. That will calm them.

With purpose, I march into the woods.

CHAPTER 26

My stomach grumbles as I push through a patch of dark green shrubs with long thorns that tear at my cloak and hair, leaving behind thin lines of seeping wounds.

I shake my head. "Those two would rather fight than search for food." I stumble on uneven ground and slip on leaves covered in snow. A bitter scent wafts to my noise.

A bushy-tailed creature, as long as a foot, runs by my head, chittering. Shiny red fur covers its body, dotted with black spots. Its long whiskers move fast as it sniffs the crooks and crannies of the tree. It climbs up and down the branches, holding onto the bark with long claws.

Out of nowhere, a red-petaled flower, the size of a toddler, snaps open from behind a bunch of green leaves and gobbles up the bushy-tailed animal, then retreats behind the leaves.

Shivering, I take a step away from the tree, fighting the urge to rescue the small critter. I know better than to interfere with nature. I can heal the animals but cannot take another's food source out of pity—that would cause more harm in the long term.

I head left when something sticky envelops me.

Yelping, I swipe off the spider web. I look over my cloak to see if the owner of the web hitched a ride on me.

Corruption Nic sniggers in my mind. "I can't believe you're afraid of spiders!"

"Then don't believe it."

I take deep breaths to calm my fast-beating heart. The only spider I've ever liked was Gwendoline. Gods, I hope she made it out alive from the Crystal Palace with her offspring.

A questing root from my pocket brushes against my hand.

"Everything is okay," I say to Mia. "It was nothing."

My stomach grumbles again.

Right. Time to look for something edible, such as wild berries or mushrooms.

With an extended arm, I wave in front of me to avoid any spider webs and continue my trek, going much slower this time.

The usual rackets of the forest: the chirping, tweeting, buzzing, chattering, leaves rustling, and branches creaking, play on my nerves. I am aware that there could be all kinds of dangers lurking behind those verdant leaves.

I scan the trees and tall shrubs until I see clumps of dark blue berries. They are the size of my thumbs, peppering a shrub with round leaves. They look ripe, ready to be picked.

My mouth salivates as I hurry toward the shrub, tripping over my own feet. With deft fingers, I reach for the closest group of wild berries.

A loud shriek sounds.

I withdraw.

A thin two-foot-long beak slams where my fingers were seconds ago.

The bird—with shiny scales covering its back that reflect the pea-green leaves of the shrub—shrieks at me and snaps its beak in an affront.

"Oh, my herbs!" I say and back away some more. "I thought those were berries."

Suddenly the shrub is full of ferocious fowls, all jabbing their beaks toward me.

I dart in the opposite direction. After a few minutes, I slow my pace.

Holding my stitching side, I look back to make sure that those birds are not following me. I peer into the cloak's pocket, but little Mia slept through the whole incident.

Corruption Nic appears, laughing. "Did you . . . try to pick . . . that bird's—"

"Don't want to talk about it!" I shudder just thinking about how I confused those berries with, well, something different.

"Maybe stick to mushrooms," Corruption Nic adds, still snorting from suppressed laughter.

"Very funny."

Though it's not a bad idea.

Picking a random direction, I hike deeper into the Forest of Loss and Darkness.

"How is that freak of nature of yours?" Corruption Nic asks. "Still alive, I hope."

My left hand curls over my pocket that houses Mia, and I trip on a dry branch.

It explodes under my boot with a deafening *Crack!*

Creatures of all sizes, along with a myriad of tiny birds, hurtle out of the trees, fleeing upward in panic. I cover my head with my arms to protect myself from them.

A cry sounds.

Something crashes through the canopy, all the way to the forest floor behind me.

I turn to see the body of a child-like humanoid inhabitant of the forest lying stunned on the ground.

"Now you killed a babe," Corruption Nic says with a shake of its head. "Well done."

I kneel by the injured youngling, who cannot be taller than three feet. Long fluffy white hair covers a feminine and purple-hued face still chubby around the cheeks—a sign of how young she must be. A ragged homespun dress covers her thin but corded body, but she does not wear anything on her bare feet. Dark brown eyes filled with tears stare at me. She holds her right arm with a bloody bone fragment jutting out of it.

"Oh, sweetheart," I say to her in a soft voice. "I can heal you, if you let me." Then I point at her injured arm.

Corruption Nic scuffs. "Why bother? That 'sweetheart' is a wild wight who will stab you in your back the second you turn away."

"Everyone deserves healing."

Her gaze studies my face, running over me, then she shows me her arm.

Engaging my A'ris magic, I go to work on the break, ensuring not to cause her any more pain than necessary.

After a long time, I sit back and wipe the sweat from my face. I reset the bone and heal the long cut until a faint pink line shows on her purple skin.

I push to my feet, then stumble. My vision blurs and a loud whining noise fills my ears—I overextended my magic.

Squeezing my eyes shut, I take deep breaths to fight it, trying not to think how often dizziness comes now after a healing.

I smile at her. "We are done. Please be careful with your arm for a while."

She tilts her head to the other side, then dashes away.

Corruption Nic sneers. "See? Too wild to even show gratitude."

"That's not why I heal."

I wonder where she lives, or how she survives in this lethal forest. Being a juvenile, does she have a small family unit or live among a bigger group? Where are the adults of her race? How come we have not met any of them?

"Maybe they are more cautious than you," Corruption Nic says.

I shrug my shoulders. Whatever is the case, her bones healed faster than most of my patients, indicating a healthy lifestyle.

Now back to gathering mushrooms—for the third time.

"You should just give up," Corruption Nic says. "I bet the men already found something to eat while you wandered around, lost and aimless."

"I doubt the men have done anything of the sort."

To my right, I discover a copse of trees with white spots on their trunk. I push through the vines toward the trees.

Their thin trunks fit between my forefinger and thumb. What looked like white spots are mushrooms with flat caps.

"They must live in a symbiotic relationship. The mushrooms must be eating bugs that would hurt the tree, while the tree provides a safe and higher place for the mushrooms, away from the dangerous forest floor."

"Boring," Corruption Nic groans.

Turning my back on it, I lean closer to observe the mushrooms. They have dark gills, which is good, as white gills often indicate that the mushroom is poisonous. Their caps are white and not red. I don't see any bulbous growth or volva around their stem—all of these make me believe that these mushrooms are, indeed, edible.

"One way to find out."

With a deep breath, I pick a mushroom off the tree and send a prayer to the Archgoddess of the Eternal Light and Order for providing sustenance.

After wiping the dirt off its cap, I take a bite.

"I didn't realize you were in such a hurry to die," Corruption Nic comments.

I wait for that telltale tingling or numbness, but it does not come. There is a pleasant taste of the mushroom and nothing else.

"Hmm, delicious!" I eat the rest. Then I fill my empty pocket with them, making sure not to pick too many from the same tree.

Finished with my task, I turn to make my way back to the men.

"How nice to see you're taking care of others," Corruption Nic says. "You never took such good care of us, now did you?"

From one step to the next, the forest disappears. I find myself back in my windowless room in the basement level of the Crystal Palace.

"Stop this!"

I blink to banish the vision that saturates everything, but it won't budge.

My nose fills with the sweet, flowery aroma of my room, mixing with fur and other animal scents. An enthusiastic chorus of barks, meows, chirps, and all kinds of screeches greets from my animals.

I run my fingers over Anton, the three-legged A'ice wolf. The wet nose of Buck presses against my arm as the old hunting dog demands my attention. Isa and Bella, the two gray cats with long fur, wind themselves around my legs. Milky cataracts glint in their mischievous eyes. Then Angie, a red bird, rubs its bent beak on my arm with affection. I smooth the feathers above her eyes, as she likes it. Bobby, a small white bear with a degenerative disease that stopped its growth when it was a cub, vies for my hand. Itty, Bitty, and Missy, three butterflies the size of small children, flicker their pastel wings in greeting.

Tears well in my eyes. "I am . . . so sorry. I didn't know . . . I should have released all of you . . . but there was no time . . ."

The animals don't care for my words. They shove at me, climbing on me.

I gasp for air, buried under them.

"Please, you are crushing me." I try to get them to leave, but I can't move a muscle. I am rooted to the spot, weighted down.

"Please, forgive me."

My pets smother me. Until I choke for air.

CHAPTER 27

"Glenna!" Angus shouts.

The disturbing vision of my animals vanishes, replaced by the Forest of Loss and Darkness.

I still can't breathe!

A branch cuts into my back as a heavy snake moves over me, sliding around my body and constricting my neck. I claw at the powerful and slippery body, but my fingers can't find purchase.

My knees give out. Dark spots dance in my vision.

A slashing metallic sound rings by my ear.

Liquid splatters on my face.

Pieces of the snake's black body drop around me.

I wheeze in air, retreating from the gruesome serpentine parts and rub my throat.

Angus clasps my shoulder. "It's over, lass." He pulls me into a hug, patting my back, until I compose myself.

"Thank you for saving me."

Shock sends shivers over my back.

The corruption has grown too powerful. It trapped me in a vision from my memory, long enough for that snake to attack me.

Corruption Nic sniggers in my mind. "You should have seen the look on your face!"

Wiping my eyes, I check on Mia. She blinks tired eyes at me, unharmed.

Angus wipes the blood off the long blade of his dagger, then sheaths it in a leather case. "Are you sure you're okay?"

I nod, avoiding the sight of the still squirming pieces of the massive snake.

"Don't worry about it. It won't hurt you, or anyone—for that matter." He hands me a bundle and adds, "Here, eat this. Sugar will help."

I untie the purple-stained handkerchief to find some round blue berries inside. "Oh, uh, I'm not sure if I should . . ." I have no idea how to explain the embarrassing incident.

Angus throws his head back, laughing. "Let me guess; You've met the Bluebells birds?"

"Maybe?"

Angus laughs harder. "It happens to all of us. After a while, you'll learn to see the difference between a wild berry and—"

"Thank you for these," I say, and shove a handful of berries into my mouth, hoping to erase the bitter taste fear left behind.

"Feeling better?"

I nod.

Together, we resume our hike back to the camp.

"I admire your courage," Angus says after a while. "You didn't let that snake shake you up. That's what my sister Aggie does, I mean, would have done. I still refer to her as if she is with us."

"Tell me more about her."

Angus smiles. "She was such a free spirit. Always looking for the next adventure. Her excitement was contagious when you were in her presence. She found goodness in everything. Trusting in life that things will turn out for the best. Until they didn't."

"She must have been wonderful," I say. "Would you tell me what happened?"

Angus sighs. "I am not sure, to be honest. Last year, I was away when the news reached me that she was hurt. I rushed home, but she passed away the night before my arrival. Her death crushed my mother. My father never looked so old and hopeless as he did on the night of her funeral. My siblings said she sneaked out to the City of Paucity on numerous occasions."

"Do you know who hurt her?"

"My family has their suspicion, but no proof. Not that the mages would care for any proof we could produce. I pray to Guardian Goddess Cyn'rha for answers every day."

I pat his arm.

"My sister always loved the city and its bustling life. I should have known she wouldn't be able to resist the temptation of it for long. Her light was stolen from us. I blame myself for what happened. I should have stayed to watch over her. I should have warned her more . . ." He falls silent, his gaze looking inward.

"I am so sorry," I say.

Angus glances at me. "Aggie loved this forest. She always brought home insects and small critters she found around our, uh, home."

"She sounds—"

"Quiet!" Angus snaps and tilts his head with a scowl. "That can't be."

"I didn't mean to—"

He lunges at me. "Down!"

We fall to the ground. He covers my body with his, staring ahead of us. I push against him, then I hear it too.

CHAPTER 28

RAGNALD

"What's taking her so long?" Ragnald winces from the pain that jabs into his jaw.

He shouldn't have fought with Angus, but he was itching to test how strong the other man was.

Now I know. The wanderer possesses more strength than I expected. He also had some training, not stumbling around like a novice street fighter. He knew where to hit for the most impact.

It took a lot of effort and concentration to match Angus, but Ragnald was relying on more than a hundred years of experience and training in physical fighting. Once he detected a pattern in Angus's movement, it was easier to overcome the wanderer.

There was a glint in Angus's eyes that warned Ragnald that the wanderer would not have any problem killing a mage.

What happened to Angus to be so prejudiced?

The methodical and often ruthless tactics of the Academia can be frightening, but Ragnald always believed that the mage elders made the right decisions necessary to maintain the magical order in the Seven Galaxies. It was never an easy task, but all the mages, including himself, were up for it.

I wish Glenna would realize what I'm doing is for the greater good.

But she is too blinded against the mages. There is so much about his past he wants to share with her, but he knows that she would not be impressed with how fast he climbed through all the ranks of mages, starting at the lowest when he was just a child of forty years—a follower. Then fifty years later he became a disciple, specializing in Fla'mma and A'qua elements, studying magical history along with galactic diplomacy. It took him another fifty years to get promoted to adherent, the last student rank before a mage focuses on one of the two paths available: track as a prowler, like that Prowler chose, or combat.

Finishing his general magic, economics, and tactics studies—first among the students—required another twenty years. He chose the combat path and took the required affinity test that revealed his triple major elementary affinity. The years flew by until he earned the mage elder rank.

Ragnald couldn't have been happier as an elder. His Mentor rejoiced with him as well.

However, the initial excitement of the Academia about his triple elemental affinity soon soured. It was replaced by petty politics and envy. The missions he was sent to became more difficult to follow through, and more taxing on his soul.

Then he disobeyed a direct order—an act he couldn't have imagined ever doing.

Glenna would get a kick out of knowing how I fell from the good graces of the mages.

"Where is she, anyway?"

Ragnald paces back and forth at the edge of the clearing. He stops to listen—outside the shrieks and titters of animals dwelling in the forest, he doesn't hear anything else.

He inhales the clean air, unlike the city. He wishes he could share his plans with her, but he knows she won't like it.

All I'm trying to do is to protect her. She's already struggling with the growing corruption and doesn't need anything more to upset her. Who knows how much longer she has?

"Angus?!" he shouts, but there is no sign of the wanderer. After their fight, they each stomped to separate corners of the abandoned village. The other man must have left.

What if Angus went to find Glenna to play the victim? What if he tries to seduce her?

Ragnald grinds his teeth. It shouldn't matter to him, but it does.

Angus has no business flirting with Glenna!

He marches into the forest while his imagination conjures images of Glenna and Angus laughing together, all happy and cozy. Engaging in activities that have nothing to do with foraging.

Furious now, he charges through the forest at a breakneck speed, following the wanderer's tracks and using his Fla'mma magic to cut a path into the overgrown foliage.

I will teach Angus what it means to cross a mage!

Then a thunderous rambling sound reaches his ears.

What on Raghild is going on?!

Ragnald steps around a row of shrubs.

Angus and Glenna clash with a swarm of black insects. The twelve-inch-long bugs assault them with their red stingers or try to bite them with wide mandibles on flat orb-like heads.

"Get down!" Ragnald shouts. Then he pulls a wide ribbon of Fla'mma to him. Twisting his hands over each other until his palms face outward, he sprays the insects with fire.

The flying swarm squeals and shrinks back from the fire, many burning to ashes as they flee.

Ragnald shuts off the fire magic and pulls Glenna to her feet. He runs his hands over her to check for injuries, noting a few bleeding scratches on her face.

Thank the gods!

He wipes the blood off her cheeks and searches her dark crimson eyes, unable to pull his hand away from her face. "Are you okay?"

There is so much he wants to say to her, but all the words vanish from his mind when her fingers touch his hand. Warm tingle sinks into his skin from her healing A'ris magic, and his bruises dissipate.

Ragnald leans down, never taking his eyes off hers.

Glenna licks her lips and rises on her tiptoes.

"You almost burned us!" Angus snaps, breaking the moment.

Glenna steps back, looking embarrassed. Ragnald curses and lets his hand fall away. Angus grins.

"Not even close," Ragnald says.

Glenna crosses her arms. "We had it under control, *mage*."

CHAPTER 29

THE VENERATOR MAGE

"What the Fla'mma balls do you think you're doing?!" the Venerator snaps at the Prowler.

After the Venerator returned from his visit with the red-haired healer, he found the Prowler missing from their camp. It took him a long time to track the other mage. When the Venerator saw what the mage was doing, he almost incinerated that sniveling Follower on the spot.

The Prowler moves his hands side to side in a hypnotic movement, his dark brown eyes glowing with an eerie yellow light from his A'nima magic.

"My job," the Prowler responds. "You have a problem with that?"

I can't let him apprehend Ragnald and the healer! He'll discover the artifact and take it for himself!

The Venerator slaps the mage's head. "Our orders were to bring them in alive." Not quite, but the Prowler wouldn't know any better.

The yellow light dims from the mage's gaze. "I thought sending the cave wasps would—"

"You are not in charge!"

The Venerator sends a Fla'mma needle to the other man's temple—a disciplinary act the mage elders favored when the young followers were getting out of control.

"There was no need for that. I already stopped using my magic."

"Now you'll learn to never take any unnecessary risks with my mission."

The Prowler rubs his temple. "You mean *our* mission."

"I lead and not you. Or did you forget, you sniveling follower?"

"No one survived calling me a follower."

The Venerator steps close to the other mage. "Are you threatening me?" He allows his Fla'mma fire to envelop his arms.

The Prowler eyes him as if undecided, then after a tense second, he turns his gaze away. "No, Venerator Mage. I, uh, meant no offense."

"Good." The Venerator turns away.

"I interfered because last night you failed to arrest the known offenders, prolonging this godsforsaken mission. I just wanted to help."

The Venerator whirls on his heel to face the mage. "How dare you meddle with my plans? Now Ragnald knows that someone is after him and he'll be more careful next time. We won't have an easy time apprehending him, thanks to your thoughtless actions. Now get out of my sight."

The Prowler shuffles away.

The Venerator stares at the back of the other man, imagining burning the mage to ashes, just to be done with him. He has no doubt that the Prowler will try something against him soon.

At least I showed him I'm still stronger than he is. That'll buy me some time to get rid of the sniveling follower and get my hands on my artifact. Then no one will stop me from becoming a mage elder.

CHAPTER 30

RAGNALD

Ragnald and the others arrive back at the oval-shaped clearing with an altar-well in the middle of it, where they slept in one of the surrounding straw-roofed cabins. Glenna limps to the edge of the clearing, looking like she'll collapse at any moment.

Ragnald channels his Fla'mma magic into her, using the magical administration as an excuse to put his hand over her shoulder to steady her without her noticing it.

She always disliked people fawning over her. She doesn't like looking vulnerable in front of anyone, let alone a mage.

Ragnald snorts under his breath.

No matter how many times she says "mage" with such distaste, I can't stop reacting to her presence.

Even now, all he wants is to kiss her.

Snap out of it! Since when are you a lovesick follower?!

With a muttered curse, he steps back, removing his hand from her shoulder. It almost kills him to separate from her.

Ragnald takes off his mage cloak and drapes it on the ground. Not a second too soon, as Glenna collapses onto it.

He glances at the dark sky with black clouds rushing by. Scents of snow, old leaves, and grass hang heavily in the air. Most of the daylight is gone—winter days never have more than six hours anyway—there is no point venturing into the forest in the nearly pitch dark for what may become another whiteout.

"I'll start on the soup," Angus says, and Ragnald nods.

The mage settles on the blanket next to Glenna, who struggles to stay upright in a seated position.

Angus makes quick work of starting a fire under a metal pot filled with water and the mushrooms Glenna gathered earlier. Then the wanderer adds a few dried vegetables and a handful of long insects.

Ragnald bumps his shoulder into Glenna, trying to prop her up, and she lets him.

She is too quiet, exhausted from the previous ordeal with insects. I hope she wasn't stung too many times—that much venom could overwhelm even a healer.

To hide his growing worry, Ragnald pulls a clean handkerchief out of his pants pocket. Using his water flask, he wets one of its corners.

"May I?" he asks.

Glenna blinks at him.

Ragnald takes it as a yes. He gently touches the handkerchief to her face, wiping off the worst of the blood.

This feels right. As if I were meant to take care of her all my life.

He moves on to her neck, but many smears of dirt seem too stubborn to come off at first try. Then he realizes that the dark spots are bruises, with scale-like imprints in them.

What on Raghild happened in that forest?!

He is about to ask Glenna when their eyes connect. All thoughts leave his mind.

Glenna smiles at him. "I never thought I'd see a mage engaging in a healer's work." Her tone sounds jovial, but her dark crimson gaze that dips to his lips is full of desire. For him.

Ragnald brushes his fingers down her cheekbone. "Someone has to take care of you." Then he tucks her dark crimson hair, with a wide streak of white in it, behind her right ear.

"I, um . . ." Glenna's voice trails off as she stares at him, mesmerized.

Ragnald leans his head down until not even a tenth of an inch separates them. He groans when she licks her lips.

Just take it easy, don't rush it.

He closes his eyes and—

"Dinner is ready!" Angus shouts. Then he thrusts two wooden bowls at them, sloshing some of the hot, green, and murky soup on Ragnald's hand.

The mage takes it with a grunt.

Glenna draws back and accepts her soup with a kind smile.

She never smiled like that at me.

Ragnald grips the wooden spoon and a pop sounds. A hairline fissure appears at the side of the handle.

Glenna hands her soup to him. "Please hold this for a moment."

Ragnald drops his spoon into his soup and takes her steaming bowl. She picks out a few seeds from her pocket and feeds them to Mia. Then takes her soup back and digs in.

Angus smirks at him with a knowing grin.

Ragnald glowers at the wanderer.

I should have beaten more sense into Angus when I had the chance.

For a few minutes they eat in silence, then Angus gathers the bowls and strides back into the forest to clean them.

Ragnald turns his attention to Glenna. She rubs her eyes but looks even more tired.

"Is everything okay?" he asks, then curses.

Of course nothing is okay! She is struggling with the growing corruption, and now she gets to deal with bug poison.

"It's just, um . . . I am, uh, bit, um, drunk . . ." She yawns, then waves a hand, tilting to the side, but he grabs her around the waist.

"No, that's not, the, um, the word . . . I'm not, uh, drunk. It's, uh, the venom. My body is just, uh, a bit, um, feverish. I'll be . . ." Her voice trails off and her eyelids shut. She lists toward him. He hugs her to his body, making sure her head is cushioned on his shoulder.

Her hair spills over her closed eyes.

Even in sleep, she looks gorgeous.

Ragnald swipes strands of hair out of her face.

She mumbles something, then scoots closer until her cold nose is buried in the crook of his neck, her soft breath tickling his skin.

Ragnald peers down at her content face.

How can someone so petite to be so fierce and beautiful at the same time?

His right arm goes numb, but Ragnald refuses to move an inch, lest he disturb her rest.

If I could use all my magic to make this moment last forever, I would in a heartbeat.

Ragnald doesn't know when or how it happened, but he knows he is lost to her. She owns his heart, and he is fine with it.

Angus steps out of the forest, and frowns when he sees Ragnald holding Glenna.

That's right. She's mine. Deal with it.

Angus inclines his chin, then puts the bowls away in his knapsack. The wanderer drops down into a cross-legged seated position in front of Ragnald with a contemplative look in his eyes. "You sure had good timing."

Ragnald raises an eyebrow. "About what?"

Does he mean Glenna?

His muscles tighten, ready to fight for her.

Angus rolls his eyes and gestures toward the forest. "Those insects were dangerous cave wasps that hate fire. If you wouldn't have come . . ." His voice trails off when he looks at the pale Glenna.

Ragnald knows what Angus means. Even now, the mage feels Glenna's heart beating too fast as her body wrestles with whatever toxin those wasps injected into her.

He points at Angus. "How is it that you have little to no scratches on you?" The wanderer looks more than well—he looks healed from their earlier fight *and* from the wasps, as if Glenna's magic had taken care of his injuries. Except Ragnald was with Glenna, and she didn't heal Angus; she was too tired.

"Never mind that. Those nasty bugs—both their bites and stings poisonous—always attack as a swarm, and don't stop until their prey is dead, or they are. Then they feast on their prey's corpse for weeks. But what's more interesting, they can be found deep inside caves. Hence the name—cave wasps."

Ragnald takes a sharp inhale. "Then how did these cave wasps appear so far from their home?"

"Isn't that the question? But that's not the worst of it, mage. They were trying to get to her."

Ragnald looks back at Glenna, the air in his lungs feeling like ice shards. "A powerful mage with major A'nima affinity drove the insects as a weapon aimed at her."

"It sure seems like it, doesn't it?"

Ragnald curls his fingers into his palm.

Whoever is following us decided to stop playing and went straight after Glenna. A mistake they should have never made. I will not rest until I find them and kill them for daring to hurt her.

"It's time to meet our pursuers," Ragnald says, already picturing tearing them apart with his bare hands.

Angus smiles, and his brown eyes flash with a predatory look. "I couldn't agree more."

CHAPTER 31

GLENNA

Lying on the ground, I dig a pebble out of my stomach and place it to the side, trying not to make any noise. I cannot see much through the branches of the wide shrub, full of round leaves with thorn-like edges that can draw blood. As they did on my arms. I resist the urge to pick at the bleeding superficial wounds. Next to me, little Mia dozes, wrapped in a moistened handkerchief, leaning against a wide branch.

After I woke up at dawn, the men filled me in on their theory that our food was poisoned by the same mage who sent the aggressive wasps, and who has been following us for some time now. They spent all morning figuring out where to set a trap, until we came across a naturally formed deep fissure in the ground, a few feet wide, just big enough to swallow up one person. The men covered the crevice with brittle branches full of leaves, making sure it blended well into the forest floor. Then Ragnald took the mage robe he lent me and hung it on a sapling, arranging it so it appeared as if I was gathering herbs. It wasn't perfect, but from a distance it did look like a person.

"Are you sure this is going to work?" I whisper to Ragnald, who lays next to me. I inhale dust and pinch my nose to stave off a sneeze.

He nods, not taking his eyes off the forest.

Angus peers from behind a tree across from us. He ignores the scrambling insects around him that run up, down, and crisscross.

"It's been at least two hours," I whisper. "Are you sure we weren't made?"

Ragnald glances at me. "Trust me, we weren't. Now quiet."

Fine! I turn away from him, staring at nothing in particular.

Corruption Nic materializes next to me. "Ooh! Another trap! How exciting! I do hope this one will work out better than the one Lilla set up in the

Spirit Realm. She let that prisoner go free, didn't she? At least you wanted to torture him. I was so proud of you!"

I try to recall what happened in the Spirit Realm, but many of the events are a hazy recollection, part of a feverish nightmare that left me with dread that I did something I shouldn't have done.

"Nothing to say?" Corruption Nic asks. "How unusual of you, my little corrupted healer."

"Just go away." I still haven't forgotten how it tried to kill me not too long ago. The corruption obeys and turns into a puff of smoke.

Something rustles.

Ragnald points ahead. Angus inclines his head and steps behind the tree, out of sight. Sweat drips into my eyes, but I dare not move to wipe it off.

A huge man strides into view, wearing a cloak covered in fur.

After a few steps, the mage stops and sniffs the air, like a wolf.

What is he waiting for?

Holding my breath, I urge the mage to take the bait.

"Are you wishing that mage harm?" Corruption Nic asks in my mind.

Technically, I am wishing for our success.

Corruption Nic sniggers. "I like how murky your moral principles are—that's why I'm getting stronger every day."

Angus takes a quick peek, then tosses a rock toward the fake Glenna.

The mage's head snaps up. His yellow-glowing gaze finds the replica, and he approaches it.

The branches give with a loud crack under the mage's feet.

The big man backpedals, swinging his arms and avoiding the trap.

Then out of nowhere, a strong gust of wind picks up, rustling the trees, hitting the mage in the back.

The yelling mage digs in his heels, fighting the wind but he can't resist it. He plummets into the deep fissure headfirst.

Then his shout cuts off.

Then the wind dissipates just as it came.

Angus strides to the trap and looks inside.

"Wait here," Ragnald says and marches toward the wanderer.

No, I will not wait. I get up and join the men.

Angus shakes his head. "Well, that mage won't ever hurt us—or anyone, for the matter."

Ragnald surveys the forest with a suspicious look in his storm-gray eyes. "I had questions."

I peek into the trap. The huge mage lies at the bottom with his head in an unnatural position.

Wiping my eyes, I turn away and send a quick prayer to the Archgoddess of the Eternal Light and Order. May the Lume accept his soul.

Angus slaps Ragnald's shoulder. "Our friend took all the answers to our questions with him into the Lume, now didn't he?"

CHAPTER 32

THE VENERATOR MAGE

Asharp pain from his right shoulder disturbs the Venerator from his sleep. He opens his eyes and yelps.

An animal the size of a large dog, with a lean body and arched back, braces itself on four legs over him. It growls at him. Its wolf-like head, full of rows of fangs in its maw, drips blood. His blood.

"For the love of Fla'mma balls!" He tries to move his arms to fight back, but ropes cut into his wrists and ankles.

That sniveling follower tied me up!

He tests the give of the rope, but it tightens even more around him, cutting off his circulation.

The beast lowers its body over its front legs, readying itself for a charge. The Venerator has no doubt that it will go for his jugular in a kill move.

Not if I can help it!

He engages his Fla'mma magic, burning through the rope in an instant. Then shoves his red flame-covered hands into the face of the animal, burning its eyes out.

The predator shrieks in a death throe, trying to escape.

The Venerator holds onto him with satisfaction.

Isn't that ironic how the hunter becomes the hunted?

Laughing, he bares his teeth at the crazed animal, watching the Lume leave it.

Then he sends a burst of Fla'mma into the creature.

Within seconds, dark ash showers over him.

Getting to his feet, the Venerator surveys the campsite.

The Prowler's belongings, a sizable black bag and a brown woolen blanket, are gone, along with the backstabbing mage.

The Venerator wipes dirt and ash from his robe. His finger touches a sore and sticky spot.

He hisses, staring at his injuries.

I hate this part.

The Venerator lifts a thin thread of Fla'mma, threading it into his fingertip. Then he takes a deep breath and channels it into his wounds.

Pain bursts from his skin.

He blacks out for a few seconds but stays upright.

Gods, I will make the Prowler pay for this!

The Venerator checks his shoulder. The bleeding stopped, leaving behind a red patch, with teeth marks around it. Then he gathers his belongings into his bag and searches for clues the Prowler left behind.

If that sniveling follower killed Ragnald's pet healer before I got my hands on my artifact, I would prolong his suffering for days!

The Venerator picks up a faint trace of A'nima magic and follows it. After a while, he catches sight of the Prowler, standing in a small area between the trees.

What is that infuriating follower doing?

The other mage looks back.

The Venerator ducks behind a wide tree, with his heart beating in his throat. Then, after a few seconds, he inches to the right side of the tree trunk and peers out.

He spots the petite healer's black cloak in the distance, in the direction where the Prowler was gawking. Right before it is an area covered with leaves and branches.

Ragnald must have set up a trap.

A rustle sounds from the imitation healer.

The Prowler strides toward her when the ground opens under his feet. The large mage fights falling in and stays clear of the trap.

The Venerator bares his teeth and engages a thick thread of his A'ris magic, shaping it into a gust of wind. Then he shoves it at the other mage's back.

The blast of air hits the Prowler, thrusting him into the opening headfirst.

The Prowler yells as he hurtles into the trap, then his shouts cut off.

That was underwhelming.

The tall man doesn't suspect anything as he checks out the trap. Ragnald, on the other hand, looks back, toward him.

The Venerator plasters his back to the tree.

Did Ragnald see me?

The Venerator readies a thick ribbon of Fla'mma magic, holding the fire in his palm, but when he peeks out again, Ragnald has his back turned to him.

The Venerator releases his magic with a quiet exhale.

Ragnald and the others exchange a few more words, then they leave.

The Venerator watches them.

One obstacle down. I'm getting closer.

CHAPTER 33

GLENNA

"I know a shortcut through the swamps," Angus declares as we come to a stop. He points to the right, at the edge of a marsh with pale green flora sticking out of it.

On our left, the endless forest, like a patchwork of green hues, continues with no clear path through it.

I take a deep breath. Decaying scents of vegetation and musty swamp permeate the air.

"I am tired of seeing trees," I say, and pull the lapels of the cloak closer. I'm glad we didn't leave it behind.

"I don't like shortcuts," Ragnald says at the same time, eying the bog.

Corruption Nic pops into existence. It looks around with distaste twisting its mouth. "The mage is right; nothing good ever comes out of a marsh."

I chuckle. "It doesn't like marshes."

Corruption Nic crosses its arms. "Laugh all you want. It's your life."

I turn to Angus. "I am all for the shortcut that will get me to the Academia quicker. Lead the way, please."

Ragnald frowns. "If that's what you want, then I will not hold you back."

Angus grins, inhaling the air with pleasure. "Step where I do, and you'll be fine."

Corruption Nic scoffs. "Somehow I doubt that."

Angus picks an invisible path and wades onto sunken land with the turbid water reaching to our ankles.

Ragnald gestures for me to go before him. I follow after Angus.

Warm water laps at my boots. I peer at it, but can't see beyond the swirling mud, with sand particles sparkling like minuscule diamonds.

"How is it that the water is not cold?" I ask, and my breath comes out in a cloud. A swirling fog evaporates from the surface of the swamp as it rises.

"There are many hot springs running through the bog, resulting in the water pleasant all year round," Angus says. He steps on dry spots, ignoring a large swath of parcel to our left, with round hills jutting out of it.

"Why aren't we going that way?" Ragnald asks.

Angus raises a hand, and we halt. He picks up a palm-size rock and pitches it at the wider land.

A bumpy triangular head, bigger than my torso, erupts out of the middle of the mound, snatching the rock out of the air, then withdraws.

"What was that?" I ask with a hand at my throat.

"That's a gnashing turtle, which calls this marsh home," Angus explains. "It prefers hiding in the hills, making a nest for its dozen offspring. It's always more aggressive during the breeding season, like now."

Ragnald shakes his head. "Better be careful."

Angus resumes trudging through the bog.

Sighing, I trail after the wanderer, with Ragnald at my back. I watch our surroundings, wondering what else is hiding under the water or behind the corroding plant life.

The greenish water extends far into the distance, devouring all the land around it with a never-ending appetite. Here and there, trees twist upward with bare branches looking half dead. Sparse shrubbery covers some of the mounds of dirt with long strips of yellowish moss clinging to their leafless limbs.

Corruption Nic crosses his arms. "I dislike how desolate everything looks."

Smirking, I look at it. "*This* desolation is bothersome?"

Corruption Nic raises its chin in response.

We keep slogging.

A racket of tweets accompanies us, along with throaty croaking.

After a while, Angus stops and gestures to the right. "It's through there. Then we're out of the marsh."

Ragnald studies the two-foot-wide patch of soil with muddy water lapping at its edges. "Are you sure? This doesn't look much different from the other places."

Angus smiles. "That's the beauty of the marsh—those who live here know the way out."

I slap an insect off my arm. "Then what are we waiting for?"

"As long as we're leaving this godsforsaken place . . ." Ragnald's voice trails off as he tramps onto the path.

I take a step too, but Angus blocks my way with an arm thrust in front of me.

"Angus?" I ask, then hear Ragnald's cursing.

"I'm stuck!" Ragnald snaps, then points at the wanderer. "I knew I shouldn't trust you!"

I push Angus's arm away from me, but he won't budge. "What's going on?"

Corruption Nic sniggers. "I told you so."

Angus looks at me. "Stay here. I have no business with you, Weaver of Life." Then he jumps on a few areas in a crisscross pattern, heading toward Ragnald.

I take a cautious step forward.

"Glenna!" Ragnald shouts. "Do not come closer!"

When nothing happens, I take another step. Then another. At the third, my foot gets stuck. The muddy water bubbles around me as I sink knee deep.

Corruption Nic scowls. "Now we're stuck. Great job."

"Angus, this is not funny anymore," I say, fighting my rising panic. This is nothing like the kind man who helped me slip into The Inn after a long night spent healing.

Angus looks at me. "I'm sorry you're caught in the middle of this."

"Middle of what?" I ask, but Angus turns away from me.

Corruption Nic mocks, "Now your stupidity will kill us all."

"Oh, shut it."

Ragnald increases his struggles to get out of the quagmire.

"The more you fight it," Angus warns, "the faster you'll sink. It's the first rule we learn."

Ragnald ceases to move, the water reaching his waist now. "What do you want?" the mage asks, straining.

The wanderer laughs. "Your magic won't work here. Don't bother."

"Angus, please let us go," I plead. "No harm done; just a bit of a mis-understanding."

The wanderer slashes out with a hand. "Stay out of this, Glenna."

Ragnald glares at the other man. "What do you want?"

Angus stalks around the mage, avoiding the edge of the sinkhole.

"Where were you a year ago?"

Ragnald grimaces. "Where I was . . . What does that have to do with anything?"

Angus slaps the mage across the face. "Answer me!"

Ragnald's head snaps to the side, and a bleeding cut appears on his lower lip.

I inhale. "Don't hurt him!" My hands itch to call for my A'ris magic and heal the mage, but the ribbons won't obey me.

The mage spits blood to the side. "That depends. I left Raghild right before winter. Why?"

Angus nods. "That means you were still here that summer. Have you ever killed anyone with your Fla'mma magic?"

Ragnald's face shuts down. A mix of emotions flash over his storm-gray irises—sadness, regret, guilt, and anger. "I'm sorry, Glenna."

Angus slaps the mage again. "That's not what I asked!"

This time a dark bruise appears on Ragnald's right cheekbone.

"Stop! Ragnald wouldn't hurt anyone!"

The wanderer laughs. "Your faith in the mage is misplaced."

"Angus," I say, "please talk to me. What do you want?"

When I dare a peer at Ragnald, Fla'mma fire flickers over his hands for a second or two before extinguishing.

Angus growls. "Tell me!" Then he slaps the mage again.

Ragnald's upper lip swells. "You know that I did. Is that what you wanted to hear?"

Corruption Nic sneers. "True!"

Ragnald watches me. I try not to show my disappointment but fail.

"When was the last time you killed someone with your Fla'mma magic? Don't try to lie; I will know it." Angus says and snaps his fingers.

Ragnald sinks another few inches, even though he didn't move.

"This is my territory. I rule here."

Corruption Nic groans. "Thank you for ensnaring us!"

Twisting my body, I try to find footing or anything to grasp, but there is nothing. I sink to my hips now. I remove Mia from my pocket and place her inside my shirt. Her roots grasp the neckline, while her vines thread around my neck as she presses close to my skin, mewling in distress. With a shaking hand, I pet her, murmuring comforting words until she calms a bit and falls asleep.

"Angus, don't do this," I say, trying to appeal to his compassionate side. "This won't bring your sister back. Please let us go."

Moisture appears in the corner of Angus's eyes. "I swore that I would find Aggie's murderer and avenge her death."

"I didn't murder your sister, Angus. I swear."

"I don't believe you!" The wanderer punches Ragnald.

The mage's head snaps back. "I was right not to trust you."

Angus snorts. "Yet here you are, in my marsh."

Corruption Nic whirls to me. "Do something!"

I gape at it. "What do you think I can do? Isn't this what you wanted all along—me dead?"

Corruption Nic wrings its hands. "No! I mean yes, but I need you to die where I can take over, not stuck deep underneath a bog where you'll be useless to my archgod!"

"I'm touched by your concern." I sink another few inches, until the warm muddy water hits my waist. I try to engage my A'ris magic again, but it sputters out of my control.

I am out of ideas.

"At least tell me why you think it was I who murdered your sister before you kill me. I deserve that much."

Angus contorts his face. "You are a mage and you will pay. But I can tell you this, I've been praying to my Guardian Goddess Cyn'rha. She showed me in my dreams—every night the same dream fragments since my sister died—that the murderer was a tall, long-haired mage with Fla'mma magic who kidnapped her and hurt her."

Ragnald's jaw drops. "There are tens of thousands of mages who fit that description."

"Angus, please. I know in my heart that it wasn't Ragnald who killed your sister. The real murderer is still out there, somewhere. We can help you—"

"Save your words for someone else," Angus says, interrupting. "If I have to kill thousands of mages to get to the murderer, then that is what I'll do. Starting with this mage, right here."

CHAPTER 34

Angus lunges at Ragnald with a right jab, but the mage counters it with a cross-jab-hook combo.

Increasing my struggle to get out of the death hold of the sinkhole, I claw at the ground. My fingers snag on fine roots.

I grasp them and pull. I make a headway of a few inches, when the roots give out and I sink even deeper, with the muddy water splashing under my breasts. Oblivious, Mia snores at my throat.

"Stop your useless wiggling," Corruption Nic says, "or both of us will perish here!"

"That might not be a bad idea."

Then DLD won't be able to use me as His Turned. But I don't want to die here. Nor do I want poor Mia to become collateral damage.

All I can do is watch Angus and Ragnald locked in a desperate fight, powerless to do anything about it.

Already Ragnald slows down, with more dark bruises darkening his skin and angular face.

Angus, panting, circles the mage.

Gods! I cannot bear to watch Ragnald die!

"There *is* something you can do," Corruption Nic says, "but you must follow my directions."

"I'm listening."

"You must combine your A'ris magic with me, I mean, with the corruption threads in you."

I gape at it.

Corruption Nic claps. "Hurry!"

Fine!

Closing my eyes, I search until I find a swirling column of blackness with lightning-like threads snapping out of it, like incensed snakes.

I grab one of the thinnest writhing serpentine threads.

"Now add your A'ris magic to it," Corruption Nic instructs. "Once combined, your magic will be disguised, and the bog won't be able to block it."

"It's not that easy." The corruption thread in my hold bucks like a wild beast trying to escape.

"Try harder!"

Focusing on the corruption-serpent, I pour my element into it. The amalgam of magic morphs into a nauseating dark-grayish-blue color, like some kind of hybrid element that is not quite A'ris but also not quite corruption anymore. It feels unnatural and nauseating.

I swallow down my bile. "Now what?" Sweat beads on my forehead, dripping into my eyes from the effort it takes to hold the hybrid magic.

"Shape half of it into a weapon," Corruption Nic says, "like a dagger, or a spear, or a sword—"

"I've seen weapons before."

Corruption Nic spreads its arms in a what-are-you-waiting-for? gesture.

Pressing on the hybrid magic thread, I separate it into halves. I grab the first half and shape it into a straight-bladed dagger.

Inhaling a deep breath, I steady my hand and throw the magic dagger toward Angus.

The dark dagger pierces Angus's shoulder, sending him to his knees. Then it dissipates, leaving behind a gushing wound.

Angus turns his head. Our eyes connect and I show him my teeth.

That's right. I won't go down without a fight.

Angus tries to get to his feet, but he staggers. Bloody bubbles form in the corner of his mouth. His lungs must have been grazed. Not good.

"If you don't want to die, get me out of here so I can heal you."

Angus shakes his head with a stubborn expression, then stumbles and falls to the ground.

For the love of mushrooms! "There is no point in all of us perishing here."

"Why bother with him?" Corruption Nic asks. "Take the second half of the magic mix and use it to get us out of this sinkhole."

I will it to disappear. It raises an eyebrow then turns into smoke.

I don't want to touch that terrible corruption magic, but there is no other option.

Grinding my teeth, I wrestle the slimy dark magic into a rope and chuck it at the closest tree on my left. It wraps around the trunk as if the magic has its own mind.

I tug on the rope—making sure not to crush Mia—and pull hand over hand, crawling out of the sinkhole one painful inch after another.

Relief floods me as the last of that strange magic mix dissipates. Though the corruption level remains too high—whatever amount I used, it didn't make an impact on the infection.

I get to my feet and step around the groaning Angus on my way to Ragnald. Then I lean down and grab the mage's hand.

"How did you do that?" Ragnald asks.

"I'll tell you later," I say to him. "Now let's get you out of here."

Holding the mage's hand between mine, I lean back and brace myself in a squat position, letting gravity assist me. Struggling for every inch of release, I pull until Ragnald gets free.

The mage turns onto his side, panting. I drop next to him onto knees, breathing hard.

Ragnald gets to his feet and swipes some of the mud off him, then helps me up.

The mage strides over to the wanderer, who lays on his back with a hand on his bleeding wound. "Give me a reason why I shouldn't kill you?"

Angus, pale from the blood loss, looks away. "Do your worst, mage. I care not anymore."

I raise a hand. "That's enough of that. There will be no killing today."

Ragnald crosses his arms. "If that's what you'd like."

I check on Angus, lifting his hand from his injury.

The bleeding wound has black edges, remnants of the corruption. I pry my pocket open, gather some herbs, and sprinkle them over the wound. It won't heal Angus but will stop the bleeding until I can access my magic.

"Where is the, uh, exit out of this place?"

The wanderer winces, then with my help stands up. He waves to the right, toward a clear and well-used path.

I lift Angus's uninjured arm over my shoulder, and we trek onto the path.

Exhaustion saps my energy. My vision tapers into the small path in front of me as I force myself to take one step after the next with Angus leaning on me—until I drag the wanderer.

I groan in relief when we reach a copse of dark green trees with solid ground under our feet.

I sigh. "I can't believe I'm saying this, but I am so happy to see the forest again."

Then I grab a thick thread of A'ris, channeling it into Angus. The corruption-tainted edges of his wound heal with the help of my A'ris, leaving behind a shiny patch of skin. Many of the dark purple bruises recede in a few moments.

Angus gestures toward the ground. I assist him to sit down.

I turn to the mage, who holds his arms by his side, with his fists covered in red and orange flames. "Ragnald, please put your fire away before you burn someone's eyes out."

The mage points at Angus. "Why did you heal him when he was ready to kill us? I should burn him to ashes!"

"Everyone deserves healing. As a healer, I swore to help others, without any discrimination."

Corruption Nic snarls in my mind. "There should be people exempt from healing, *especially* the ones who tried to kill us."

Ragnald extinguishes his fire with reluctance. "I do not agree with your philosophy."

"I'm not surprised," I say, and step to the mage, channeling my A'ris magic into his forearm, healing his bruises and a few cracked ribs along the way.

Angus drags a hand through his hair. "The mage is not wrong, Glenna. I, uh, let my vengeance take all my reason. I just wanted to interrogate him. But I allowed my animosity toward mages cloud my judgment and, well, I got carried away."

Ragnald raises an eyebrow. "That's not a good enough explanation."

I wipe my hands. "I cannot know what you've gone through, but I can relate to your feelings toward the mages. I once felt the same way and did something impulsive out of desperation, compromising my healer's oath."

I glance at Ragnald. It seems the mage remembers too.

"I've since learned from that mistake," I continue, "and I have no doubt that you will too. You deserve a second chance to right your wrongs."

Angus hunches his wide shoulders forward. "You humble me with your benevolence, Weaver of Light, though I do not deserve it. I'll strive to live up to it and learn patience for I know my Guardian Goddess Cyn'rha will lead me to the true culprit. I must trust her to reveal the murderer when the time is right."

Ragnald rolls his eyes.

Angus clears his throat. "Mage, I got to know you. Deep down I knew you were not a ruthless murderer. For all the hurt I caused you and Glenna, I ask your forgiveness."

"I can't say I am happy with you right now," Ragnald says, "or that I will ever trust you . . ." his voice trails off. He sees my pointed look and adds, "However, I can understand your motivation. I may have done the same if someone had hurt Gle—I guess this means you're forgiven. But do not cross me again."

Angus nods. "I understand." Then he jumps to his feet, wearing his old jovial smile, and says, "I decided that I will go to the Academia as well. I'll have better luck finding the killer there."

Ragnald raises a hand. "You can't come with us."

I smile at the wanderer. "By all means, join us."

Both Ragnald, and Corruption Nic in my mind, groan.

Angus rubs his hands. "Then let us go! I am excited at the prospect of finding the murderer."

Ragnald shakes his head and leads the way into the forest.

Above the tree crowns, on top of the mountain plateau, an imposing gray fortress towers over its surroundings—our destination.

After a while, Ragnald comes to a sudden halt.

I bump into his back. "What now?"

Ragnald turns to the side to reveal a hundred light-purple-skinned dwellers with sharp spears.

CHAPTER 35

I gape at the short purple beings, who cannot be taller than four feet. White tufts of hair cover their heads. A pair of long horns curve downward, ending by their jawlines. Their eyes burn with a red light as they glare at us. Homespun clothing covers their lower body in various sizes like loincloths, or shorts, or full-length pants. Rolled ribbons cross their toned chests, sometimes twice. Instead of boots, they wear the same cloth ribbons wrapped around their feet and around their calves.

They jab their wooden spears at us, their corded and muscular arms not wavering.

"Not the Drearies!" Angus and Ragnald say in unison. Then the men curse under their breath.

"What is that?" I ask and take a step closer to Ragnald.

Spears poke in my direction.

Corruption Nic appears next to me. "How do you get yourself into jeopardy without even trying?"

I'd like to know the answer to that question too.

"They are very dangerous," Angus says from the corner of his mouth, "and territorial. I thought we were far away from their village's border, but it seems they extended their land, now bordering mine—the marshes. Do not smile at them; they take that as a challenge for a fight."

I wipe the beginning of a pacifying smile off my face. Instead, I pat the silky red petals of Mia, who still dozes around my neck.

More spears prod at me, and my hand freezes.

"For the love of corruption, stop fidgeting!" Corruption Nic snaps.

"Also, if they smile at us," Angus continues, "that's bad as well. We might be as good as dead."

Ragnald adds, "That's why they're called the Drearies—they always glower, until they smile as they kill you. Frowning means they approve of you. Though I am not sure."

"There is a small chance," Angus says, "that they are cannibals. I can't recall if they prefer their own for food, or those unlucky ones who get lost in their territory. As you can imagine, not many have survived to tell that tale."

Corruption Nic doubles over, laughing. "Cannibals! Of all the things you can run into, you found cannibals!"

I hope their cannibalism is a myth.

Ragnald continues, "The Academia have known of their existence, but we tend to avoid them. They are, well, not intelligent enough to reason with."

Angus cuts a sharp look at the mage. "How dare you judge them? What if the Drearies consider all the mages prancing around as primitives?"

"We don't *prance*, I will have you know."

I resist the urge to cover my face. "This is not the time to bicker like children."

Both glare at me.

Corruption Nic snickers. "You are so dead!"

The Drearies advance, forcing us to start walking. We march deeper into the forest as the afternoon sunlight gives way to the night. Hunks of dried mud flake off our clothing, leaving behind a pungent smell of putrid swamp.

Ragnald frowns at the wanderer. "How do we know this wasn't another trap of yours?"

Angus spreads his hands. "I deserve that, I do. But think mage—if this is another trap, why am I right in the middle of it too?"

Ragnald nods. "That might be so. But what did you mean earlier when you said your 'territory?' Who are you?"

Angus shrugs. "It's, uh, not important."

Ragnald cuts a look at the wanderer. "This is not how you earn my trust, whoever you are."

Angus curses under his breath.

Then our group pauses in the middle of a glade with small dirt mounds, and a lot of purple grasses with white flowers.

Angus grimaces. "This is not good."

CHAPTER 36

RAGNALD

Ragnald looks around the glade. The dirt mounds, covered in purple blades of grass, also house burrows. Hundreds more purple dwellers spill from their underground homes, lining up on either side of the main dirt path that cuts through the area, chattering among themselves.

Ragnald inhales. Aromas of baked bread drift on the breeze, along with scents of fire and spiced meat. His stomach grumbles from hunger, though he suspects *he* might be their dinner.

Butts of spears prod Ragnald's back.

He resumes shuffling across the little village along with the others.

He tries not to worry about Glenna.

Maybe I can threaten them with my Fla'mma fire or bury the warriors in the ground with my T'erra magic so we can make our escape.

He doesn't care whether Angus keeps up with them. Nothing but saving Glenna matters.

Soon they leave the village behind and enter a wide meadow. Millions of tiny butterflies with sparkling wings illuminate the dark night. More purple grass with white tufts of flowers bend in the wind and crumple under their feet.

"Look how the Drearies blend among the flowers," Glenna says with awe. "They are so cute!"

Ragnald groans and discards all his plans involving magic that might hurt the Drearies in any way.

She would never forgive me.

They cut through the field, then stop at the edge of a hundred-foot-wide crater. The spear-wielding Drearies line up around them, crowding all around the perimeter of the deep basin.

This does not bode well, but I don't want to scare Glenna.

Glenna turns to him. "Ragnald, did you see how the Drearies exude peace? Well, if you ignore the spears, that is. They're just so calm. Isn't that splendid? Though it might be this charming pasture that makes me feel so content."

Angus bursts into laughter but covers it up with a cough.

Ragnald sighs, not feeling at peace whatsoever. "I imagine they will *calmly* kill us, then *calmly* bury us, then, I assume, because by then I won't be alive to witness it, they will *calmly* resume their lives, as if nothing happened. How is that for 'splendid'?"

Angus guffaws.

Glenna pouts. "That was not funny, *mage*."

"But your mage is right," Angus says. "It's not probable we'll come out of this alive. Though I have one thing I can try to get us out of this fiasco."

Without warning, Angus's visage shatters, falling off him like shards of a broken mirror. An eight-foot-tall, wide-shouldered and robust troll, with long green braided hair that resembles roots from the swamp, straightens up. More root-like veins cover his muscular chest, even sticking out from his thick forearms. Long claws tip his fingers and bare feet. His sturdy legs are covered in remnants of brown pants. His handsome face that still has hints of Angus sports thick eyebrows. A pair of fangs jut upward from his lower lip, while a multitude of green tusks stick out of his jawline.

Gaping, Glenna studies the monster, first with fear, then with wonder.

Angus's dark brown gaze takes in the Drearies, then he lifts his head and bellows. The predatory sound reverberates, destroying the quiet of the night.

Ragnald's ears ring and the hair rises on the back of his neck. He knows what Angus is, though he never thought to meet his kind.

None of the Drearies flees in fear. Instead, they lift their spears, ready to fight the humongous troll.

That's just great.

Angus shrugs a massive shoulder. "It was worth a try. Your turn, mage."

Glenna snaps her head up. "Don't you dare hurt them with your magic!" Then she points at Angus and asks, "Who are you?"

Angus bows his huge head toward her. "I am Angus the Wanderer, sixth son of Chieftain Angar of the Swamp Trolls."

Glenna's eyes widen. "Swamp troll?"

"There are many troll types, but swamp trolls reside on Raghild. I used glamour to disguise my true self. It's a nonmagical skill, unique to us. We developed glamour as defense against the mages when they came to Raghild hundreds of years ago. The mages hunted us to near oblivion. But we outsmarted them, retreating deep into the Forest of Loss and Darkness, calling the Marsh of Misery our home."

Ragnald looks Angus up and down. "I couldn't sense your, uh, troll state at all."

"That's the whole point, mage."

Angus reengages his glamour. A shimmer runs over him as he returns to his wanderer self. "Then I guess this is it. Start praying to your preferred god or goddess for a safe trip to Lume."

There must be something I can do!

A commotion sounds.

Across from them, a crowd parts to give way to an older female Dreary who sits on a wooden chair with poles on either side, carried by younger Drearies.

Must be their matriarch. This is really, really, *not good.*

The Drearies around them holler in greeting. Then they hit the butts of their spears on the ground. Rocks roll into the yawning crater.

Fla'mma fire leaps onto Ragnald's fingers.

This is my chance to burn a path through them!

Though he'll have to drag Glenna away kicking and screaming, for she'll want to heal anyone who gets burned.

Multiple spots of pain burst in the back of Ragnald's head and back.

His magic extinguishes.

The mage turns back to see five Drearies holding their spears, butts first, on him. He has a feeling next time they'll prod him; it will be with the pointy end of their spears.

A youngling bursts onto the ledge, next to the matriarch, with something wrapped around her arm.

Ragnald squints.

Is that a splint?

The young Dreary chatters, pointing toward Glenna, then at her arm.

When did she have the time to heal that youngling?!

Ragnald turns to Glenna, who pretends to be engrossed at her feet.

The matriarch smiles, showing fang-like teeth, and says something. Those piercing fangs make Ragnald sure that the rumors of cannibalism might not have been exaggerated.

Then all the Drearies smile, and throw their spears in the air, catching them with great dexterity, then slam their weapons into the ground.

Angus chuckles. "I believe our little Weaver of Life just saved our hides. Now, that's what I'd call splendid!"

CHAPTER 37

GLENNA

The Drearies escort us away from the crater. Instead of cutting through the flowering meadow as before, they circle the edge of it, heading right.

After a while, we reach a stone-tiled circular clearing similar to the ones where we'd made our camps over the past few days. There are no abandoned structures or huts nearby, just the usual arch with a well underneath it, placed in the middle of the tiles.

The matriarch turns to us and gestures with both hands, palms down, toward the ground.

Everyone, including us, drops into a seated position.

"Maybe instead of killing you," Corruption Nic says, "they will sacrifice you to their gods, then eat your flesh." It leans back onto its elbows next to me.

"That's still killing," I point out. I lift the sleeping Mia off my neck and remoisten her dry handkerchief. Then I place her back into my pocket. A few of her roots twitch, and one vine curls around my finger for a moment.

Smiling, I note that she's had another growth spurt, as more of her roots stick out of the hem of my pocket. Soon I will have to find a place for her—she can't live in my pocket forever.

The matriarch hobbles to the well and begins speaking. Her words are clear. Must be this sacred place that allows me to understand her.

"Once, in the beginning of time, there were three ancient giants who walked Rag'a'hild, caring for us in the name of our Guardian Goddess Cyn'rha. We lived in harmony and lacked nothing. Our sun warmed our land. Our animals ran free. Life was plentiful and simple. Not a dark cloud marred our blue sky. We were happy."

The Drearies murmur agreement and hit their palms on the ground.

The matriarch continues, "Then the mages came. They brought greed, want, and anger. Our sky darkened. Our sun weakened. Our fields gave no more. Winter came. Then darkness came. Our guardian goddess slept. Her giants retreated. But we don't forget. We give thanks every day. We hope every day. We pray for their return every day."

The Drearies jump up, yelling their agreement.

I glance at the dark sky, with clouds rolling over the moon and wonder what the mages have done to this world to sicken it like this.

The matriarch clasps her hands palms up and holds them in front of her. A young Dreary hurries to the matriarch and deposits pebbles into her weathered hand.

The matriarch says, "We give thanks to the Mountain Giant who built this land and these mountains for our Guardian Goddess Cyn'rha." She throws the pebbles into the well.

I wait for the telltale splash, but not a sound can be heard.

Another dreary, this time a warrior, hands the matriarch a wooden mug full of clear liquid. "We give thanks to the Sea Giant who made our rivers, streams, and seas for our Guardian Goddess Cyn'rha, nourishing this land and us." She pours the liquid into the well, then hands the mug back.

A third Dreary brings a small canvas bag the size of my hand to the matriarch. "We give thanks to the Wind Giant who brings mild seasons as our Guardian Goddess Cyn'rha wishes, so we can plant and harvest." She empties the bag's contents—dried flowers and grass—into the well.

Two Dreary warriors carry a carcass of a goat-like animal with six legs. "Finally, we give thanks to our Guardian Goddess Cyn'rha, who takes care of us, provides food for us, and protects us."

Corruption Nic shakes his head. "How pitiful. They should be praying to my archgod instead. He will win at the end."

"Not if I can help it," I mutter and focus on the corruption to leave. It crosses its arms but complies.

The matriarch hobbles back to her chair, and all the other Drearies line up. They take their preferred items out of pouches that hang on their belts and repeat the process in quick succession. Many have a bone fragment or a fur patch to sacrifice to their goddess.

When the Drearies finished, they head away from the clearing.

A strange pull draws me to the well. It's similar to the one I visited a few days ago, but there is a warmth emitting from its smooth, gray stones.

Closing my eyes, I pray for Rag'a'hild to heal the damage the mages did to this world. I pray for my family, who never had a chance against the mages. I pray for all the healers whose lives the mages destroyed.

Tears blur my vision and fall into the well.

A warm breeze drifts up from the well, caressing my face and drying my tears. Comfort spreads through me.

With a sigh, I return to the waiting men.

Ragnald makes a face. "I had no idea how our presence affected Raghild, I mean, Rag'a'hild."

Angus slaps the mage's back. "That was the wisest comment I've ever heard a mage utter."

CHAPTER 38

I laugh along with the smiling Drearies, sitting on the grassy ground. We watch others twirl and dance around the burrows back in the village. The spears have been replaced by handmade flutes and palm-size string instruments. Everyone sings, claps, or drums their feet, creating quite a musical festival.

It turns out the Drearies like smiling, and they don't take offense to our smiles now that we're all friends.

Corruption Nic steps out of a puff of smoke and sits next to me. "Who knew you had so much in common with these primitive creatures—both of you were defeated by the mages."

I turn away from it.

The matriarch takes a seat in an elevated wooden chair. She grins showing off white teeth with a few missing, while nodding along to the music. Next to her, long tables hold clay trays piled high with vegetables, rolls, dried and cooked meats, while bowls brim with stews and soups. Tantalizing scents of food and spices mix with grass and dust, saturating the air. Many Drearies line up by the tables, going for their second or third servings.

Thank the healing herbs the Drearies are not cannibals. Though what happened to their previous visitors is still a mystery.

Angus and Ragnald have their plates piled high with their fourth helping. I rub my full stomach—I ate too much.

The youngling with her arm in a splint sits down next to me.

"How is your arm?" The moment we left the sacred clearing, none of us could understand the Drearies anymore.

She stares at me.

I point at her splint, raise my eyebrows, and lift my arm up and down.

She responds in her guttural language with a big smile.

"Why you care about her is beyond me," Corruption Nic says.

Ignoring the corruption, I take it that she is doing well.

She gestures toward my pocket from which quite a few roots poke out.

"Oh, that's just Mia," I say and pull the hem of the pocket to the side. The young Dreary leans close, looks inside, and her eyes go wide. She makes snapping motions with her fingers, similar to how the adult flowers chomp their prey.

I shake my head and take out a few seeds. "This is what Mia eats now." She shrugs her shoulders.

"Why are you called Drearies?" I ask and make a sad face. "When you all enjoy smiling." I point at my own smile.

She tilts her head, then looks around. She leans close to a bunch of purple grass and pulls a long one out. Then she shoves it under my nose.

"Would you like me to smell it?" I ask and sniff it. It smells like, uh, grass.

She grimaces. Instead, she lifts the grass and points at her chest, talking fast in her own language. Then she makes a sad face and shakes her head.

Oh! "You're not called the Drearies."

She chatters in agreement, and points to her fluffy hair, then at the grass that has the beginning of a similar fluff.

"Instead, you're called Stalks?" The noun, I hope, and not the verb.

"Here comes your wanderer," Corruption Nic says, pointing at the approaching Angus.

When Angus reaches me, he extends a hand. "Care to dance?"

I place my hand in his. "Sure."

He pulls me to my feet and twirls me in a circle, following the rhythm of the song the Stalks are playing.

"I wanted to apologize to you," Angus says. When I raise an eyebrow in question, he adds, "You know, for the, uh, misunderstanding earlier."

Corruption Nic snickers. "Misunderstanding? That's a mild description!"

"You already apologized." I swipe clean strands of hair out of my face. I'm glad the Stalks showed us a hot stream of spring water when we reached their village a few hours ago. We took turns washing the mud off. Then Ragnald dried our clothing with his Fla'mma magic.

"I, uh, didn't tell you all of it," Angus says with a deep exhale. "I knew you were a healer and that you came to The Inn with a mage. I followed you and waited for you for days. When you almost got caught, I stepped in to help you, so I could earn your trust. I didn't expect you to become my friend. Can you ever forgive me?"

Corruption Nic laughs. "Your mage was right about him all along."

I see Angus in a whole new light. No wonder he earned my trust—his actions were all designed to achieve just that.

"You manipulated me," I say.

Angus winces. "I did, lass."

I glance away from him. His betrayal hurts like a physical wound that won't stop bleeding. While I understand with my logic why he did it, my heart aches—I was not a friend but a means to achieve his goal.

Corruption Nic shakes his head. "You'd be a fool to forgive him. How do you know he won't deceive you again?"

I don't know that; not anymore. Yet I can't help but wonder what I would have done in his place.

My initial reaction is to tell him that I can never forgive him or trust him, but that's too harsh. It comes from a place of hurt feelings. All it would accomplish is to hurt him back.

Corruption Nic scoffs. "What are you waiting for? Just send him away and be done with him. He is not your friend."

I close my eyes and force the corruption to disappear, which it does.

Nothing is as simple as right or wrong. There are shades of each. If anything, I can relate to that. It was the hardest lesson I had to learn, and it almost cost my friendship with Lilla. Not to mention how I endangered Ragnald too. But now I know better.

"I forgive you," I say, and mean it. "You could have kept this to yourself, and I wouldn't have been the wiser. But you decided to be honest with me. I won't lie and tell you that it does not hurt to be used, but I empathize as to why you did it. As I said before, you deserve a second chance to prove yourself. All that matters are your actions going forward. Just promise me that you won't take advantage of anyone else in your search for the murderer."

"I promise you, Weaver of Light. Your friendship means a lot to me."

"What are you going to do once you have your revenge?"

"I'll have to think about that," Angus says. "When I go to sleep, vengeance is my last thought. When I wake up, vengeance is my first thought. All I want is to find whoever hurt my little sister, so she can rest in Lume. That's all I care for now."

"I hope you'll find your peace too," I say, "and protect yourself from vengeance consuming you."

"It's not consuming—"

"May I cut in?" Ragnald asks, already taking my hand from Angus.

Angus nods and heads toward a nearby table. I hope he'll consider my advice. He'll need a new purpose in life once he completes his quest.

"Did you know the Drearies are called Stalks?" I ask.

Ragnald places my other hand on his shoulder. "Is that so?" Then he grasps my waist and leads me into a slower dance.

I feel self-conscious all of a sudden—I was never a good dancer. Yet, in the mage's arms, I dance as gracefully as if the opposite is true.

"You are, um, very skilled," I say to him, ignoring the blush heating my face.

"Are you surprised? In my two hundred years, I have acquired a few talents here and there." He pulls me into his body.

Unable to resist anymore, I lift my hand off his shoulder and trace his cheekbone.

Ragnald's gaze darkens, and he tilts his head into my palm. "I love when you touch me." Then he covers my hand with his.

"I like touching you," I admit in a husky voice.

"A mage and a charlatan? Is that a good idea?"

I have a second to tell him to stop, but I can't recall why.

Ragnald leans closer, until our breaths mingle. His gaze dips to my lips. Then his mouth is on mine. His lips move sensually, igniting a fire in me.

I return his kiss, sliding my hand from his face onto the back of his neck and into his hair. I tug on the silver strands, asking for more. Asking all of him.

Ragnald growls and deepens our kiss, slowing down until we're barely dancing.

I let him in. I don't want our kiss to end. Ever.

A small hand taps my back, shattering the moment.

I pull away from Ragnald, and he releases me.

Looking away, I hide my surprise at how easily I gave in. How I kissed him back.

"Glenna," Ragnald says, but I pretend I don't hear him. Instead, I smile at the female Stalk who grabs my hands. Then she twirls me toward an older Stalk, while a youngling pulls the mage in the other direction.

Soon we engage in a quick and spirited frolic, getting lost in the crowd of dancing Stalks. Happiness is contagious, and I find myself laughing out loud.

My lips tingle, as if the mage's kiss left a brand on my mouth. Kissing him felt like tasting the forbidden star pears of Evander—a fruit that looks delicious with its gleaming yellow skin, though a bite from it is lethal.

Even now, all I think of is Ragnald. How it felt to be in his embrace. When what I should think of is ending this fling before it's too late. I'm putting his life in danger since I can become Turned at any moment. Yet I can't convince myself to discontinue this foolishness. What is wrong with me?

"You were always selfish like that," Corruption Nic says in my mind, "caring about your own happiness and nothing else, didn't you?"

That can't be true!

Then Angus shouts, "Fire!"

CHAPTER 39

RAGNALD

Wildfire rings the village, shutting them in. It shoots seven feet tall, then inches closer and closer.

The Stalks retreat from the flames, huddling around their matriarch.

"Get water and bring it here!" Angus yells. "Hurry!"

The Stalks obey, and line up where Angus points. Glenna joins the front of the line, throwing buckets of water at the wall-like fire.

It makes the flames burst taller.

The yellow-reddish light of the fire illuminates the dark sky with sparks surging into the air, blinking out of existence the next instant.

Ragnald, rooted to the spot, stares at the blaze. The skin on his face too warm from the blaze.

In his mind, he sees a terrified young girl with blue eyes, in another place, with the night sky behind her unnaturally bright. Terrible crackling sounds as the burning fire consumes everything in its way, spreading unrelentingly. Buildings burn, imploding. Lanky people with dark blue hued skin scream, running from danger, many with their clothing already on fire.

His heart beats in his throat. His nostrils struggle to inhale the air that's saturated with scents of smoke, ash, and charred meat. He gapes at his Fla'mma-covered palms.

When he looks up, he finds the young girl's blackened body at his feet.

What have I done?

"Ragnald!" Glenna shouts, breaking into his thoughts and erasing the fragments of memories from his past. "Do something!"

Ragnald stares at her for a moment, then looks around at the nightmarish scene. It's as if his past found a way to come to life, with the fire spreading violently on top of the grassy mounds and burrows, destroying the homes of the Stalks and threatening the villagers' lives.

Ragnald hesitates. "I can't—"

Glenna cups his cheek. "Please help us."

Ragnald nods, her words cutting through his doubt. Her belief fueling his magic.

She steps back with an encouraging smile.

Ragnald strides to the closest burning wall of fire that threatens the Stalks. As he watches it, he realizes that it does not behave as a natural wildfire, but more like controlled Fla'mma fire.

He knows it will take a bit more effort to combat it, but he will not rest until it's done.

With newfound energy, Ragnald waves his arms in a circle, engaging his A'qua element, and shaping it into clouds above the flames encircling the village.

Then he pulls on his T'erra magic, reversing the movements of his arms. Once a thick thread obeys his call, he drops down on one knee and slams a hand on the ground. His magic rushes into the soil, opening it up until a shallow trench runs the circumference of the glade in front of the fire. He tugs on the A'qua thread of the clouds, and rain showers down.

Then Ragnald flows to his feet, circling his hands, one over the other, pulling on the fire in front of him.

The roaring fire bucks against the rain, raging. It jars to a halt in the T'erra trenches. Then dissipates as the Fla'mma threads are pulled from it.

Ragnald strides along the border of the fire until nothing is left of it but ash and black, curling smoke.

Exhaustion presses him down. He gulps in smoke-saturated air.

After a long moment, Ragnald straightens. He circles his arms, threading his T'erra magic into the trenches and restoring the destruction.

Finished, he glances around.

I couldn't save that village from devastation, but at least these villagers escaped the same fate.

Glenna steps to him and touches his back. "Nicely done, mage."

CHAPTER 40

GLENNA

I cut through the rising black smoke, though the ground and the burrows are restored, thanks to Ragnald and his magic.

The Stalks scurry around, helping others with burn injuries.

I raise my hand. "Let me heal you. Please."

Corruption Nic appears by my side. "Please do. I love your long-winded healing sessions. Again, I don't understand why you waste your talents on these—"

"I've told you many times before. Everyone deserves healing."

I gesture toward the Stalks. The youngling, with her arm in soot-covered splint, waves her people closer, chattering in their guttural language and coordinating the patients.

The next few hours go by in a blur as I heal all the injuries—various degrees of burn wounds, a few sprained ankles, a couple of broken bones, and some bleeding cuts.

"Without Ragnald's intervention," Angus says and hands me a wooden mug of water, "we would not be here."

I take a sip. "The mage saved us all." Then I peer into my pocket and splash a bit of water on the handkerchief covering the sleeping Mia's roots and hand the cup back to him.

"Where is Ragnald anyway?" I ask and pat my face to rid myself of the wooziness. I used up too much of my A'ris magic.

Angus points to the left, toward a large group of Stalks with the mage in the middle. "He just escorted a grateful matriarch to her home."

I head over to Ragnald. "Thank you."

The mage turns to me, surprised. "That's the first I've heard you . . . of course."

Grasping my shoulders, Ragnald looks me up and down with an impersonal attention the best healers give to their patients, too busy determining the diagnosis to carry on with small talk.

"I'm fine," I say, hiding my smile.

He slides his hands down my arm. "Are you sure? You tend to ignore your own well-being—"

"Ragnald, I'm *fine*." I lick my thumb and rub a large smear of ash off his right cheek.

"Oh, how cute," Corruption Nic says, sniggering. "You are in the touchy-feely phase of dating."

A muscle jumps under my eye, but I don't argue with it.

Ragnald pulls me to him. "That you are—fine, and more."

I giggle, while Corruption Nic rolls its eyes.

Then I recall how the mage stood frozen, staring at his hands. "What happened?" I ask, interrupting Ragnald from leaning down his head. I am not sure if I can handle another one of his kisses.

"I don't follow."

With a sigh, I step back from the mage. "You seemed lost in thought when the fire was threatening the Stalks' village. Why?"

"Nothing of import," Ragnald says and points at the sky. "It's dawn. We should resume our trek toward the Academia and make up for lost time."

I want to pry more but instead I nod.

Angus strides to us, carrying bags. "Ready to go?"

"Yes," Ragnald says.

Two Stalks dart to us, holding food packages wrapped in leaves, and half a dozen leather water flasks. We put away our rations and smile in thanks.

Then we bow to the Stalks and leave their village. Angus leads as usual, with Ragnald at my back.

I glance over my shoulder, but the mage avoids my gaze.

Biting my lower lip, I worry about Ragnald. It shouldn't bother me that he closed himself off to me, but it does. I want to know what caused him such distress. I want to comfort him. I want to . . . feel his arms around me again.

I shake my head.

I can't have anyone else's death on my conscience.

Corruption Nic snickers. "It is a long list of deaths already. But what's a few more?"

"Go away," I mutter. It obeys right away for once.

Pushing vines out of my way, I duck under branches.

I won't think about the mage. In fact, I won't think about anything. That will help me get through the day.

Not even a few minutes goes by, when our kiss pops into my mind uninvited. How natural his body felt against mine. How good it felt when . . .

Shoving fronds of a plant away from my face, I curse.

I can't waste energy on this crush. I must spend more time figuring out how to get rid of the corruption. That's a good plan.

"It's not a little crush," Corruption Nic says in my mind.

I know my heart better than anyone.

Exhaustion from the sleepless night catches up with me. With each step, fatigue bears down on me. The trees blend into a blur.

The sky darkens and night falls.

"We'll make camp here," Angus says and I almost cry from relief.

CHAPTER 41

VENERATOR MAGE

The Venerator pours his Fla'mma magic into the fire that encircles the village of the Drearies.

Ragnald, paralyzed, doesn't even react to the new threat, just as the Venerator suspected would happen.

Ragnald always took the easy way out, leaving me to take care of his messes. But I did what the mage elders ordered and cleansed that village.

Those dark-blue villagers never should have used magic without the mage elders' permission. They ignored the mages' warning. It was no surprise to him when the mage elders ordered a group of them, including the newly minted Mage Elder Ragnald, to take care of them.

There wasn't a single one of the villagers left to tell anyone what happened. Just as there won't be anyone left to tell what happened to Ragnald and his pet healer.

The Venerator is more than sure that the artifact under the healer's skin won't get damaged by Fla'mma. Many of these artifacts survived fires, blizzards, floods, and even volcano eruptions.

His trap set, the Venerator paces back and forth, waiting. His fingers can feel the artifact, and the anticipation is almost too much for him to bear.

To his surprise, he hears the healer's shout.

When the Venerator looks, he finds Ragnald attacking the Fla'mma circle with his triple elemental affinity.

The Venerator stumbles back.

I'm not going to give up!

He shoves his arms forward, palms up, and strains to add more Fla'mma into the seven-foot-tall blaze.

Guttural shrieks sound behind him.

The Venerator whirls to find a group of Drearies springing toward him with wooden spears raised high.

Gods! How many patrols do the Drearies have?! I already avoided two!

The Venerator dives to the side to avoid the shower of weapons. One of the spears catches in his mage robe, grazing his ribs, while another one slashes his right thigh.

Pain bursts from his injuries.

Godsdammit! How can that sniveling ex-elder Ragnald always get so lucky?!

The Venerator races away, as fast as his injured leg allows.

I'll come back another time. No one escapes me once I begin hunting them.

He engages his Fla'mma magic and throws fireballs back toward his pursuers.

The Drearies dodge the blazing shots, hiding behind trees.

When the mage peers over his shoulder, the Drearies are still trailing him.

The Venerator reaches for his A'ris magic, and sends puffs of wind at the Drearies, shoving them off their feet. Then he pumps his legs faster, until the air burns in his throat.

After a while, he stops and turns back, but the forest lays quiet. No sign of the Drearies.

The Venerator smirks.

I was always the fastest and smartest of all the followers.

The Venerator vacillates whether he should go back for the artifact. But he decides against it. His Fla'mma magic is depleted, and he needs to regenerate it. His A'ris magic has already been used twice in such a short time—he'll need days before he can use it again.

He takes a few deep inhales.

This was not a failure. Now I know I cannot face Ragnald on my own in direct conflict. I will need assistance.

He already knows who to turn to.

Cracks of dry twigs sound to the right of him.

His head snaps up as he turns to face the new threat.

CHAPTER 42

GLENNA

A feeling of unease jars me awake. I open my eyes and find eight men standing around the slumbering Angus and me.

Glaring, they stand more than six feet tall, muscular, wearing the black mage cloaks with the six light elements embroidered on them. Their hands glow with their magic, ranging from bright red to yellow.

I poke the wanderer with my foot. "Angus, wake up!"

Angus sits up with his hands raised, though a predatory light flashes over his brown eyes.

Pushing the blanket off, I sit up too and glance around, but don't see Ragnald.

"No need to act rashly," the closest mage with wide shoulders says. His dark brown gaze, full of confidence, studies us. He drags a hand through his short dark brown hair that frames an oval face with a straight nose and a straight mouth. His cloak gapes open, revealing that he wears no shirt under it, just black pants tucked into matching boots. "Hands where I can see them," he adds in a calm voice.

"Who are you?" I ask, making sure my empty hands are visible. I have no plans doing anything impulsive. Not against eight mages.

Corruption Nic appears standing next to the leader. "I'll bet you do something crazy soon. You just can't help it."

My gaze flickers to the corruption, but I ignore it otherwise.

"Just to be clear, girl," another mage says and pushes long blond strands off his shoulder. "We are the ones asking questions here." His green eyes glint coldly in a tanned square face. Then he crosses his thick arms, muscles bulging like boulders.

Girl? Me?

Corruption Nic laughs. "They have no idea who they're dealing with!"

The blond mage adds, "We asked you a question. Answer Athol, my mage brother."

I pinch my forearm to see if this is a surreal dream, but the pain reassures me that it is, indeed, not a dream. More like a living nightmare.

"Uh, what was the question?" I ask and Corruption Nic hoots in laughter.

Athol raises a hand. "Blair, no need to scare her."

Another mage, from the back, steps forward and asks, "Where is Ragnald? Huh?" Dark brown eyes glare at Angus and me. Long black hair frames an angular face with sharp cheekbones. He raises his hands, covered in Fla'mma fire.

Athol gestures to the black-haired mage. "No need to be snappy, Arkibald. I'll handle her."

Handle me? Are they afraid of me?

Blair says, "We are mages. We dictate."

Angus eyes the mages quietly. Too quietly.

"No need to be rude, Blair," Athol says, then smiles at me as he adds, "Just tell us where Ragnald is. No one will hurt you or your travel companion."

The other mages laugh.

Somehow I doubt that.

A handsome tawny-haired mage raises a hand and waits.

Athol pinches his nose bridge. "No need to raise your hand, Craig. We discussed this."

Craig nods. "I just want to say that I don't trust strangers. What if they killed Ragnald? And why does she have roots sticking out of her pocket?" He shifts his weight from one muscular leg to the other.

I gape at the mage, speechless.

Corruption Nic slaps his leg. "This is too much!"

Athol sighs. "You don't trust anyone, Craig."

"My name is Dand," a mage with a long black beard says. "I know that if I ask you nicely, my beauty, then you'd be inclined to answer. Sweet, can you tell us where Ragnald is?" He raises his voice to a shouting level at his last question.

My ears ring, and I wince.

Athol shakes his head. "No need to yell, Dand. She is not deaf."

Dand frowns. "How do you know, Athol?"

Athol snorts. "Because she looked disgusted—obviously understanding you, mage brother."

The other mages chuckle.

Craig raises his hand. "I just want to say that we should tie them up. Then we can go search for Ragnald. I bet she is the healer who took advantage of Ragnald's good side, tricking him into helping her." He nods toward Angus and adds, "This other one must not have much acumen judging by his blank stare. Must be a poor relative burdening her."

Corruption Nic gives up and drops to the ground, laughing with tears running down his face.

I exchange a glance with Angus. He mouths, "burdening"?

The brush rustles.

Ragnald strides out of the forest. He takes in the scene, and his expression turns furious. "Put your magic away this instant."

All eight mages comply.

Impressed, I look at Ragnald, the real leader of these mages.

Athol grins and slaps Ragnald's back. "No need to bark at us. It's been too long, mage brother!" The other mages repeat the greeting, forgetting all about us.

Ragnald settles on the ground. "Thank you, mage brothers, for coming to my aid. I need all your magic to create a disguise for my, uh, healer friend. One that stands the test of the Academia guards."

The other mages sit down as well.

Blair frowns. "Is that all? Would you like us to conjure you a kingdom or two while we're at it?"

Athol raises an eyebrow. "No need to mouth off, Blair. All of us came running when you needed extraction from a delicate situation involving an empress and her jealous wife. Or have you forgotten already?"

Blair grumbles under his breath, "That was different, nothing like this one."

Arkibald juggles fireballs between his palms. "Why should we help a healer? Huh?"

All eight mages snap their gazes to me.

"Yes, Ragnald, why should they help a lowly healer?" I ask. "Answer Dand's question."

"His name is Arkibald," Ragnald and Athol say in unison.

"You should help *me* help her, not because she is a healer," Ragnald replies, "but because we have a unique opportunity on our hands—she is infected with corruption."

Now the eight mages glower at me.

Angus pats my back. "You poor lass, that explains so much, you have no idea."

Grinding my teeth, I rub the tear-shaped scar on my left arm for comfort.

Corruption Nic sits up. "You should be proud that the Archgod of Chaos and Destruction found you worthy of His—"

I force the corruption to vanish. With a glare, it retreats into my mind.

Craig raises a hand. "I just want to know why you came back to Raghild, brother. After the mage elders stripped you from your elder rank—"

Athol interrupts him, "Craig, no need to air our dirty magic in front of strangers."

Arkibald puts his forearm on his knee. "Are you sure the mage elders will greet you with open arms, huh?"

Blair flicks his wrist toward Angus. "Are we supposed to disguise him as well?"

"That *he* has a name, and it's Angus," the wanderer says. "Also, I will not require any mage's help."

Craig raises a hand again. "I just want to say that if Ragnald needs our help, then we should help our mage brother."

The others murmur agreement.

Ragnald flows to his feet. "Then let us proceed with haste, my brothers. Time is not on our side."

CHAPTER 43

RAGNALD

Ragnald and the eight mages surround an uneasy-looking Glenna in a circle. Angus watches them from a safe distance, holding a fidgeting Mia in his large hands.

The small field where they gather is perfect for what Ragnald has in mind. Even the late morning sun peeks through the dark gray clouds in swaths of light, hopeful in the otherwise stark and cold day.

This should be enough to disguise her A'ris magic from the Academia guards.

He ignores the pesky thoughts about how no one has ever done anything like this before. The Academia always caught A'ris magic users.

Ragnald nods at his oldest mage brother, Athol, with feigned composure. He trusts Athol with his life knowing that if anyone, it's this mage who has the knowledge and practice to cast such high-level magic.

There is one way and that's forward.

He glances at Glenna. She nods.

The urge to stride to her and take her into his arms almost overwhelms Ragnald, but Athol steps forward, saying, "Let us all combine—"

"I have a question," Angus says.

Athol frowns. "Yes?"

"Is this safe for her?" Angus asks.

"I'd like to know the same," Glenna adds.

Ragnald crosses his arms. "I wouldn't let this ceremony proceed—"

Athol turns to Ragnald. "No need to overreact, mage brother. Allow me to answer."

Ragnald inclines his head. "By all means."

Athol turns to Angus. "Just like with any surgery—"

"This is nothing like surgery," Glenna grumbles.

"—there is a small chance that things won't work as anticipated—"

"Not with *my* surgeries," Glenna says.

"—but that is a very small chance," Athol continues. "I do not think we should worry about it."

Craig raises a hand.

Athol rubs his eyes. "Craig, no need . . . we discussed . . . what is it?"

"I just want to ask," Craig says, "what happens if this doesn't work? Will we all die because of her?"

Ragnald lunges toward Craig, but Athol stops him with a muscular arm thrust across Ragnald's chest. "There is no need for violence," the other mage says, then turns to the tawny-haired mage. "Craig, I will talk to you later. Right now, we need to take advantage of the sunlight—it's an essential part of the process."

Blair turns to Athol. "We want to know the answer to Craig's question. We are the ones who'll bear the brunt if this misfires."

Ragnald raises a fist covered in Fla'mma fire. "I'll give you something to bear!"

Athol sighs. "Blair, no need to worry. While I cannot guarantee that this will work, just like there was no guarantee of our safe getaway from the Silk Ribbon Empire after your, um, sensitive situation with its empress, that won't stop us from trying. *Now* can we proceed?"

Blair curses but does not argue.

Arkibald plays with a small flame running across his fingers. "Why do we—"

Athol claps his hands. "Glad we had a chat!" Then he raises his arms and adds, "Now let us all combine our elemental magic into a congenial stratum with the aid of this ancient ceremony that will allow Glenna to stay hidden under our elements. May the Archgoddess of the Eternal Light and Order shine Her benevolent light on Glenna!"

"May the Archgoddess of the Eternal Light and Order shine Her benevolent light on Glenna!" Ragnald and the others repeat.

Athol continues, "Let us layer our major elements in the order based on major and minor affinity in our seniority of our brotherhood. Start with the primary element, then move to the secondary one. When I call the element, place it shaped like a net over Glenna."

Ragnald and the others nod, raising their arms up.

"Fla'mma!"

Ragnald steps forward, moving his arms in a circle, until his hands are covered in flames and his silver hair floats around his face. He shapes his Fla'mma element into a six-foot-tall rectangular net and places it over Glenna. The magical net settles over her like a soft blanket. He steps back into place.

Glenna shivers.

Athol, Arkibald, Blair, and one more of his mage brothers repeat the process. Then Blair, Dand, and another mage brother follow with their secondary major element.

"T'erra!"

Ragnald steps forward again. He slams his palms together, once, twice, until his palms are covered in loose soil. He shapes it into a net and places it over Glenna. Then he steps back into the circle. Dand and one other of his mage brothers follow after him. Then Athol and Craig repeat it for the secondary element.

"A'qua!"

Ragnald steps forward the third time. He twirls his hands over each other until his palms are covered in sloshing water. He shapes his magic into a net and deposits it over Glenna, then steps back. Blair and Craig are next, then Arkibald and two of his mage brothers follow for the secondary element.

Athol clasps his hands and walks around Glenna seven times, muttering something in an ancient language. Sweat drips from the mage's face as he says, "It is done."

Ragnald strides to Glenna, while the others disperse from the circle.

"My magic feels so . . . muted," Glenna says and hugs her middle.

Athol shakes his hands out. "No need to worry. We have done what we've set out to do—disguising your magic, allowing you to get inside the Academia. It will dissipate on its own after a few days."

Ragnald puts on his second pair of orange glasses—the first one he seemed to have misplaced back on Uhna. He cannot see any signs of layered magic or A'ris magic on Glenna.

Ragnald puts away his glasses. "The disguise worked."

Gods, I hope this will stand the test of those Academia guards.

Angus hands Mia back to Glenna. She places the flower into her pocket with trembling hands.

Athol grins. "No one will know she is a healer. When the Academia guards test her, all they will find is a whirling and unfocused mix of Fla'mma, T'erra, and a little bit of A'qua—the usual mixture that would swirl around any untrained followers applying to the Academia of Mages. I'm glad you called for our help—this ceremony must be done by nine mages, where the elements are present as primary and secondary major affinity. Thanks to you, we have covered all the requirements."

Ragnald clasps his mage brother's forearm. "I am grateful you came."

Athol slaps Ragnald's back. "Always, mage brother."

"Arkibald, Dugald, Fraser, and Ewan," Ragnald says to four of his mage brothers, "you go ahead to the Academia and find safe living quarters for Glenna and me. Somewhere on the followers levels should do. We'll join you later."

The four mages incline their heads and stride away from the field.

"Good idea, Ragnald," Athol says. "No need for the nine of us to show up at the Academia's door. We should avoid any suspicion, if possible. That reminds me." He takes a few steps toward a tree and picks up a black knapsack. He pulls out a few folded articles of clothing in a dark brown color, then hands them to Glenna. "This will help you look like a runaway follower we just apprehended."

Glenna accepts the clothes with a grimace. "How are you going to explain that it required five mages to catch me?"

Athol scoffs. "Elementalist battle mages have no need to explain anything."

Glenna eyes Athol. "Is that so?"

Ragnald says, "What Athol meant to say is that it's not uncommon for a group of four or five mages to band together, returning to the Academia from their posts off-world."

"I see," Glenna says, then unfolds the shapeless pants and shirt, with distaste twisting her lips. "I guess I better change into these." She heads toward a tall shrub and ducks behind it.

Ragnald turns to Athol. "Is running away still a problem?"

"No one would admit this, but it's gotten worse. I believe it's because the Academia has tripled the amount of magically inclined children arriving every day."

"Why does the Academia require such a surplus of followers?" Ragnald asks.

Athol shrugs. "No one knows. Our esteemed mage leader, you know how he is, does not interfere with the mage elders, ignoring the surge of new students. As if that's not enough, the squabbles among the prowler and venerator ranks have gotten worse as well. They too hunger to be promoted to an elder. The mage elders are not in a hurry to fill that one spot, seeing how you repaid them."

They will have to add one more—me.

Athol continues, "Not to complain, but the mage leader has been even worse of a hermit these days, avoiding everyone and hiding out in the library most of the time—a trait you two have in common, I believe."

I used to hide in the library, but now I have reason to stay outside of it.

As if his thoughts conjured Glenna, she returns, looking gorgeous in the borrowed clothing. She hangs the black mage cloak on a tree branch and pulls on the brown cloak the followers wear. Then she joins Craig, Blair, and Dand. It doesn't take long before she chimes into the mages' conversation. She even laughs at Craig's puns, though it seems the joke is at the expense of the mage and not on purpose.

"No mage has stared at a healer like you," Athol says. "Did you lose your sanity on that pirate world, what was its name? Ubba? Utnah?"

Ragnald crosses his arms. "It was Uhna, and no. I am saner than I ever was."

Athol smirks. "No need to be snappy. I would be blind not to notice how infatuated you are with her. Don't try to deny it."

"I won't."

Athol chuckles. "No one will believe me when I say that the infamous Ragnald fell hard for a woman after being single for so long."

"It was bound to happen sooner or later."

I'm glad it was for her.

Glenna snaps at Blair, muttering. The next second she smiles as if nothing happened. The other mages study her.

Ragnald glances at Athol, just as the smile disappears from the other mage's face. "I'm not one for panicking, but I have to ask—how far gone is she?"

Ragnald recounts the symptoms Glenna has been having, but Athol raises a hand to stop him.

"No need to continue, even I recognize that those are scroll-scribed signs of late stage Turning. You know that, don't you?"

Ragnald's fingers curl into his palms. "I won't give up on her!"

"No need to argue with me, mage brother. I'm on your side, remember?"

"Yes, of course." Ragnald drags a hand through his long hair and adds, "She is still herself. I must get the elders' help to rid her of the corruption. I have no doubt that forty-one elders—including me—can handle it. I just need to convince the old mage to support me, then the rest will follow."

Athol shoves Ragnald's shoulder. "No one needs luck more than you, if you are to pull off this impossible task. I hope you'll succeed, mage brother."

CHAPTER 44

GLENNA

Rubbing my temple to ease a headache that buzzes behind my eyes, I crane my neck to stare at the formidable fortress.

A long line of people snakes toward the gray brick and flat-roofed Academia of Mages. Sitting on top of a hill, one side of it is a sheer drop into a canyon below, while the other side is an even steeper drop into the ocean. A dirt road cuts through an open area with visibility for a few hundred feet—the Academia's location seems perfect and impenetrable from any attack.

We spent most of the day hiking through the forest, until we reached the wide dirt road leading to the Academia of Mages. None of the tired and hopeless-looking people seemed bothered by our sudden appearance. Instead, many held their heads bowed with a magical passport stamp glinting on their forehead, averting their eyes, and keeping their distance from us as they shuffled their feet, kicking clouds of dirt into the air.

Our line makes a bit of headway toward a ten-foot-tall metal gate manned by mage guards.

I take a few steps forward. "It's, um, even more imposing than I thought." I check on Mia, who dozes in a makeshift bag made of a scarf Craig lent me. She has grown so much that she does not fit into my pocket anymore. I will have to find her a suitable home soon.

Next to me, Ragnald smiles. "It's magnificent, isn't it?"

Angus and I exchange a look. The wanderer rolls his eyes and turns back to the road.

"That's not the first word that comes to mind," I mutter.

While the Academia of Mages does seem to be a well-built fortress, it somehow lacks any architectural beauty as if it were built with two goals in mind—practicality and intimidation. Not a single buttress or any other adornment decorates it. Thin barred windows break up the monotony of the sheer brick walls.

"The word 'unimaginative' works fine," Angus says, earning a frown from Athol.

Ragnald points ahead. "Those two wings stand where the original Academia was first built, but a wildfire destroyed most of the buildings four hundred years ago. It took years to rebuild it into an even bigger and more spacious fortress, with the addition of the hundred-foot-tall Elders' Tower in the center." He gestures lower and adds, "Those concentric courtyards are the ones I spent many decades practicing my magic as a follower, than as a disciple."

Athol chuckles. "No need to bore poor Glenna with those old stories, mage brother. What's important is that the nine of us became a brotherhood right around that time."

Corruption Nic appears leaning on Athol's wide shoulder. "Misery does love—"

"It's not boring," I say, interrupting the corruption. "It must have taken quite a bit of discipline to last through decades of magical studies like that."

Angus snorts. "That's their job—to study magic. How hard can it be?"

Ragnald brushes his hand to mine.

A blush stings my face. I do my best not to think of our kiss. It was the last one anyway; it didn't mean anything.

Corruption Nic smirks. "I just love how pretentious you are—an endless source of self-placating lies."

A scream sounds ahead, then cuts off. We take a few more steps forward.

Grinding my teeth, it takes all my effort to disregard the mage guards killing anyone who has the smallest amount of A'ris magic.

"Maybe you'll be next," Corruption Nic whispers.

Blair pulls his long blond hair into a ponytail. "We should push to the front of the line and be done with this nonsense."

Craig raises a hand, then lowers it when Athol glares at him. "I just want to say that it was nice being one of your mage brothers. You know, in case we don't—"

Athol interrupts him, "No need for alarm, Craig. It's too late to turn back anyway."

"We'll stay in line and not take any unnecessary risks," Ragnald says.

Dand combs his long black beard and glances at me. "Sweet, I hope you'll make it. I think I like you."

"Um, thank you?"

Dand winks. "Any time, my beauty."

Ragnald narrows his eyes at Dand, who stops smiling and raises both of his hands. "No offense meant, mage brother."

Blair's stomach makes a loud noise. "Gods, I'm starving! We have the best meals in the Academia, Glenna. Anything you can imagine—roasts, stews, chowders, soups. And the bread! Freshly baked daily, crusty but soft inside to mop up the juices."

My mouth salivates. "It would be nice to eat a home-cooked meal." One can only tolerate mushrooms, root vegetables, and seeds for so long.

Corruption Nic tries to pull Dand's beard, but its fingers pass through the black hairs. "First, you'll have to get inside, remember?"

Another scream sounds. We take a few more steps forward.

I cover my mouth to hold my nausea at bay. "Why are so many people risking their lives to come here? Shouldn't they already be safe now that they have their passports?"

Athol frowns at Ragnald. "No need for secrecy, mage brother."

Ragnald curses.

Athol turns to me. "Not to scare you, but the magical passport is the first step to getting into the Academia. The second and final step is to pass the inspection at the gate."

Corruption Nic sniggers. "Here it comes."

A chill washes over my spine. "What inspection?"

"She may not have to do the inspection as a runaway follower," Ragnald says. "We mages can enter without any hassle, thanks to our magical insignia tattooed on our wrist."

"What insignia?" I ask.

Ragnald and his mage brothers present their bare right wrist, then make their insignia visible by threading a bit of magic into it.

Angus studies the insignia and replicates it with perfection in his glamor. The mage brothers blink in surprise, then test it and nod with an impressed expression.

Athol nods. "No need to have any concerns then."

We take a few more steps, almost at the gate.

"Will one of you tell me what kind of inspection?" I demand.

All five mages shush me.

The two petitioners ahead of us enter through the gate on trembling legs. They give a wide berth to the piles of ash on the left.

Corruption Nic sniffs the air with pleasure.

Glaring at it, I cover my nose to block the scents of smoke that pervades the air, mixing with the smell of garbage that leaks in a dirty stream down the cobblestone street of the Academia.

Four men with long hair and wearing dark orange cloaks with the mage circle embroidered on their chests, glare at us.

"Next!" one of them shouts and gestures toward us with an impatient wave.

Ragnald places a hand at the small of my back. I take comfort in his touch and together we step in front of the guards.

"We apprehended a runaway follower," Ragnald says, gesturing to me and the five mages—Angus's glamour gives him the perfect disguise as just another mage. I wish it would have been that simple for me—but the ancient ceremony mimics the wild amalgam of a runaway follower and not the complicated mage insignia.

Athol adds, "No need to hold us up any longer."

Blair says, "We are all weary from the hunt."

Craig raises a hand, but Athol shoves it down.

The closest guard eyes our group. "Is that so?"

Ragnald raises his chin, then moves to enter the Academia.

The second guard thrusts his hands out, covered in fire. "Not so fast!"

Ragnald scoffs. "What's the holdup?"

The third and tallest mage guard says, "We have to test your runaway first."

Ragnald narrows his eyes. "Since when?"

The mage guard grunts. "Since now."

I gulp, trying my best not to look scared.

"This is going to be interesting," Corruption Nic says.

Ragnald gives me a reassuring smile, but I detect worry deep in his gaze.

I stop fidgeting with the borrowed cloak, and instead I recall one of my happiest memories, collecting herbs from the little garden my family had, hoping to steady my frayed nerves.

The tall mage guard lifts his fist, then uncurls his fingers. A black orb flips open in the middle of his palm, the size of a marble. Black ribbon-like metal threads around his fingers, covering them like an incomplete glove.

"Hold still," the guard says.

White light swirls in his hand, coming from the glove-like device. The guard shines the light over me, tracking it from head to toe, then back.

Sweat drips into my eyes.

Corruption Nic rubs his hands. "What will it be? Will they find you guilty?"

I tighten my shaking stomach muscles, hoping this ordeal will be over soon.

The light blinks out and the device retracts back into the orb.

The tall guard flicks his wrist. "Proceed to enter."

CHAPTER 45

Dazed, I enter through the metal gates. Ragnald follows close behind. Athol, Angus, and the three other mages don't have to complete the test, and soon they join us.

Corruption Nic traipses on my right. "I was so sure they would find you out."

"Be quiet," I mutter and rub the teardrop-shaped scar on my left arm. My headache progresses into a full-blown migraine and my eyes water.

Fla'mma-infused lampposts light our way as the sun sets on the horizon. We trek the twisting cobblestone streets that branch in all directions. Muted chatter breaks the otherwise quiet Academia grounds. To my surprise, the streets are clean; not an errant piece of garbage rolls around.

All the citizens hurry with hunched shoulders, as if trying to be invisible, paying no attention to our presence.

Adjusting the sling with Mia, I groan as the buzzing sensation in my head worsens. To take my mind off the headache, I watch mage men and women hurry past us, often in groups of two or three, focused on their purpose. In many open spaces, a dozen followers practice a variety of elements like Fla'mma, A'qua, or T'erra without any mage instructing them. We pass single-story buildings on the left and right, part of the inner town with tradesmen such as blacksmiths, bakers, and clothesmakers.

Everywhere I look, I see mages. I try not to fidget being around so many of them, but none of the mages pays us any heed.

"So much superiority," Angus grumbles. "I bet they don't know the meaning of humble."

Athol shoves at Angus's shoulder. "No need to be judgmental."

Blair adds, "We mages take pride in our profession and don't hide it from others. Unlike you, whatever you are."

Angus studies Blair. "That might be so." He hoists his bag up his shoulder and adds, "I won't burden you any longer. It's time for us to go on our separate paths. Glenna, swift travels and much happiness upon reaching your destination."

I repeat the traditional salutation. Then he strides away.

We near the twenty-foot-tall wooden double doors of the keep. No guards glare at this entrance. We head inside, blending into the crowd of mages and passport-holding visitors without any trouble.

The cooler air inside smells stale but clean. Fla'mma torches light the cavernous main hall. Most of the civilians head right, toward an open area with wooden benches crowded with many visitors waiting for their turn.

Some of the mages in front of us take the stairs across from the entrance, climbing up, while others take one of the two long corridors that branch left and right.

I look around, though there's not much to see in the sparsely decorated Academia.

The interior underwhelms me just as the exterior did—not a single painting or tapestry adorns the stone-tiled walls of the cavernous hall. I wonder if they are afraid of decorations—maybe they think it would make them seem less intimidating?

At the Healers' College, every wall had something to showcase, such as portraits of famous healers, special herb mixes, and so on.

Craig raises a hand. "I just want to say I always believed Athol could make this work."

Athol sighs. "Craig, no need to . . . yes, thank you, mage brother."

Ragnald leads me to another stairway—one going downward. "Arkibald and the others should have a place secured by now."

I grind my teeth against the sharp headache as we climb down the wide stairs. With each windowless level, the pressure grows from the heavy stone walls and tons of soil that surround me as if I am in an ancient tomb.

Or in that dungeon, where we battled DLD under the Crystal Palace. The archgod killed so many, including my Nic.

Corruption Nic hops off the stairs like a kid. "Now you think of them. What you mistake as grief is in fact guilt, but you are too selfish to recognize the difference, aren't you?"

"It's a lie," I mutter. "I do grieve everyone who died in that battle."

Corruption Nic shrugs a shoulder. "If you say so. You haven't even thought of me, I mean Nic, for days now. I find that curious."

That can't be true, can it?

After what seems like twenty levels down, we enter a long corridor. We follow it twisting and turning to the right, until Athol stops in front of a closed wooden door.

Glancing in both directions down the Fla'mma-torch-lit corridor, Athol raps his knuckles on the wood in a pattern.

A tall mage with thick forearms opens it.

"Dugald!" Athol says and slaps the other mage's shoulder.

"Took you long enough," Dugald says in a deep baritone, then avoids my gaze as he steps aside.

We cram into a small room barely big enough for two, let alone for seven.

Ragnald sits at the foot of the bed, while I take a seat next to him. I pretend to be enthralled by the white blanket and not bothered by how close his body is to mine. I pat the pillow and place the scarf holding the dozing Mia in the middle of it.

Blair and Craig take the two chairs, Dand leans on the wall by the door, while Dugald leaves with a curt nod.

Athol perches at the edge of the table and pushes a wrapped woolen cloth toward me. "No need to leave this room—there is food and drink in here for three days."

"I wasn't planning on walking around," I say, then raise a finger. "Did you say three days?"

Is he suggesting that I need to stay in this suffocating tomb for three days?!

Ragnald gets up and squats by me, taking my hands into his. "You'll be fine. No one will search for you here, at the follower's level." He looks to the side, then adds, "You won't be alone. I promise."

Athol frowns. "No need to make hasty decisions, mage brother."

Ragnald doesn't respond as he gets to his feet. He waves his arms in circles by his side, each circle smaller until his hands meet in front of him, cupped outward.

Blair's eyes widen. "We don't invoke that spell, ever, mage brother!"

Craig raises a hand. "I just want to ask, is this safe? Should we leave before Ragnald kills us?"

Athol jumps to his feet, facing Ragnald. "Stop!"

"What's happening?" I ask, but the men don't respond.

A bright orange and red flame grows in the center of Ragnald's hand, then dark brown minuscule rocks swirl next to it, and a blue twirling water joins the other two.

Athol throws up his hands. "Now you've done it!"

Ragnald tosses the raw elements onto the table, then doubles over, breathing hard. "I know what I'm doing."

Athol sputters, while Blair, Craig, and Dand, struck with shock and awe, crowd around the table.

What has these mages acting so strangely?

I get up and elbow the men to the side. "What are we looking at?" I eye the three groups of raw elements. Then the fire spirals upward, followed by the rock, then the water, until miniature figures standing two feet tall form out of them.

"Would you look at that," I say, studying the elemental golems with well-formed arms and legs. The fire and rock golems are shaped like males—the former tall and wide-shouldered, the latter robust, while the water one has feminine curves and long chains of bubbles for hair. Though they have no facial features, it's obvious they watch their conjurer, waiting.

Ragnald points at me. "Protect her with your lives."

The three elemental golems turn toward me and nod.

Blair curses under his breath. Craig raises a hand, but Athol shoves it down as he says, "No one can know about this, mage brothers."

Dand shoves a hand through his hair. "The beauty of this healer must have gone to Ragnald's head."

"No need to be melodramatic, Dand," Athol says, then turns to Ragnald. "This is forbidden magic, mage brother, and you know it. This won't help you further your goals."

"That's not why I did it," Ragnald says, looking at me. "If I can't be here to protect you, then I'll leave you with the next best thing."

"No one has ever done anything like this for me," I say.

Ragnald brushes a few strands of hair off my face. "You deserve the best."

"Those are abominations," Blair says and takes a step toward me.

All the elementals' heads snap toward the mage. Palpable danger hangs in the air, directed toward the blond mage.

Ragnald crosses his arms. "I would lower my voice and step away from Glenna if I were you, mage brother."

Blair glowers at the elemental golems, then backs away.

Corruption Nic sniggers. "That's so adorable! Too bad all elemental golems turn on their conjurers sooner or later."

"That won't happen," I mutter and squat in front of the table. Leaning on my elbows, I smile at the golems.

The fire golem shoots flames in front of him then catches the blaze, absorbing it. The rock golem lifts his hands with a thin line of dust falling from it, while the water golem creates a wave under her feet, letting it lift her up, so she can look me in the eyes.

"They are adorable," I say.

All three golems preen.

Athol turns to Ragnald. "No need to waste any more time here. Go seek out your Mentor. We'll leave too. We don't want to attract any attention to Glenna. But don't worry, mage brother, we'll watch over her."

Ragnald clasps Athol's forearm, then the other mages' too. He watches them leave, then turns to me. "I best go too."

He hesitates, as if wanting to say more, then marches out the door.

I try not to think about why I'm here, amid all the mages, the archenemies of healers.

Corruption Nic snickers. "This will be your downfall."

"Go away," I mutter and it disappears.

I hug my middle, fighting unease.

I must get rid of the corruption one way or another. I believe in Ragnald. I know he'll find a way to convince the mages to help me. All it will take is some time.

"Which you don't have in abundance," Corruption Nic whispers in my mind.

With a deep exhale, I pull out a chair and sit at the table. The three elementals approach until they reach the edge of the table. The rock golem shoulders the fire golem to the side, while the water golem waves.

I smile at them. "Now what shall I name you, little cuties?"

CHAPTER 46

RAGNALD

Ragnald pushes the heavy wooden door open and enters the enormous library at the heart of the Academia of Mages. For a second, all he can do is stare into the round main hall. His gaze tracks the circular levels with overburdened dark brown bookcases visible over the metal railing.

Beyond those circular levels, dozens of corridors branch off, creating a maze. In the past, Ragnald explored them with his Mentor, searching for answers to the mysteries of elements, archgods, and era wars.

Knowing where his Mentor would be, Ragnald crosses the pine-colored hardwood floor polished to a mirror-like shine, striding toward a narrow stairway that leads to the third floor. He passes dusty tomes, torn ancient scrolls shoved on top of the books, and bookcases that lost their dark brown color. He strides along the low, ornate metal railing that runs along the perimeter of a square-shaped inner courtyard, then heads left at a corridor until it dead ends. He turns right, cutting through the neat row of black shelves with thick leather tomes containing knowledge about the past six era wars.

He finds his Mentor by a wooden table, bending over a pile of old books and scrolls.

Ragnald notes the deep wrinkles on the weathered face of his Mentor. The fuzz of hair sticking up seems to have thinned. The lines cutting by the corner of his Mentor's mouth had deepened, but the intelligence shining in the dark brown eyes of his oval face did not dim.

Ragnald pushes the scroll down in front of the Mentor. "You're still trying to untangle the mysteries of the Seven Galaxies, I see."

The old mage squints at him. "And you still interrupt me at the worst possible time. How good to see you with my old cataract-ridden eyes! Come closer, son."

Ragnald steps around the corner of the table until he stands in front of his Mentor.

The old mage grasps his forearms in his arthritic fingers and looks up into Ragnald's face. "What are you doing here, son?"

"I need your help, Mentor."

The old mage huffs. "I already helped you after you botched your important appointment on Uhna. Failing to report back the rising levels of corruption and the presence of the Archgod of Chaos and Destruction could have earned you a death sentence."

"I told the mage elders that there was no time but to react."

"Son, you went on an adventure with the Sybil in this new Era War."

Ragnald grimaces. "As I said—"

The old man flicks a thin hand. "Yes, yes! You had no time to do your duty. Bah!"

Ragnald exhales. "I followed your training. The Sybil had no control or any understanding of her Lumenian magic. It was vital that I represented the Academia and ensured she would not make a mistake."

The Mentor unrolls a worn scroll. "What was it like to meet the Archgod of Chaos and Destruction?"

Ragnald curls his fingers into his palms. "It was my worst nightmare come true. The archgod exuded unlimited power—even in mortal form. With one look, He infected hundreds with His corruption, which is why I am here."

Ragnald takes a deep breath, unable to continue. Fear, like nothing he experienced before grips him.

What if there is nothing we can do to help Glenna? What if it's already too late for her?

The Mentor raises an eyebrow. "Please continue."

"I need the help of the full mage elders' circle—all forty-one of them and the leader—to eradicate corruption from my uh from a person who suffers from it."

The Mentor shakes his head. "If you are here to get your elder rank back, the mage elders won't give it to you—it was a one-time promotion."

"I don't care about getting my elder rank back!" Ragnald snaps. "I just want to help this person."

"You shouldn't have come back here, son."

The Mentor turns to leave, but Ragnald stops the old mage with a hand on his thin shoulder. "Please."

The old mage exhales, irritated. "Follow me."

They head back between two rows of bookcases, all the way to a dead end. The Mentor points at an overflowing bookshelf burdened with scrolls and books of all sizes. "These tell us about the first Era War when the Turned appeared." The old mage points at the second shelf and adds, "These scrolls contain knowledge of the corruption. Once the seed of the corruption takes root in a magic user, they will progress through three stages until they become Turned."

The Mentor unrolls a large scroll and points to the illustrations depicting the stages. "Many have tried different approaches to eradicate the corruption, but it all resulted in speeding it up. See here?" he asks and gestures at the top right corner image with fire burning a city and a Turned centered in the destruction.

The Mentor lets the scroll roll back into itself. "There is nothing I can do to help you."

The sound of the library door opening and shutting breaks the silence.

Ragnald crosses his arms. "There must be something the mage circle can do."

"The mage collective, before they were called the mage circle, thought to reverse the curse of corruption in mages, but they often ended up dead when the Turned fought back and escaped. After that, the collective refused to allow any assistance lest they play into the hands of the Archgod, allowing His Turned to wreak havoc."

Ragnald slams his fist on the bookcase, rattling the books. "There must have been something they discovered! Anything!"

I cannot give up hope about helping Glenna, for there lies a dreadful reality, one where she is lost to me forever. I cannot live without her. I love her!

The Mentor looks away. "You are a son to me, Ragnald, and I cannot lie to you."

Rhythmic footsteps sound on the nearby staircase, getting closer.

"You have brought trouble to my Academia, son."

Six mage guards march to Ragnald. He fights to get away, but the guards restrain him.

"What have you done, Mentor?"

I have to get back to Glenna!

The Mentor pats Ragnald's face.

"What I should have done when you first showed your rogue tendencies, son. I cannot allow you to destroy my Academia."

The old mage glances at the guards. "Take him away."

CHAPTER 47

GLENNA

I pace up and down the small windowless room beneath the Academia. I struggle to tune out the relentless buzzing sensation in my head.

My golems—whom I named Flame, Pebble, and River—trail behind me like puppies. Mia found a home on Pebble, who allowed her to sink her roots into his wide back and thick right arm, seemingly unharmed by the flower entwining with him. She also stopped sleeping so much, becoming more alert as if she knows she can grow with room to spare. She purrs, holding seeds in her vine hands, munching on them from time to time.

"Why do I have to stay behind every time?" I ask my three elementals. "It's not fair."

Flame makes a sizzling sound, expressing his distaste just as Pebble hits his right fist into his left palm. River nods her head in agreement, then combs her flowing long bubble hair with an elegant hand.

"I'm just worried about Ragnald."

Corruption Nic materializes by the bed and drops down on the white blanket. "You do care about the mage."

I open my mouth to deny it but snap it closed when I realize that it wouldn't be true. I *do* care about Ragnald.

Corruption Nic morphs into Lilla. "I can't believe you're cheating on my dear brother like that! How can you move on when he'll never love anyone else? He will never experience life again. You are so cruel!"

I turn away from the corruption. "It's not like that."

Something tugs on the hem of my shirt. I look down.

Pebble gazes up with concern clear on his featureless face. Mia mewls on his shoulder, one of her vines reaches up to touch my hand. Behind him

Flame and River smile.

I marvel at the connections between the elemental golems and me.

The three golems turn their head to stare at the corruption as if they can see it too.

"Leave me," I mutter. It rolls its eyes but disappears.

Pebble waves his arms, grunting.

"I don't want to wait here and do nothing either."

The other two golems nod.

"Did you all grow another foot?" They now stand a little over three feet. I add, "Anyway, there must be something for me to do."

I pace a few more steps. "In fact, Lilla would always go to the library when she needed answers. What do you think?"

Flame shakes his head. Pebbles raises an arm, and River nods, putting her hands on her hips, while Mia snaps her vines.

"That's three against one. It's decided then."

I leave the small room and shut the door.

A heavy hand lands on my shoulder.

I turn to face a hooded mage.

"I'm afraid your studies must be delayed, follower. The mage elders have summoned you."

Corruption Nic whispers in my mind, "The end is near."

"Oh, shut it," I say.

The hooded mage digs his fingers into my shoulder. "I will do no such thing. You can come with me the easy way, or I can drag you by your hair. Which will it be?"

Does this mage know that I am a healer? Or is this just a routine summons? If I fight back, I might reveal who I am. It's best to go along until I know more. Until Ragnald is back.

Corruption Nic laughs in my mind with glee.

I raise my hands. "Lead the way."

CHAPTER 48

The hooded mage and I enter a wide circular room through a stone doorway. The black ceiling hangs twelve feet above a glass wall. Not a single piece of furniture clutters the voluminous room.

Our footsteps echo as we stop in the middle of the mosaic-covered floor, with the six light elements depicted under my boots.

From somewhere, a burst of wind flutters the black robes of forty mages standing in front of me. They glare with disapproval. These must be the mage elders whom I need to help me.

Oh, my herbs.

A bird flies into the room from the right. One of the mages shoots it with a Fla'mma ball, burning it to ashes.

"Irritating vermin," an older mage elder grumbles from the second row.

My eyes widen as I realize that nothing but thin air separates us from the hundred-foot drop below.

The hooded mage puts both his hands on my shoulders, his fingers digging in and preventing me from escaping. "How do you like the mosaic, huh? It's made from the crushed stones we took from those annoying altars the locals built to their guardian goddess and her giants."

I shrug, though I cannot dislodge his hands off me. "It's as foul as your Academia."

"You know nothing!" the hooded mage snaps. "We burned their villages down, showing them how powerful the Academia is. Now they are so scared, they hide in the Forest of Loss and Darkness. It's where they belong anyway—into that wild and untamable place. How is that for foul, huh?"

"That's the very definition of 'foul,'" I say. "At least they are free from the oppression of the Academia."

Corruption Nic materializes in front of me. "I rejoice. Your doom nears."

Ignoring it, I turn my attention to the mage elders. They all seem quite advanced in age, at least seven hundred years old or older. They vary in height—some tall, while others short. Most of them are lanky, but there are a few with round bellies. However, they all have an unhealthy grayish tone to their pale skin, reminding me of a disease I saw before.

A tall mage elder with a long gray beard says, "You are not a follower, but an impostor and a healer."

They know!

"At least I am not afraid of A'ris and healers, like you cowards!"

The hooded mage shakes me by my shoulders. "Show more respect!"

I struggle against his hold. "Never!"

Where is Ragnald? Is he safe? I dare not ask after him—that might betray his presence to these elders with ruthless dark eyes. They all stand unmoving; not even a finger fidgets. An air of anticipation hangs around them.

What are they waiting for?

Then the heavy stone door behind me bursts open and a commotion sounds.

CHAPTER 49

RAGNALD

Ragnald, pushed by one of the six guards, stumbles inside the circle. He glances around, noting that all the mage elders preside. On his left, Glenna is held by a hooded mage he doesn't recognize.

Reverberating footsteps sound from the doorway. Fifty mage guards march into the circle, taking positions behind the mage elders.

That's unusual.

He surveys the elders he hasn't seen for more than a year. They've changed so much—looking pale, as if they avoided the sun for a long time.

The mage leader is not yet here—that does not bode well for me.

Then his mage brothers Athol, Blair, Dand, and Craig, shoved by more guards, shuffle inside the circle, coming to a halt next to Ragnald.

"Are you okay?" Glenna asks him, and Ragnald nods. He wants to explain to her what happened, but his Mentor strides across the mosaic-decorated floor and turns to face him.

All the mage elders bow their heads toward the Mentor.

"Mage Leader, you bless us with your unexpected presence," they say in unison.

Blair snorts. "That's another way to say, 'What the heck is he doing outside the library?'"

Craig raises a hand, but Athol shakes his head at him. "No need to get involved, Craig."

The Mentor gestures with his thin hand. "Yes, yes. As you were."

The mage elders turn their piercing gaze on Ragnald again.

The Mentor says, "Elementalist Battle Mage Ragnald, you have broken our laws and brought a corruption-infected magic user into the Academia, thus bringing danger to us."

"Mentor, please let me explain . . ."

"No, son. I taught you to always have the interests of the Academia at the forefront of your mind. I taught you that all your actions should be in service to the Academia. Yet here you are trying to regain your elder rank while risking our lives with that almost-Turned."

How did I ever think that my Mentor was on my side? All the old mage ever cared about was the Academia.

The mage elders exclaim.

"I told you that I don't want that anymore!" Ragnald snaps, but his words get lost in the noise.

Glenna's shocked gaze flashes with pain, then anger.

The Mentor lifts a hand. The mage elders quiet down.

"What phase is she?" the Mentor asks, examining Glenna as if she were a specimen and not a person with feelings. "Judging by the wide streak of white in her red hair, and how twitchy she is, I'd wager that she is at the end of the second phase."

"With forty-two elders and you—"

The Mentor interrupts him, "Give up, son. There is no way any one of us would vote for you to get another promotion. Even if she wasn't corrupted, you still brought a healer without a passport to the Academia—just breaking these laws could get you imprisoned. For all these crimes, I find you guilty. Your punishment is immediate banishment from Raghild. Thus our peace and safety will be restored."

I've failed her!

"No!" Ragnald shouts.

Glenna glares at him with tears shining in her dark crimson eyes. "This was your plan all along—to regain your lost rank. You never wanted to help me."

Ragnald curses. "That's not true, I—"

Glenna turns her head away. "I can't believe I was worried about you, *mage*!"

CHAPTER 50

GLENNA

"I will not cry," I mutter, fighting tears. Ragnald's betrayal cut a deep hole in my heart.

Buzzing intensifies in my mind. Tens of thousands of pinpoints bombard me, like bugs marching under my skull.

I clutch my head.

"Stop moving around, you sniveling follower!" the hooded mage behind me snaps. "I'd hate to retaliate."

His nails dig into my neck, drawing blood.

With a hiss of pain, I lower my hands, my vision turning red.

"That's it," Corruption Nic says. "You've just entered the third and final phase of Turning."

"Leave me alone."

Ragnald curses, then turns to the older mage with white hair sticking up. "We must band together and reverse the corruption in her before—"

"It is already too late, son," the older mage says. "Hear her muttering. See how the insanity glints in her eyes. She is beyond our help."

Corruption Nic sniggers. "See? I told you, I'll win."

"Be quiet!" I snap.

The mage elders gasp in outrage.

Long Beard clasps his gnarled hands. "That was entertaining, Mage Leader Alaisdair, but it's time to get serious. Banishment is not enough for such severe crimes."

Alaisdair's white eyebrows draw together. "Is that so, Elder Gangas?"

Gangas smiles. "Rest assured; they won't leave the Academia. At least not any time soon."

The mage elders chortle.

Alaisdair frowns. "Imprisonment is too—"

Gangas sneers. "I wasn't talking about imprisonment."

Alaisdair blinks at the other mage. "I don't understand—"

Gangas's smile grows wider, showing tips of his sharp teeth. "You've spent too much time hiding in your library, Mage Leader, away from reality."

Alaisdair takes a step back. "What reality is that?"

"One where you are not the mage leader anymore," Gangas says.

Alaisdair points at the other mage. "You can't do this!"

"Oh, but I can," Gangas says. "I have been voted to mage leader. Also, I simplified our punishment system into one sentence."

Alaisdair gapes.

Gangas smirks. "It's death to all who disobey."

Alaisdair swipes at the pale mage, but two mage guards take hold of him. "You always wanted more power than what you had, Gangas."

"You cannot execute Glenna!" Ragnald shouts.

Fire stings my shoulders.

"Don't test me," the hooded mage says, "or she'll pay the price."

Ragnald raises his hands in fists. "I will kill you for this!"

The stone door opens.

A stocky mage guard marches in. He winks at me, then addresses the mage behind me. "I bring news."

"What do you want?"

"I want you," the mage guard says. His image shimmers, revealing Angus. "Guardian Goddess Cyn'rha guided me to you, murderer. You killed my sister. I will not let you harm Glenna too."

He leaps at the hooded mage, shoving me out of the way.

CHAPTER 51

RAGNALD

Angus punches the hooded mage with an uppercut.

Before Ragnald could join Angus, mage guards rush toward him.

Ragnald takes a few steps back until he bumps into his mage brother Athol. They turn back to back, with Blair, Dand, and Craig joining them as they face dozens of mage guards. The mage brothers engage their elemental magic, attacking the guards.

The guards retaliate with their own magic or deflect with Fla'mma shields.

Glenna, using her A'ris magic on rocks she had in her pocket, slingshots the closest mage guards until three restrain her.

A new wave of mage guards advances on Ragnald and his mage brothers. Athol and Blair get buried under nine guards. Dand gets tackled and forced to kneel with his hands bound in front of him. Craig struggles under a heavy T'erra net.

Ragnald shoves off two guards, turning to help his mage brothers when a Fla'mma arrow pierces his right shoulder. He clenches his teeth to prevent the shout of pain in and takes one more step.

Eight mage guards surround Ragnald, pummeling him with their fists enhanced by T'erra magic.

Ragnald deflects the blows with his A'qua shield. Then three more guards lunge at him. They restrain him, tying his hands behind his back with an A'qua glove-like clamp, preventing Ragnald from summoning any more of his magic.

Angus releases his glamour and towers over the mages in his swamp troll form, avoiding the magical attacks with supernatural dexterity. Then he slips in an A'qua puddle, and a mage guard binds him with Fla'mma rope.

Ragnald glowers at the approaching Gangas.

"Someone let a swamp troll into the Academia," Gangas says and points at four mage guards. "Go kill the guards at the gate and replace them."

The guards bow their heads and hurry out of the circle.

Alaisdair grabs the arm of Gangas. "You can't kill them for such a minor mistake!"

Gangas disregards the older mage and nods toward two guards.

They take hold of Alaisdair, dragging the mage leader to the side.

"I should have pushed out of the tower," Gangas muses. "But then you won't see how this all ends."

Alaisdair's wrinkled face turns red. "What is wrong with you?"

"Nothing," Gangas says. "Everything is as it should be."

The hooded mage releases me and pushes to the front. A gust of cold wind shoves the hood off the mage's head.

Ragnald curses. "Arkibald?!" His eighth mage brother was the one who brought Glenna in front of the elders.

But why?

Arkibald gives Ragnald a condescending look. "Took you long enough to recognize me, huh?" Then the ex-mage brother strides to Glenna, waves the guards off, and grabs her left arm. "I've completed your order and brought Ragnald with his pet healer to you. Now let me have her."

Ragnald roars. "Get your hands off her!"

Gangas shuffles over to Arkibald. "What is it that I sense about this corrupted healer?"

Glenna tries to kick Gangas, but the ex-mage brother pulls her back before her foot can connect with the elder's shin.

Arkibald grimaces. "It's, uh, nothing. Her grandfather stole something from me and I want it back."

Glenna gasps. "You lie! My grandfather never stole anything from a *mage*! It's a family heirloom and useless anyway."

Gangas lifts Glenna's left arm and sniffs it. "It's just a cheap trinket. It will perish with her." Then the elder drops her arm and throws a Fla'mma net over her.

Glenna recoils as the net singes her.

"Glenna," Ragnald says, "stop moving or it will burn you."

She nods with moisture in her eyes but obeys.

Arkibald scowls. "But you promised—"

Gangas slaps Arkibald across the face. "I promised you nothing."

Ragnald shakes his head. "Is that why you betrayed me? For the elder rank?"

"You just figured this all out, huh?" Arkibald asks. "Tell me, do you still dream about that village? Do you blame yourself for all their deaths?"

Glenna's head snaps up and the Fla'mma net burns her cheeks. "What village?"

Ragnald clenches his teeth.

The village that haunts me in my dreams.

"You can't answer her question, huh?" Arkibald asks. "You never had what it took to be an elder. *I* took care of the village, while *you* froze."

Relief washes over Ragnald.

I wasn't the cause of their death. I couldn't save them, but I will save Glenna.

"My name is Angus Wanderer," he says as he gets to his feet. "You murdered my sister. Prepare to pay for her death!"

"Not with that again," Arkibald says and shrugs. "It's not murder to get rid of *pests*."

Angus bellows and lunges at Arkibald. Five more guards dart to him, bombarding him with Fla'mma balls until the wanderer falls onto his knees.

"Stop hurting him!" Glenna shouts, reaching toward Angus, then yelps from pain.

Alaisdair places a hand on Gangas's arm. "Please stop."

Gangas shakes Alaisdair's arthritic hand off his arm. "You were always an old fool and missed our ascension."

Alaisdair draws his gray eyebrows together. "Ascension?"

All forty mage elders, including Gangas, drop their robes to reveal a grotesque visage of withered bodies with thick black veins crisscrossing their skin, visible through the holes in their ragged clothing.

The scent of rotting garbage hits Ragnald. He and his mage brothers gag.

"They are almost fully Turned!" Glenna cries.

But it's still not too late to stop them.

"This is not ascension," Ragnald says and gathers Fla'mma and T'erra magic into his palms.

I need a distraction to shatter the A'qua glove.

Ragnald nods at his mage brothers. They incline their heads in understanding.

Athol winces. "No one should side with the Archgod of Chaos and Destruction for power."

Ragnald searches for an opening, a crack in the A'qua glove, but it feels too smooth.

Blair adds, "We always fought against the archgod in the era wars. How could you let your greed lead you to Him?"

Ragnald hides his smile when he finds the tiniest fissure and hammers his T'erra magic into the fissure until it becomes a hair-thin crack.

Dand says, "That's why you stripped Ragnald of his elder rank—you couldn't stand someone younger and more powerful among you."

Ragnald combines his Fla'mma magic with T'erra and threads the mix into the crack to widen it. He cannot go too fast, or the A'qua glove would activate, shutting him off from his magic. He blinks away sweat dripping from his forehead.

Craig raises his hand. "I just want to know, was it worth it to sell yourself to the archgod?"

The A' qua glove opens up and Ragnald absorbs the threads, adding them to his magic, waiting.

Gangas smiles, showing blackened sharp teeth. "It's you who have sided with the enemy—the Archgoddess of the Eternal Light and Order and Her Sybil."

The stone door bangs open.

Dozens of Turned mages of all ranks crowd into the circle, filling up the cavernous room.

CHAPTER 52

GLENNA

The Turned surround us. Even the mage guards get rid of their robes to reveal they too have become Turned.

Corruption Nic grins. "You've lost."

No! There must be something we can do!

Keeping my breath steady under the Fla'mma net, I try to comprehend this many almost Turned. How did DLD get to them?

Corruption Nic glances around. "This is one of my master's brilliant plans—He has been tempting the elders for years and no one was the wiser. Now behold the fruits of His efforts."

I gulp.

One fully Turned can level a city. What would this many Turned do if they roamed free?

"You could be one of them," Corruption Nic says. "Powerful and—"

"Don't be a complete ignoramus," I say. "I will never serve DLD."

Corruption Nic crosses its arms. "You have no other options left. Your mage betrayed you, using you for his own purposes. You can't escape from this tower. You are out of time."

I look away from it and my gaze lands on Ragnald. His betrayal hurts so much.

Corruption Nic tilts his head to the side. "Then why do you still worry about him?"

I shouldn't worry about Ragnald, but I do.

Gangas looks around, his eyes turning black. "Soon the Seven Galaxies will be remade in the image of my master, the Archgod of Chaos and Destruction. We will be at the forefront of bringing peace to all who suffer from the oppression of the Archgoddess of the Eternal Light and Order," he says and points at us. "But before we can do that, we must get rid of Her maggots."

Black Fla'mma, Diseased A'nima, Barren T'erra, and Murky A'qua light up the hands of the Turned as they focus on us.

"Not so fast!" a black-haired mage with green eyes shouts as he bursts into the circle. I recognize him as Ragnald's sixth mage brother, Dugald. Followed by two other mage brothers, the brown-haired Ewan and Fraser, dozens of other mages, and my three elemental golems, who have grown to seven feet tall—with a blooming Mia perched on Pebble. She lashes out with her vines and snaps her thorny maw at the Turned near her.

Ewan throws powder into the air, then using his A'qua magic he sprays the mix over me.

The Fla'mma net vanishes.

I shove away from Arkibald, then sidekick the Turned guard on my right.

Another Turned rushes at me.

I kick him in the groin.

My three elementals snarl, cutting a path to me. Flame guards my front, with Pebble and Mia behind me, while River stands at my side.

Ragnald joins his seven mage brothers, fighting like a whirlwind against the tide of Turned mages.

Angus tackles Arkibald, trying to gain the upper hand against the Fla'mma-using mage.

Five Turned elders attack us.

Flame takes the first, deflecting the torrent of Black Fla'mma. Pebble lunges at the second and third Turned elders, shielding me with T'erra magic, while Mia immobilizes them with her vines. River battles the fourth, leaving the fifth female Turned mage to me.

The Turned tries to claw at my eyes, but I duck under her twisted hands. I stomp on the side of her knee. The Turned's leg buckles and River envelops her with an A'qua bubble.

The rest of the Turned raise their hands, glowing with their corrupted magic, renewing their attack on us.

Gangas approaches, blasting Black Fla'mma mixed with Murky A'qua torrents at Flame and Pebble.

The two elementals stumble to the side.

River pounces on Gangas, but he hits her in the chest with a Black Fla'mma orb. She crumbles to the ground.

"No!" I shout.

Using my A'ris magic, I slingshot Gangas with rocks.

The Turned elder bats them away. He retaliates with a shower of Black Fla'mma balls.

I duck and pivot out of the way of the corrupt magic.

When I straighten, Gangas reaches for me with his clawed hands.

I kick out, but he avoids it. I send a cross-jab combo to his face, but he leans out of the way. He shoots me with a Murky A'qua torrent.

I jump to the right and shoot him with my slingshot.

Gangas bats it away and advances on me.

I back away from him.

Then thin and oozing arms grab me, restraining my arms by my side.

"Let me go!" I yell, struggling to get out of the hold of the Turned behind me, while avoiding the claws of Gangas.

Corruption Nic cackles. "Stop fighting the inevitable."

"No!" I cry out.

The elemental magic of Fla'mma, T'erra, A'qua, and A'nima sings to me.

Desperate, I grab the threads without thinking.

For a moment I don't know what to do with the magical threads—they are unfamiliar to me, bucking under my control. Then the skin on my right wrist where the tear-shaped heirloom is buried becomes hot, as if asking to be used.

I thread the slippery elements into it. The heirloom swallows it like a black hole.

That's not helpful!

Gangas grasps my chin. "It's time to finish your transition into Turned."

Corruption Nic rubs its hands. "Yes!"

I try to tear my head out of Gangas's hold, but his black nails cut into my skin.

Recalling one of the lessons Ragnald had with Lilla on how to shape her magic into a weapon, I form my A'ris element into a sharp disc, then whirl it at Gangas.

The A'ris disc cuts the Turned elder's arm off. His dirty fingers drop from my chin.

Then I form my A'ris magic into a spear and jab it backward, into the Turned behind me.

The Turned's hold disappears.

I dance away from it.

"I never thought I'd ever see you cause harm to another being," Corruption Nic says.

"I didn't," I say.

The elemental magic of Fla'mma, T'erra, A'qua, and A'nima still flows to me. Unsure what to do with them, I thread them into the heirloom again.

Corruption Nic smirks. "Are you so sure about that?"

"Gangas doesn't count; he is Turned."

Corruption Nic points behind me.

Frowning, I look over my shoulder. Then my heart sinks seeing my elementals trembling in pain, including Mia. Then I realize that the elemental magic threads are coming from them, given freely.

I cut the flow and rush to their side.

"I'm so sorry! I didn't know what I was doing!"

I hug Pebble and River to me. Flame pats my back. "I promise on my life that I will never hurt you like this again."

Corruption Nic laughs. "Now you know another reason why the mages forbid making the elementals—they are walking magic batteries."

Turned guards encircle us. One of them shouts, "Stay down!"

I turn to attack, but then I notice the capture of Ragnald and his seven mage brothers.

"Glenna," Ragnald says and wipes blood off his forehead, "forgive me. I just wanted to help you."

Truth rings in his words and I nod.

"Where is Angus?" I ask. Ragnald points to the left. Angus lies unmoving on the ground with Arkibald standing over him.

Gods! I hope that mage didn't kill the wanderer!

Corruption Nic surveys us. "As far as effort goes, it's admirable. But you never had a chance." It looks at me and adds, "Now all these men will die because of you."

Tears roll down my cheeks. It is right—we never had a chance.

My legs buckle and I land on my knees.

"Are you crying?" Corruption Nic asks. "It's pointless."

I shake my head, but I can't stem the tears. They land on the colorful mosaic of the ground.

Closing my eyes, I pray to the Archgoddess of the Eternal Light and Order and to Guardian Goddess Cyn'rha to save Ragnald, his mage brothers, and Angus. I pray for all the innocent mages and students who had nothing to do with the archgod. I pray for the Turned who are lost now. I pray for the children trapped in the Academia and on Raghild. I pray for Raghild the mages ruined. Then I pray for the love Ragnald and I never had.

Lighting strikes around the tower. It illuminates the gray sky outside the circular wall-less room. Thunder reverberates inside. Cracks form in the high ceiling and in the marble floor under my knees.

Then a humongous pair of dark brown eyes from a rock-and moss-covered face peer inside the tower.

CHAPTER 53

$$\approx$$

BACK TO NOW—GLENNA

"Don't worry, Weaver of Light," an ancient voice booms in my head, gentle but chock-full of power. "You made sacrifices at the altars of my guardian goddess, and you prayed to my goddess. We heard you."

I gape at the Mountain Giant, recognizing it from the tales the Stalks shared with us.

The Mountain Giant glares at the Turned. "You have wreaked destruction and chaos. You poisoned our beautiful world, Rag'a'hild, for long enough. Guardian Goddess Cyn'rha will tolerate you no more."

The Mountain Giant slams his fist into the roof of the tower, punching off the top. Then he spreads his arms wide and brings his fists into the tower somewhere below us.

An explosion shakes the tower. It topples to the side.

Ragnald lunges toward me, but he cannot reach me in time.

The floor slips from under my feet and I plummet.

Pebble grabs my hand and Mia pulls me close to him with her vines. The rock golem hunches over me, shielding me. Flame holds Pebble's left shoulder, burning the showering debris around us. River shoots water ahead of us to slow our descent.

Then we crash to the ground.

Pebble shatters on impact, but re-forms the next instant with Mia still attached to his back. I land on my right shoulder, dislocating it.

Agony jabs into my body. I suck in a breath through my teeth.

Flame picks me up, with River shielding us as we sprint away from the rubble bombarding the ground.

We stop in an upper courtyard some distance from the imploding tower.

Mages, both Turned and nonturned, flow out of the building in a flood.

Breathing hard, I hold my right arm close to my body to prevent jarring it.

The Mountain Giant batters the left and right wings of the Academia until the buildings shatter with an ear-piercing boom. Fire breaks out just as the giant withdraws into the clouds.

My gaze searches for the survivors, but I can't find Ragnald, Angus, or the seven mage brothers anywhere.

Corruption Nic stands next to me. "You killed them."

"No!" I yell, grasping my head against the incessant pinpricks.

Thousands of Turned mages, including many elders, rush outside, unscathed.

How can we win against them?

Corruption Nic scoffs. "You can't."

More explosions rock the Academia, shaking the ground. I fall to my knees and sink inches into the cold mud but cannot force myself to get up. Exhaustion beyond the physical presses down on me.

Corruption Nic's visage morphs into that of my late adoptive father, Great Healer Robley. "So many innocents died today because of you, my dear Glenna," he says and his wise hazel eyes in his wizened face glint with sadness. "Atone for your acts and for breaking your healer's oath."

I never broke my oath!

But the corruption doesn't budge. It reverts to a laughing Corruption Nic.

I smash my fists in the mud and scream.

Freezing wind tangles with my once-crimson-now-white hair, blowing it across my eyes, with a few long strands sticking in the blood seeping from my left eyebrow. Cold cuts through my bloody cloak.

Fighting rages everywhere I look.

The dark and imposing fortress collapses behind me with a strident boom.

Screams of pain and anger add to the cacophony and chaos as wreckage hails all around us, burying many. But it doesn't stop the Turned. They swarm coming like sandroaches that flock to the dead to feast on their carcasses. Mages and followers who escaped the corruption and the falling debris, battle with the Turned, but there aren't enough of them against the corrupted.

In my mind's eye I see all who passed in the skirmish with DLD on Uhna: Nic, Great Healer Robley, my pets, and all the innocent people who were at the wrong place at the wrong time. Their deaths bear down on me and I cannot get enough air into my lungs.

Then I hear my real adoptive father's voice in my mind, "People die, no matter what we do. No matter how hard we try to prevent it, my dear Glenna. It will hurt more than you can imagine, but do not carry that responsibility or it will destroy you."

Closing my eyes, I cherish the memory from long ago, when I first practiced healing under his tutelage. I had forgotten his advice. I blamed myself for those deaths because it was easier to find fault in myself than to accept the pain that came with the knowledge that they were gone. I forbade myself to succumb to grief.

Corruption Nic grins. "Look who decided to join us." It points to the right.

Gangas, missing his right arm, along with dozens of Turned elders march toward my elemental golems and me.

Athol's shout rings out on the far left. He fights side by side with a bleeding Ragnald and the other mage brothers, along with Angus.

Ragnald is not dead after all!

I exhale in relief.

Corruption Nic smirks. "It doesn't matter. Your mage will never know how you feel about him. Because you pushed him away. Now it's too late."

"It's never too late," I say, and my gaze follows Ragnald as he attacks the Turned, cutting a path through them, trying to reach me.

"I *did* push him away," I say, wishing I could say this to him. "I thought I was doing Ragnald a favor protecting him from the danger that my corrupted state posed to him. But in truth, I was protecting myself from getting hurt by loving someone again."

That's why I was so mean to poor Ragnald in the beginning, taking every chance I had to snap at him.

I look back at the corruption. "I won't die to atone for whatever fictional sin you think I committed. I will fight till I have no breath in my body."

Dizziness overtakes me. I fall forward onto my left hand, sinking all the way to my elbow in the cold mud.

The insistent buzzing almost overwhelms my mind, growing even louder. For the first time, I can feel their location, deep under the ground, coming from decomposing bodies.

Corruption Nic smirks. "That's where you belong, my sweet love, with the dead."

The corruption level inside me rises.

I choke, unable to breathe.

Gangas and the Turned elders claw at me.

"Glenna!" Ragnald roars. "Watch out!"

CHAPTER 54

RAGNALD

I must get to her! Hurry!

A group of four Turned lunges at Ragnald.

He throws a dozen Fla'mma balls at the two nearest Turned mages. They drop to the ground. Then a female Turned pounces on Ragnald, lobbing Black Fla'mma orbs at his head.

Ragnald ducks under the corrupted fire and buries her into the ground with his T'erra magic.

The last male Turned throws an A'qua spear at Ragnald's chest, but he dances out of the way. It scrapes his ribs, drawing blood. Then Ragnald sinks the male Turned into the ground as well.

Glenna's scream cuts into his heart.

"Glenna!" he roars, hurrying to her. But he cannot make headway—three more Turned attack him with Barren T'erra, trying to bury Ragnald, but he leaps over the cracks and burns them to ashes with a Fla'mma torrent.

Helplessly, Ragnald watches Gangas and a dozen Turned advance on Glenna. *Gods, let me get to her in time!*

A young Turned lashes at Ragnald with Murky A'qua chains. One cuts into Ragnald's left arm, but he shakes it off. Forming a Fla'mma tornado, he picks up the Turned along with six others and throws them out of his way.

"Son, behind you!" Alaisdair yells.

Ragnald whirls to see Alaisdair crumble to his knees with a Black Fla'mma sword sticking out of the middle of the mentor's thin chest.

"No!" Ragnald shouts and drowns the huge Turned guard with an A'qua deluge.

The mentor falls to his side.

Ragnald drops to his knees by the older man, pressing a hand on the gushing wound to stave off the bleeding.

Alaisdair tries to smile, but pain distorts his face. "My ignorance will be my undoing," he says with bloody bubbles forming at the corner of his wrinkled mouth.

Cold washes over Ragnald. "Save your energy. Let me——"

Alaisdair places a bloody hand over his. "It's already too late for me, son. This is all my fault . . . I ignored what the other mage elders were doing . . . letting them run disorganized . . . I knew how they were . . . I just never realized . . . how far they were willing to go . . ."

Alaisdair coughs and more blood spills from his mouth. "You must stop them, son . . . promise me."

"I promise, Mentor."

Alaisdair squeezes Ragnald's hand. "I wish I was more help to you, son . . . I regret betraying your confidence and . . . refusing to assist you in your time of need . . . Please forgive me."

"It's forgiven," he says just as the light fades from the older mage's gaze.

Ragnald whispers a quick prayer for his mentor and gently closes his eyes.

Getting to his feet, he looks around, searching for Glenna.

To his right, Angus in his large swamp troll form fights Arkibald, whose left arm hangs by his side.

Fury replaces grief seeing his once mage brother Arkibald.

I should have seen your betrayal coming, but I trusted you. We've been studying together for more than a hundred years, following the orders of the Academia. We shared the same experiences. How could you turn out to be this jealous and selfish? All because of the promise of the elder rank?

Ragnald shakes his head.

I almost became you—chasing that cursed elder rank. I thought I wanted it to help Glenna, but in truth I wanted it for myself. To validate and justify my past actions. When all I had to do was accept who I am, with my past and all. Otherwise I will become just like you—a broken shell of a man. A cold-blooded murderer. A mindless puppet of the Academia.

Then Ragnald's gaze finds Glenna and he staggers at the weight of the love he feels for her.

I regret lying to you. I regret not being honest with you. I would give up being a mage if it could save you.

Ragnald kicks a crawling Turned guard away from him.

Gods, let me prove it to her how much she means to me! Let me be the one who saves her! She was the one I was waiting for. It was always her.

With a newfound energy, Ragnald battles his way toward Glenna.

CHAPTER 55

GLENNA

Gasping for air, I scratch at my throat with my uninjured left hand, but there is no air. I collapse onto my back into the frigid muck, with black spots swimming in my vision.

Corruption Nic leans over me. "You're almost there!"

The dozen Turned mages and guards fight my elemental golems. Gangas sinks his claws into my shoulders, flooding me with agony as he presses me deeper into the mud.

The buzzing intensifies in my mind as the dead call to me from deep underground. They reach for me with their skeletal hands, begging me to help them. Begging me to heal them.

"I . . . cannot . . . heal . . . the dead," I gasp. Their call is insistent.

"You were always a lousy healer," Corruption Nic says. "Don't bother wasting what little magical energy you have left."

"Everyone . . . deserves . . . healing."

Then mud covers my face and the tide of corruption cascades over me.

Blackness takes over. To give in is to become Turned.

I battle against the corruption as the pressure builds. But it saps my energy as it infiltrates my cells and blood, killing everything in its path.

The heirloom under my skin pulsates, beckoning, just as the dead cry for me even now.

With nothing left to lose, I channel my A'ris magic into the heirloom.

For the first time, I can feel a neutral storage of magic that still has hints of Fla'mma, A'qua, T'erra, and A'nima waiting to be added to my magic.

I realize that the heirloom must have needed these five light elements to activate it. That's why it stored the borrowed magic from my family and me, and then from my elementals. Its function must be to turn the foreign elements outside of my own magic into a neutral magical power, one that is now compatible with A'ris, acting like a huge boost of magical fuel.

Then my air runs out.

My lungs burn.

Panicking, I grab onto the enormous magical power and add it to my A'ris magic. Then I grasp the rising corruption, and wrestle it while mixing my magic into it, just as Corruption Nic taught me in the swamp. This time my boosted magical power outweighs the heavy corruption, and I can take control of it.

The dead beg louder in my mind.

Saturating it with my A'ris magic, I prune the magical mix until the only characteristic of the corruption that's left is the animation part—one that DLD uses to reanimate the dead into dark servants. Then I shove the burgeoning magical mixture into the ground.

The torrent blasts into the dead, who soak it up. They burst to the surface, lifting me out of the mud. Thousands of skeletal dead in various states of decomposition rise all around us, like my very own army.

I wipe my face and gasp for air.

The magical mixture still floods into the ground, into the waiting dead, spreading in all directions under the Academia for miles. The heirloom, like magical storage, fuels the neutralized threads, enabling my A'ris magic to not run out while I grapple the corruption under my control, ridding myself of it.

"No! Don't kill me!" Corruption Nic begs.

I face it. "You were wrong—I am a great healer."

Corruption Nic howls in pain and lunges at me. Its hands go through my body without causing any damage.

I channel the cleansed-corruption into the dead, reanimating more of them. "Everyone deserves healing—"

Corruption Nic falls to its knees, interrupting me, "Stop! Please!"

"—including me," I say and shove the last of the corruption mix into the ground.

With a death keen, Corruption Nic shatters.

Gangas backs away from me. "What have you done?!"

"Help us," the risen dead plead, though they have no voice. Yet I understand what they need.

I point at the Turned. "Now is your chance to right the wrong that was done to you. Now is your chance to heal your soul and move on to Lume! Avenge yourself!"

Then I cut the magical connection.

I have no control over them or over their actions anymore, which is how it should be. I have no right to take advantage of their suffering and use them for my own gains.

"You were not supposed to be able to do that!" Gangas screeches. "Commanding the dead is a lost skill from before the era wars. I will kill you for this, necromancer!" He dives at me with Black Fla'mma covering his gnarled hands.

I duck under his attack.

"I am not a necromancer, but the Weaver of Light and Healer of All, including the dead, whose souls cannot move on thanks to you and your corrupted kind."

Gangas lashes out with a flare of Black Fla'mma.

Flame jumps in front of me, taking the brunt of the dark-fiery stream. My fire golem absorbs the corrupted magic inside of him, burning through it and becoming stronger.

Then Pebbles punches Gangas, preventing the corrupted mage elder to use any more of his chaos magic.

Mia spits poison on Gangas, paralyzing him.

Then River sprays the Turned elder with a flood of water, sinking him into the mud.

Before Gangas can get to his gnarled feet, Flame burns the corrupted elder into black ashes.

I shake my head. "No one is going to miss him."

My elemental golems nod, then surround me in a protective circle. We turn to face the battlefield.

The wave of dead overwhelms the Turned mages and guards, taking out many corrupted elders as they stampede across the courtyards.

Ragnald and his mage brothers stare at me in shock or in surprise, then back away from the thousands of undead that shuffle around them with arms stretched out. But the newly risen focus their attention on the Turned mages. They attack the corrupted, skipping around Ragnald and his mage brothers.

With disgusted looks on their faces, Ragnald and his mage brothers leave the undead alone and instead join the fight alongside the risen.

Many nonturned mages attack the skeletal army, but the undead do not care about them. After a few minutes, the mages stop their assault and fight the Turned instead.

Some of the undead are more intact—they must have been murdered by the corrupted mage elders. At least now they have a chance to avenge their deaths on the minions of DLD and thus on the archgod Himself.

Other deceased are showing an advanced state of decay, often leaving them with a porous skeleton. They stumble around, taking down the Turned zealously. I wonder if they might be leftovers from the previous era wars.

The waves of departed maul the Turned, swallowing up the corrupted like an unliving wave.

Within minutes, most of the Turned are gone. Except for the seven Turned mage elders who escaped by turning into a column of smoke and rising to the sky out of reach at the last second. A fact I have to let Lilla know, so we can prevent the Turned from reuniting with DLD.

Once the undead avenged their deaths, they have nothing else left to do. They drop to the ground, turning into dust. A bright light rises from their ashes, full of gratitude and happiness. They sparkle once, then they float upward, heading to Lume. Healed once again.

I smile. "For what is the most ultimate healing if not saving one's soul." I send a prayer for their souls to the Archgoddess of the Eternal Light and Order.

Dizziness makes me sway. I drop to the ground, jarring my dislocated shoulder. White hot pain pierces me.

The wrongness that I've felt on Raghild remains, lodged deep in the ground. The slow-burning corruption must have infected the world itself.

I grab what's left of my amplified A'ris magic. "I was trained to treat poisoning." Then I channel it into the ground, seeking out the corruption. When I find it, I neutralize it.

The grayness recedes from the soil, from the plants, and even from the sky. Strong sunlight of late morning shines through the dissipating dark gray clouds.

I inhale the clean and crisp air, wrestling with fatigue.

I feel Ragnald's intent gaze on me. I turn my head to look at him.

He stands among his seven mage brothers, one of them supporting Angus's huge swamp troll form, with Arkibald's motionless body at their feet.

"Well done, Weaver of Light," the Mountain Giant's voice booms in my head. I can almost see its tremendous silhouette in the air across from me. "You healed the citizens, past and current, and you also healed Ra'ga'hild. We thank you for that."

"Don't mention it," I say and lay back before I faint.

River sits behind me and lifts my head onto her thigh, making sure to support my injured shoulder. Flame and Pebble stand guard over us, with Mia snapping her vines in the air victoriously.

Ragnald strides to me and drops down to his knees. Then he pulls me into his arms. "Glenna, are you okay?" He checks on me, running his hand over my body.

I wince when he touches my injured shoulder. "I'm fine."

Ragnald closes his eyes for a moment, then says, "When I couldn't get to you, I worried that I'd lose you. Then that army of undead arrived; I assume that's your doing?"

I nod. "They needed some healing."

Ragnald laughs. "Of course they did." He swipes a long strand of hair out of my face. "Whatever you did with the dead, it seems you got rid of the corruption. There is a thin strip of white left in your hair."

I'm about to agree with him when I sense the tiniest seed of corruption in me, dormant.

"That's not the case, mage. I should have known it won't be so easy to get rid of it all."

Then unconsciousness takes over.

CHAPTER 56

RAGNALD

As the sun sets, Ragnald places Glenna's unconscious body on the bed inside a small wooden hut that once belonged to his mentor. He is grateful that it is far away from the Academia, though it is near the edge of the Forest of Darkness and Loss. Somehow the forest looks a lot less dark and a lot more cheerful with colorful flowers blooming everywhere on evergreen trees.

The golems, along with Glenna's vegetarian carnivore flower, guard the cabin outside from a distance. His mage brothers sent Ragnald away to take care of Glenna while they searched for survivors. They planned to meet the following morning to discuss what's next for the Academia.

Ragnald kneels by the side of the bed and looks at the pale Glenna. He knows this battle took a lot out of her.

How I wish I had A'ris magic to heal her!

But there is nothing he can do for her other than make her comfortable and pray to the Archgoddess of the Eternal Light and Order for help.

Ragnald touches her cheek, which feels too cold. "Please don't die. I shouldn't have brought you to the Academia, into danger."

Using his A'qua magic, he cleans the blood and mud off her face. Then using his T'erra magic, he lifts off all the dirt and mud caked on her clothing. He returns it into elemental magic form and adds it to his own magic.

Ragnald lifts Glenna's hand and kisses her fingertips.

"I have so much to tell you," he says, and his voice buckles. "I thought I had more time . . . that you could forgive me . . . and love me after all of this . . ."

Ragnald exhales, cursing.

"I was a fool for wasting all that time and not showing you how much I loved you. I was a coward. The truth is, I loved you the moment I saw you at the royal wedding of Lilla's father. I only took one look at you, with your fiery hair and your dark crimson gaze flashing with spunk that I fell for you in that instant. Before I could have asked you out on a date, that boomberry wine incident happened and, well, I overreacted. I closed myself off."

Ragnald lowers his forehead on their clasped hands.

"When the Archgod of Chaos and Destruction infected you with His corruption, I secretly cherished it. While I hated seeing you suffer and struggle, at least I could be near you. I thought that would be enough. But it wasn't."

Ragnald lifts his head and rubs a circle on the back of Glenna's hand.

"I tried to show you with my actions how much I liked you, hoping you'd like me back too. But you pushed me away at every chance you had. I didn't know what to do with you."

Try as he might, Ragnald cannot let go of Glenna's hand, worried he'll lose her.

Then he smiles, recalling how she made him sleep on the floor when they were on the Teryn ship and then later, on Callum's home world.

"You made helping you as difficult as you could. Maybe you were testing my resolve and commitment to you. But I didn't mind."

Ragnald swallows. "I love you, Glenna. You hear me? I love you so much. Please come back to me. Don't leave me!"

He kisses Glenna's hand again and turns his face, laying his cheek on it, fighting grief.

Then he feels the softest touch on his hair.

CHAPTER 57

GLENNA

I float in blackness. Pain does not batter me anymore. Warmth blankets me, coming from a bright light far ahead of me.

"Stay for a bit," a beautiful voice says. The blackness morphs into a gorgeous summer day with bright blue ocean water lapping at the softest beige sand. A snow-covered mountain—with a hint of an ancient face in the rocks—curves around the beach. An attractive woman with long black hair covering her slender naked body dips her toes into the water, while a flower-perfumed wind plays with her long strands.

She turns to me and smiles. "My giants and I are awake, thanks to you."

I return her smile, knowing who she is. "I'm glad to hear that, Guardian Goddess Cyn'rha."

"You healed my world, Ra'ga'hild, and us." She sashays to me, then hugs me, kissing my forehead. Warmth spreads from the place where her lips touched my skin, healing all my aches, wounds, and my dislocated shoulder. Though it cannot rid me of the corruption seed.

"Even I cannot take that from you. But now you know what to do with it."

I nod.

An urgent male voice echoes around us. "I love you, Glenna. You hear me? I love you so much! Please come back to me. Don't leave me!"

The guardian goddess touches my face. "Go to him. You deserve happiness."

The beach disappears.

My fingers bury into silky strands of hair, and I open my eyes. I find myself in a wooden hut, feeling healed and energized.

Ragnald lifts his head and looks at me with his storm-gray gaze swimming in moisture. "Glenna?"

"I'm not dead, mage. Don't grieve over me yet."

He sits on the edge of my bed. "I confessed my love to you, and you complain. Is there anything I can do to please you?"

My heart picks up its pace. "I have a few suggestions."

Ragnald blinks. "But you were dying a mere moment ago."

Grasping a long silver strand of hair, I pull him closer. "What are you waiting for, *mage*?"

As if my words lit a fire in him, his whole demeanor changes.

Gone is the calm and collected mage.

Gone is the logical and methodical man.

Ragnald worships me with his every kiss and touch. I return it with all my heart. Embracing him and welcoming him. Giving him all I am. All my love.

I've never thought I would love anyone after my Nic. I didn't dare give my heart to another man. I was so scared of getting it broken again. But Ragnald never gave up. No matter how horribly I treated him. No matter how hard I pushed him away, he always came back to me.

My stubborn mage.

After, as we lay next to each other on our sides, I touch his face. "I love you, too. You hear me? I love you so much!"

Ragnald turns his head to kiss my palm. "You had me when you poisoned me."

CHAPTER 58

RAGNALD

Next morning, Ragnald strides through a door into a brick building, located at a lower courtyard. A round wooden table covered in scrolls takes up most of the room, with his seven mage brothers standing around it, conversing in low voices.

Blair grins. "We are sure glad you could tear yourself away from Glenna long enough to spare a minute for us."

Athol slaps the back of Blair's blond head. "No need to be jealous, mage brother."

Craig raises a hand. "I just want to ask, what are we going to do now that there is no more Academia?"

Dugald averts his eyes from Ragnald. "How is, um, your healer doing, mage brother?"

Ragnald remembers how "well" Glenna felt a few minutes ago and clears his throat. "She is much better."

Blair puts his hands on the table. "Less than forty percent of all mage ranks survived the battle. We have no reports yet from the mages off world, but our numbers are decimated."

The mood turns solemn.

Ragnald and the others bow their heads, sending prayers for those who perished.

Athol nods. "No need to panic yet, but we need to decide what we'll do before word of the Academia's destruction spreads in the Seven Galaxies."

Craig raises a hand and waits.

Athol wipes his forehead. "Craig, there is *really* no need to . . . just ask whatever it is, mage brother."

"I just want to know now that the mage elders are, um, gone, does that mean we all got promoted to elder rank?"

Ragnald taps his chin. "That's a good question. I—"

A respectful knock interrupts him.

One of his mage brothers opens the door.

A gangly Devotee Zorion in a blue robe, and a tall, wide-shouldered monk wearing a hooded red cloak step through the doorway.

When the other monk takes the hood off to reveal his bald head, Ragnald recognizes him.

"Devotee Zavier, it's been a while," Ragnald says and introduces the monks to his mage brothers. "What are you two doing here?"

"Fifty years is not that long," Devotee Zavier says. "I see you are faring well, as much as possible after the obliteration of your Academia. Devotee Zimon warned this might happen, and he was right."

Devotee Zimon bobs his head, covered with short brown hair. "I did foresee it, didn't I?"

Ragnald frowns at the monks. "If you foresaw this, then why didn't you come to fight against the Turned?"

Devotee Zavier shakes his head. "That was not our part to play."

Athol grunts. "Not to be rude, but what on Raghild are you here for then?"

Devotee Zimon grins. "We are here to assist you."

Blair pinches the bridge of his nose. "With what? We have this under control, *monks*."

Ragnald turns to Devotee Zavier. "Are you here to rebuild the Academia?"

Devotee Zavier raises his eyebrows. "Not quite."

Blair groans. "Will one of you Pada monks explain why you came? Other than to frustrate us, that is."

Devotee Zavier clasps his hands in front of his red cloak. "Let's gather the survivors so we can begin." Then he turns to Ragnald and asks, "Aren't you supposed to be somewhere else?"

EPILOGUE

GLENNA

Ragnald lands the small shuttlecraft we borrowed from Devotee Zavier on the far side of Cathal as per the monk's instruction, the location of Lilla's new mission as a sybil.

"I still don't understand why that Pada monk insisted to land so far away from Lilla," I say, unable to hide my impatience to rejoin my best friend and to tell her all that's happened.

Behind me, Angus stretches. "Took long enough to get here, wherever here is."

Ragnald flicks off a multitude of switches. "Are you inferring, wanderer, that my piloting skills are not to your liking?"

Angus chuckles. "If the spaceship fits . . ."

Ragnald scoffs. "Then why did you come with us?"

Angus shrugs a shoulder. "I had nothing better to do—"

"—than to annoy me." Ragnald finishes the wanderer's sentence, then ducks his head when he sees my pointed look. Then he reaches out with a hand and adds, "Why don't we go and see for ourselves the wisdom of Devotee Zavier?"

Taking his hand, I smile at him. Along with Angus, my three elemental golems, and a blooming Mia, we stride to the back of the ship.

Oppressive heat and humidity slap us across the face the second the back of the ship opens. The landing platform slides out, revealing a wild and dripping orange-green jungle. Smells of decaying undergrowth mix with flower scents.

Angus inhales with pleasure. "Smells like home, though a bit too humid." Then he adjusts his bag's strap on his wide shoulder and leaps off the platform.

Ragnald jumps off, then lifts me off the platform. He pulls me to his body and steals a kiss from my lips before he removes his hands from my waist.

Angus stares ahead with tilted head, and a predatory look flashes across his eyes. "I changed my mind. I don't like this place anymore."

I glance around but don't see anything out of the ordinary. "Why?"

"It's a bit too quiet, isn't it?" Angus asks, then sniffs the air. "There is something off . . ."

I look around again.

The lush green and orange jungle drips water to the ground. Not a sound of animals or insects can be heard. Unnatural silence settles around us, broken by the clattering and clicking noise our ship makes as it cools.

I hug my middle. "Is this normal for a jungle?"

Ragnald glances around too, trying to hide his unease, but I catch the way the muscles tighten on his jaw. "I'm sure it is," he says in a reassuring voice, but nods toward Angus, who releases his glamour.

The swamp troll ambles in front of me, my elementals next to me, while Ragnald takes up a position behind me, with his Fla'mma fire covering the mage's hands.

The hair on the back of my neck stands up.

Suddenly a rustle comes from our right.

We whirl toward it.

The men curse.

My eyes go wide. "Oh, my gods! What happened here?!"

ACKNOWLEDGEMENT

I'm so happy to present you, dear readers, the fourth installment in the Last Lumenian book series.

A lot of teamwork goes into creating a book. I would like to thank these wonderful individuals who helped bring this book to life:

Thank you, Matt, for your understanding my hectic schedule. You balance out my "bad" author habits.

Thank you, Julie and William, for the skilled editing you both provided. You help make this series amazing. I appreciate you both very much.

Thank you, Dan and Natasha, from NY Book Editors. I know I can always count on you.

Thank you, Jenny and Kelly, for the great support and enthusiasm you show for this series. So happy to have you on board.

Thank you, Doug, Jackson and Henry, for the wonderful content you create for this series. I appreciate your creativity.

Thank you, Mario, for your continued support for this book series. It means a lot.

Thank you, Ed and Don, the best PR guys in the whole Galaxy One.

Thank you, Melissa, the best creative director, and friend in the whole Galaxy Two.

Thank you, Clif, the best map illustrator in the whole Galaxy Three.

Thank you, Tim, the best cover artist extraordinaire in the whole Galaxy Four.

Thank you, Lukas, the best illustrator in the whole Galaxy Five.

Thank you, Ray and Abigail, the best web design wizards in the whole Galaxy Six.

Thank You, dear readers, for being the BEST READERS in the whole Seven Galaxies. It was a pleasure to meet many of you this year during events. Your support means the world to me!

Last but not least, thank you God, for this amazing writing journey. I can't wait to see what else is in store.

Family–see dedication page. (I love you but no need to be attention hogs.)

GLOSSARY

A

Academia of Mages
Where the mages reside. It's quite spacious.

Aggie the Wanderer
Angus's younger sister who passed away.

Alaisdair, Mage Leader
He is the leader of the mages.

Altars, Sacred
There are many of these altars in the Forest of Loss and Darkness, built for Guardian Goddess Cyn'rha and her three giant protectors.

Amel'ee
Healer and mother to Glenna.

Ancient Powers
They ruled the Seven Galaxies before the Omnipower took over.

A'nima, element
Nature magic.

A'qua, element
Water magic.

Archgod of Chaos and Destruction

The other ruling archgod. He is ageless. He possesses the dark elements and corrupts others into dark servants or Turned, if they have magic.

Archgoddess of the Eternal Light and Order

One of the ruling archgods. She is ageless and fights on the side of Light and Order in the Era War. Lilla is her sybil. She is the mother of all Lumenians. Her acolyte is Aisla.

A'ris, element

Air magic.

Arkibald, Mage Brother

A tall, black-haired mage. He can be a bit arrogant.

Athol, Mage Brother

A tall mage with dark brown hair and eyes. He prefers to wear his mage cloak shirtless.

B

Ban

The ban on healers means they could not step foot on Raghild.

Blair, Mage Brother

Blond mage with green eyes. He has very muscular arms.

Bluebells birds

Large, ferocious fowls who hide among the leaves of shrubs. It's easy to confuse wild blue- berries with their, well, bells.

Bruth, Prowler Mage

A mountain of a mage with affinity to A'nima. He is not very nice.

C

Caderyn, a'ruun
An imposing and large, but fit, older warrior who is the emperor of the Teryn Empire. Callum's and Rhona's father. He has a well-established beard.

Cathal, planet
Orange-green jungle planet with a peaceful atmosphere. It is the location of Lilla's second mission as a sybil.

Cave wasps
Twelve-inch-long nasty insects that live in caves. They assault their prey with their red stingers and bite with their wide mandibles. They are afraid of fire.

Circle, Mage Elders'
It consists of forty-one mage elders and the mage leaders. It used to be called Mage Collective.

City of Paucity
It's a major city on Raghild with many twisting muddy streets, rickety buildings, and a seaport.

Corruption Nic
Mysterious man who has a lot of opinions to share. Usually, unprompted.

Craig, Mage Brother
Tawny-haired and handsome mage. He likes to ask questions.

Crystal Palace
Home of Lilla and Glenna, who also worked there as a healer. It was destroyed by the Archgod of Chaos and Destruction.

Cyn'rha, Guardian Goddess

The original guardian goddess of Raghild. The mages forbid the citizens to pray for her. She is sleeping now.

D

Dand, Mage Brother

Tall mage with a long black beard.

Dark fiends

They are creations of the Archgod of Chaos and Destruction. They tend to be monstrous.

Dark servants

They are creations of the Archgod of Chaos and Destruction. They don't like Lumenians or anything alive, to be honest.

Deidre, Head Chef

Head chef and mother figure for Lilla. Friend to Glenna. DLD killed her.

Device, mysterious

The Mage Elders acquired this mysterious device that allows its user to detect the most minuscule amount of A'ris magic in anyone. It's a black orb the size of a marble.

Devotee, Pada

Devotee is the second highest rank among the Pada monks.

Disciples, Mages

Second lowest student rank at the Academia of Mages.

DLD

Shortened version of the Dark Lord of Destruction, a nickname the Archgod of Chaos and Destruction prefers to use. It does drive the point home, if I may say so.

Drearies
Strange and aggressive dwellers who live in the Forest of Loss and Darkness.

Dreary village
Grassy field with burrows where the Drearies live.

E

Elders, Mage
They are part of the governing body of the Academia, along with the Mage leader. There are forty of them, with one spot open to be filled.

Elements, chaos
They are six chaos elements that are the domain of the Archgod of Chaos and Destruction. There are six of them— Dusky A'ris, Murky A'qua, Barren T'erra, Black Fla'mma, Diseased A'nima, and Acerbus.

Elements, light
There are six light elements that are the domain of the Archgoddess of the Eternal Light and Order—A'ris, A'qua, T'erra, Fla'mma, A'nima, and Lume.

Era War, the
A devastating and recurring galactic war between the two ruling archgods that happens when the imbalance of power between them becomes too great. Like now.

Evander Forest, Galaxy Six
Where Glenna's family lived for a while.

F

Flame
Fla'mma elemental golem.

Fla'mma, element

Fire magic, one of six light elements. Fun fact: can be formed into fireballs!

Flower, Carnivorous

It is a flower hybrid that is carnivorous.

Follower

Lowest rank of student mage in the Academia.

Forest of Loss and Darkness

A foreboding forest. It earned its name thanks to all those who never came back, or if they did, they were lost to darkness, meaning insanity.

G

Gangas, Mage Elder

He is a 701-year-old mage elder with a long gray beard.

Giant protectors, three

There are three of them: the Mountain Giant, the Wind Giant, and the Sea Giant. They are sleeping as well.

Glenna, healer

She is the twenty-three-year-old petite best friend of Lilla. Talented healer. Has beautiful dark crimson hair with white strands and dark crimson eyes.

Glenna's pets

Anton, a three-legged A'ice wolf; an old hunting dog, Buck; two gray cats, Isa and Bella; Gwendoline, a spider; a redbird named Angie; Bobby, a small white bear; and Itty, Bitty, and Missy, three butterflies.

Gnashing turtle

It lives in the Swamp of Misery, making its nest in the hills. It is a huge turtle-like animal that can turn to be aggressive during breeding season.

Great Healer Robley
Glenna's adoptive father. He achieved the highest healer rank on Uhna. He perished in the battle against the archgod.

Guards, Mage
They guard the entrance to the Academia of Mages and wear orange cloaks instead of black.

H

H'rarh Dynasty, Galaxy Six
It's where Ragnald studied under a Pada monk a long time ago.

Haulers
They bring chained children who have magic to the Academia from all over the Seven Galaxies.

Healer's college
Where all the healers study.

Heirloom
A teardrop-shaped ancient heirloom passed down many generations to Glenna. Her father inserted it under the skin of her left wrist.

Higher Ranks, Mages
There are four: Prowler, Combat, Venerator, and Elementalist Battle Mage.

I

Inn, The
A dilapidated four-story building, named The Drinks and Damages Inn but everyone calls it The Inn.

Innkeeper
An oversized and obnoxious man who kowtows to the mages.

J

Jo'nah

A young kitchen servant boy who spilled boiling water on his stomach. Luckily, Glenna healed him.

Josh'ua

Healer and father to Glenna.

K

Known offender

People who go against the wishes of the Academia of Mages earn this stigma. It's not good.

L

Lady, The

It is the favored nickname of the Archgoddess of the Eternal Light and Order.

Leah'na

An eighteen-year-old woman who works at The Inn as a kitchen servant.

Lilla, Sybil

A nineteen-year-old ex-princess-turned-rebel-turned-sybil. She is also the best friend of Glenna.

Lume, element

Powerful magic of light and energy.

Lumenian, legendary

A legendary race that the Archgoddess of the Eternal Light and Order created. There is only one left now—Lilla.

M

Mages
They rule Raghild, though they do not care to keep the streets safe from crime.

Magical Cleanse, War
A war between the mages and the Pax Septum Coalition due to the high taxes the mages wanted to implement on the worlds. It ended with the mages being banned, until Lilla's father, the king, invited a mage, Ragnald, to reestablish diplomatic channels. It didn't turn out so well.

Matriarch
The Drearies have a matriarch ruling them. She usually sits on an elevated wooden chair, carried by four warriors.

Mentor, Mage
An older mage who mentored Ragnald and helped him when Ragnald disobeyed an order.

Mia
Glenna rescues the vegetarian carnivorous hybrid flower babe.

N

Nic
Lilla's stepbrother and Glenna's love. He was killed.

O

Omnipower
An unknown power that governs the Seven Galaxies with balance in focus.

Other mage brothers
Dugald, Fraser, and Ewan. They are tall, handsome, and powerful but didn't have a big role in this story. They are also good fighters.

P

Pada, Galaxy Six
It is the name of the lush, green world and of the monk-like people who reside there. They are mysterious and highly magical. They are also the first world the Teryn Praelium conquered. Without a fight, I might add.

Passport, magical
Visitors of the Academia of Mages are required to petition for the magical passport. It is a magical stamp on the forehead. Only those who do not have any traces of A'ris element are eligible for it.

Pebble
T'erra elemental golem.

Port of Souls
Where wooden ships dock and bring crates of wares from other local cities.

Praelor, Teryn
Title, meaning emperor.

Praelium, Teryn
Name of the Teryn Empire.

Pumy
A foamy and beer-like purple drink the locals accidently discovered. It originates from the fermented stomach content of large vermin. The purple color is due to the grains changing color from the stomach acid of the creature.

Q

There are no "Q" words in this book, other than quiet, quieter, quietly, quick, quicker, quality, quite, question, questioning, questions, quaffs, quest, questing, quagmire, quarters, and queue. But that's all!

R

Rag'a'hild
The original name of Raghild.

Raghild
Home of the Academia of Mages. It's an overwhelmingly gray and disheartening world.

Ragnald, Elementalist Mage
A loyal friend of and ally to Lilla. He is a two-hundred-year-old handsome mage expert in magic. He has triple elemental affinity in T'erra, Fla'mma, and A'qua elements. On occasion he is known to build stairs for himself out of rubble by using his T'erra magic.

Reh'ba
A twenty-one-year-old woman who works at The Inn as a kitchen servant.

River
A'qua elemental golem.

S

Servant, kitchen
Many children and young adults who were kicked out of the Academia end up working at The Inn as kitchen servants. They are treated badly.

Seven Galaxies
Where this story plays out. It has (you guessed it!) seven galaxies in it.

Skills, magical
These skills originate from many-generations-dulled minor affinities.

Spies
The mages deploy many spies to keep their fingers on the "pulse" of Raghild.

Spirit Realm
Glenna has visited this realm in Book 2: *True Teryn*. She doesn't remember much that happened there.

Student Ranks, Mages
There are three: followers, disciples, and adherents.

Swamp of Misery
It is deep in the Forest of Loss and Darkness. Also, home of the swamp trolls.

Swamp troll
A mysterious creature who calls the Swamp of Misery its home.

Sybil
Right hand, avatar, and general to the Archgoddess of Eternal Light and Order. Lilla holds the honor of being the current one.

T

Tag
A young man who used to be a follower but now is a thief. He is a good friend of Ragnald.

Tears of ancients
The dying tears of the ancient powers became artifacts, scattered all over the Seven Galaxies.

T'erra, element
Ground magic.

Teryn, Galaxy Six
Name of the planet and its people.

Thieves
Raghild is plagued by many of them, all part of guilds and eager to make a living under the forgiving eye of the mage elders.

Tier One factions
Seven worlds that the Teryns conquered first. These are Pada, Marauders Syndicate, Industrial Conglomerate, Farmers' Partnership, Miners' Coalition, Merchants' Verde, and Free Traders.

Turned, Mages
A corrupted magic user who is bent on destroying everyone and everything in their way. Blood-thirsty and ruthless.

U

Uhna, Galaxy Five
The oceanic home world of Lilla. Name of the planet and its people.

V

Venerator Mage
A mysterious Fla'mma-wielding mage who was ordered to apprehend Ragnald and Glenna.

W

Warship, Teryn
A tremendous, black, and rectangular ship. Its size is so massive it could easily double for a small city. Its jagged surface is covered with world-erasing cannons, space missiles, and energy-shield piercing arrays. In other words, very dangerous.

Weaver of Life
This is the name healers are called by the locals of Raghild.

X

Ex, like ex-mage. There is one in this book.

Y

A letter in the ABC. Also, short for why.

Z

Zavier, Devotee

A bald and wise Pada monk who taught Ragnald. He wears a dark blue robe with two sashes running in front of it—one sky blue for A'ris and the other dark brown for T'erra.

Zimon, Devotee

Dark-haired Pada monk dressed in a red robe with A'nima yellow and A'ris blue sashes on its front. He is lanky and can be a bit chatty.

AWARDS

2020 Annual Best Book Awards
Winner: Best Cover for Fiction

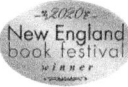

2020 New England Book Festival
Winner: Science Fiction
Honorable Mention: General Fiction

2020 New York Book Festival
Winner: Romance
Honorable Mention: Science Fiction

2020 San Francisco Book Festival
Winner: Science Fiction

2021 Cygnus Book Awards
Finalist: Science Fiction

2021 eLit Awards
Winner: Science Fiction/Fantasy
Winner: Romance
Winner: Book website for fiction

2021 Eric Hoffer Award - First Horizon Award
Finalist

2021 Eric Hoffer Award - Da Vinci Eye Award
Finalist

2021 Eric Hoffer Award - Grand Prize
Short List

2021 Eric Hoffer Award
Honorable mention: Science Fiction/Fantasy

2021 Firebird Book Award
Winner: Sci-Fi Fiction

2021 Independent Author Network
Finalist: First Novel, Fiction: Science Fiction

2021 IAN Book of the Year Awards
Finalist in First Novel over 80,000 words
Finalist in Science Fiction

2021 Independent Press Award
Distinguished Favorite: Fantasy

2021 Los Angeles Book Festival
Runner-Up: Romance and
Honorable Mention: Science Fiction

2021 Readers Favorite Book Award
Romance - Fantasy/Sci-fi

2021 Speak Up Radio Firebird Award
Winner: Cover Design for fiction

2022 Beach Book Festival
Runner-Up: Science Fiction

2022 Best Book Awards
Finalist: Best Cover Design: Fiction
Finalist: Fiction: Fantasy
Finalist: Fiction: Science Fiction

2022 Bookfest Book Awards
Winner: Fiction > Romance - Science Fiction | Fiction
> Sci-Fi - Action & Adventure | Fiction > Women's -
Fantasy

2022 Cygnus Book Awards
Grand Prize: Science Fiction
Finalist: Science Fiction

2022 Chatelaine CIBAs
Finalist: Romantic Fiction

2022 eLit Book Awards
Silver: Best Book Website: True Teryn

2022 IAN Book of the Year Awards
Finalist: Action/Adventure and Science Fiction

2022 Independent Press Award
Winner: Best Cover for Sci-fi Fiction
Distinguished Favorite: Fantasy

2022 Independent Publisher Book Awards
Silver: Book/Author/Publisher Website

2022 Indie Ink Awards
Finalist: This Book Made Me Hungry/Thirsty

2022 International Book Awards
Finalist: Fiction: Fantasy
Finalist: Fiction: Science Fiction

2022 London Book Festival
Runner Up: Science Fiction

2022 Los Angeles Book Festival
Honorable Mention: Science Fiction

2022 National Indie Excellence Awards
Finalist: Book Cover Design: Fiction
Finalist: Science Fiction

2022 New England Book Festival
Honorable Mention: General Fiction

2022 NYC Big Book Award
Distinguished Favorite: Fantasy

2022 New York Book Festival
Honorable Mention: Science Fiction/Horror

2022 Ozma CIBAs
Finalist: Fantasy Fiction

2022 Readers Favorite Book Awards
Finalist: Fiction - Adventure

2022 San Francisco Book Festival
Honorable Mention: Science Fiction

2022 The Wishing Shelf Book Awards
Finalist: Books for Adults

2023 San Francisco Book Festival
Runner Up: Science Fiction

2023 Wishing Shelf Book Awards
Gold: Books for Adults
Finalist: Science Fiction

KEEP THE MAGIC ALIVE.
IT'S JUST THE BEGINNING!

THE
LAST
LUMENIAN

S.G. Blaise

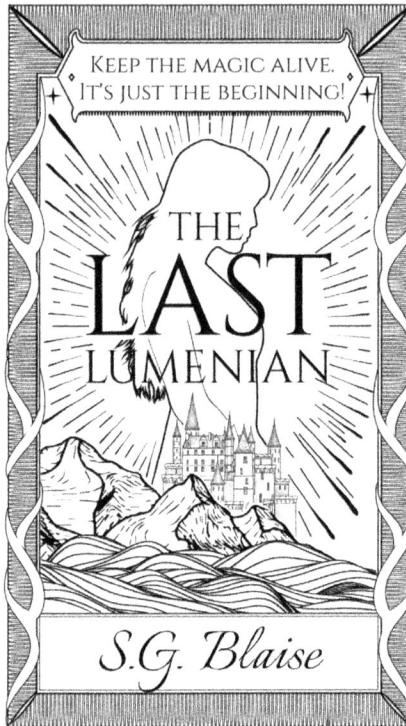

🐦 @SGBlaiseAuthor
f /thelastlumenian
📷 sgblaiseofficial

www.sgblaise.com

To receive exclusive content sign up for the S.G. Blaise newsletter at
sgblaisenews.com

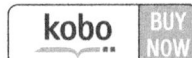

Printed in Great Britain
by Amazon

44177298R00138